Lacey

Also by Janis Susan May

Family of Strangers
The Devil of Dragon House
Heritage of Shadows

Lacey

*A romance of Regency England
in which
three couples discover
that love
does conquer all*

Janis Susan May

Walker and Company
New York

First published in the United States of America in 1987 by the
Walker Publishing Company, Inc.

Published simultaneously in Canada by John Wiley & Sons
Canada, Limited, Rexdale, Ontario.

Library of Congress Cataloging-in-Publication Data

May, Janis Susan, 1946–
    The last laugh.
    I. Title.
PS3563.A9418L37   1987   813'.54   86-34013
ISBN 0-8027-0955-9

Printed in the United States of America

10 9 8 7 6 5 4 3 2 1

For my brother
Robert A. "Bob" May
and his wife Juanita . . .
with love.

Lacey

=1=

"MOTHER, THAT IS the most shocking thing I've ever heard! You can't be serious—"

"I fail to see the objection. It was your father who forbade the mention of Charlotte's name in this house after she eloped, not I. Nineteen years ago . . ." For a moment the aged voice faltered. "Anyway, as I have told you, I instituted a search for Charlotte's child." The faded blue eyes, their calm now tinged with ice, swept to the inappropriately-clad woman, pained that the creature still affected fashions and behaviour more suited to her daughter. Leonora has always been a tragedienne, Lady Chyngford thought with scant charity. The moment her will was crossed the matter became a national emergency with enough histrionics for an entire grand-opera troupe.

"I started enquiries the day your father died," her ladyship continued placidly. "Just to assuage your minds, I left instructions in my will that it was to be done just so if I were to predecease Homer. Charlotte's child will have what is due her. After all, Charlotte was your sister."

"Yes, she was, and a great deal of embarrassment she caused me, too," Leonora pouted, a wave of anger against her pretty sister rising to the fore with a totally disproportionate violence. "Running away like a common trollop, bringing disgrace and gossip on us all."

Sir Cicero Chyngford detached himself from the mantel against which he had been leaning. The eldest of the Chyngford progeny and the only male, he followed in his

1

father's footsteps taking his duties as Head of the Family quite seriously so long as they did not interfere with his own pursuit of pleasure. With a purposeful step he advanced toward the tiny, white-haired lady, adopting the stride and stance so often seen in his late father and, in doing so, unconsciously alienating any slight sympathy he might have engendered.

There's nothing of me in him, the old lady thought with sudden sadness. *He is merely a younger version of his father and has become the same kind of man his father was.* He *underestimated me, too.*

Sir Cicero puffed out his chest, making its girth almost equal to that of his midriff. "But try to see reason, Mother dear," purred the son and heir to the Chyngford fortunes. "Perhaps we can help Charlotte's child, but is it necessary to bring her into our home, or push her into a society for which she is not prepared? After all, she has been raised in a totally different world and has doubtless learned a different mode of conduct, one which would be embarrassing to the Chyngford name." Sir Cicero relaxed, pleased with his idea. Just the thing—protect the family image, keep that harpy of a sister off his back, and satisfy his mother. Perhaps the Americas; he had heard they had shockingly low standards over there, and the girl might even make a decent marriage.

Lady Chyngford's back became even more erect. "So it is the Chyngford name about which you are worried, Cicero."

"It is an old and honourable name, Mother."

Old it is indeed, Lady Chyngford mused with a rancour she had thought long dead, *but how honourable after your father's usage of it, and how will it be when you no longer wear it?* "In that case, the worry should be more with the child, for she is a double Chyngford—an honour which neither of you possesses. Doubtless you were carefully prevented from knowing all the facts, but the man with whom your sister eloped was Barton Chyngford, the son of your father's own cousin Laurence—"

"The chit has our name," moaned Leonora, Lady Dunfield, to no one in particular. "We won't even be able to say we don't know her."

"As to her being raised in a different atmosphere, that is true, but it needn't worry us. Indeed, it cannot but be beneficial for both of you to be exposed to someone from a vicarage. Your unfortunate reputation, Cicero, has reached us here at Greathills, far as it is from London. Just as your father's did," she added, surprised that the old bitterness should still linger. Sir Homer had disliked the estate; it was a good enough place to park his wife and children, but too dull and too far from the varied lures of London for a bon vivant such as he.

"Now you both listen to me," the old woman went on. "It is time you married again, Cicero. If you're so concerned about the Chyngford name, you'd best start doing something to perpetuate it. It's been six years since your Diana died, and though Helvetia is a lovely child, an eight-year-old girl is not an heir! Besides, she needs a mother and brothers and sisters. She is too much alone here. And as for you, Leonora, it's about time you found another husband while you still can. I know you and your daughter have been living on capital, and that won't last long. And perhaps if Elizabeth had a father behind her, there would be a better chance of her making an advantageous match."

In unaccustomed unity, brother and sister exchanged despairing glances. Who would have expected such decisiveness from the old lady? During their father's lifetime she had been scarcely more than a cipher, with nothing to say for herself; her agreement to whatever he said had been expected without question.

"Charlotte is dead now," her ladyship continued, the old pain familiar in her bosom. She had thought she might die of it, but the promise of Charlotte's child had kept her going. "I intend that her child shall have all the advantages that are rightfully hers. She is on her way here now."

"Mother! I have a very important deal coming up about that bay stallion . . . . Lord Piedmont is coming here!"

"And he'll never offer for Elizabeth if he sees she has a vicarage brat for a cousin," Leonora added.

The thin lips curved into a smile. She had told Homer Chyngford he would regret his treatment of her and Charlotte, that in the end she would triumph. When he had banished her to the country, away from the only life she had ever known, making sure that her bitter exile should not interfere with his pleasures in town, she had accepted because she was his wife and because the only one to whom she might have reached out was now forever beyond her reach.

She had borne her burdens with the dignity expected from one of her breeding, accepting her duty, but the treatment meted out by her husband to their dreamy, romantic daughter had created an insurrection in her bosom. It had been a quiet insurrection, to be sure, with no outward signs—she had learned both early and painfully that Sir Homer would retaliate without mercy to any contravention of his will—but she had sworn she would win. Opposition now only made the aged back stiffer, and had either of her children cared to look—really look— closely at her, they would have seen that she looked younger than she had in years. A ghost of roses lingered in the waxy cheeks, the faded blue eyes glowed with life and depth; Lady Chyngford, née Louisa Anne Hampstead, was more than ready for a battle.

"To think of a child like that—dragged up in parsonages and God knows where else—mingling with my Elizabeth! It would make her the laughingstock of town! Who knows where that girl might have been, what sort of ideas and manners she might have picked up . . . . She might even have some dreadful disease!" Leonora's solid shoulders gave a good imitation of a maiden's terrified quaking.

"In this matter I thoroughly agree with Leonora, Mother. You cannot make mock of the Chyngford name . . ." Cicero's voice failed too late at the sight of his mother's fiery eyes.

"I hope that you and your father are never called to an accounting for your treatment of the sacred Chyngford name!

"Well, my dears, I cannot say that I expected your approval. You do not have to fall in with my scheme, but I think that you shall."

"Never," replied two personalities with one voice.

"Very well. I shall have to sponsor a London season myself for Louisa Anne—yes, Leonora, Charlotte named her daughter after me, which neither you nor your brother chose to do."

Sir Cicero looked uncomfortable, and Lady Dunfield flushed a brilliant pink, which clashed sadly with her gown of startling primrose. "Dear George wanted Elizabeth named after his mother—"

"If you are going to tell a whisker, daughter, at least make it a good one! Dear George never took two looks at his child after he discovered it was a female!" In full control of the situation, Lady Chyngford rose and walked the short distance to the window, the rustling of her silk mourning clearly audible in the thick silence.

The home park stretched away from beneath the window, rolling in rich green grass to a line of trees now fuzzy to her ladyship's vision. Off to the right, at the bottom of the gentle slope, was the pond that Sir Homer's mother had designed and installed. The coping had been constructed in a careful counterfeit of crumbling masonry, which, combined with the shattered columns rising from the water, formed the impression of a Delphic pool stolen from its oracle and magically transported from the misty shores of Greece to the prosaic English countryside. The surrounding gardens, rich with roses and honeysuckle, had been designed by that same earlier Lady Chyngford, who had spent most of her short life tending them. Sadly, the present lady wondered if that other one, too, had been parked here at Greathills to be out of her husband's way.

"Mother, that is impossible," came a strangled voice hard to recognise as the bombastic Sir Cicero's. "I forbid it."

"You are scarcely in a position to forbid anything, Cicero," said his mother. "Do not think that I know nothing of those rumours about my death which your father put about and of which you have said nothing! At the time I fell in with his deception. I preferred to live quietly in the country, where I should not be forced to look on your father's philanderings, but there are a few people in London who know me still and would welcome me back to the ton. That would be quite an embarrassment, wouldn't it, Cicero? Besides, since Louisa Anne is to inherit most, if not all, of my private fortune, perhaps she should have a grandmother active in Society."

That was a severe blow to both her children; Sir Cicero, well versed in his father's habits of horses, women, and cards—and, unfortunately, heir to his father's habit of losing—knew that at the moment his mother's personal monies were the mainstay of the Chyngford fortune. If she should die suddenly and this vicarage-born upstart should withdraw her inheritance, the Chyngford estates would crumble.

Lady Dunfield, however, saw the threat more personally. The late and largely unlamented Lord George Dunfield had passed to his reward some years before, leaving almost nothing behind to comfort his widow and helpless child save an ancient and spotless name and reputation, neither of which were particularly merchandisable items. The Dunfield jointure was scarcely sufficient to promote the most marginal life in London, even if her ladyship did economise by spending a great deal of time at Greathills— at her mother's expense—under the guise of visiting.

"Mother! How cruel can you be? For years you've promised that to Elizabeth!"

"No, my dear. I promised that it was for my neediest granddaughter. Now, this is my plan, which I have no doubt that you will convince yourselves is in your best interest to follow. Leonora, it is high time that daughter of yours was married. Cicero, you prate a great deal about the honour of the Chyngford name; it is about time you lived up to such high ideals. I propose that we reopen the house in London; you two and the two girls will move in. It will be entirely proper for a family—even one such as ours—to live there together. Cicero, you will look after your sister and nieces. Leonora, you will chaperone both Louisa Anne and Elizabeth through a first-class Season . . . all at my expense, of course."

Cupidity vied with stubborn selfishness, waging an heroic war in the ample bosom of Lady Dunfield. It was all she had ever dreamed of—a full, no-expense-spared Season for Elizabeth, and perhaps a chance for herself to meet someone whose wealth and gentility was sufficient for her to consider leaving the lonely confines of widowhood. But, on the other hand, to be saddled with that tiresome girl . . . Still, if one were clever, something acceptable might be managed. . . .

Sir Cicero was less easily swayed. "That is impossible, Mother."

"You needn't worry, my dear son. I shouldn't then need to leave Greathills. You would not have the burden of protecting your father's fiction about my death."

Damnation, he thought, *she can read my mind!* Like his father, he had found life much more convenient to manage as a widower, but to admit it so baldly hardly cast a flattering light over both of them. "That's not it at all, but—"

"Cicero, let me put some facts before you. Greathills is entailed and therefore your property, but the little manor at Dobbing Green is mine personally. I can remove to there at any time."

The baronet looked confused. "I don't understand."

"I love Helvie, but I am getting old," said Lady Chyngford with just the correct soupçon of pathos. "She has lived here since her mother died. It would be a shame to uproot her. I'm sure you could find someone—"

"You mean you would go off and desert Helvie? That is a monstrous way to treat her. It . . . it's unnatural! She is your granddaughter!"

"Exactly!" retorted her ladyship, and it was some time after she swept from the room that her son worked out in his mind exactly how neatly he had been trapped.

= 2 =

ALREADY THE COUNTRY was changing. Through the carriage windows Lacey Chyngford watched the harsh, bitter moors of the North Country give way to the softer, more rolling, somehow friendlier country of the South. The land became greener, and even the sunshine seemed brighter each mile they travelled, banishing the grey shadows of Yorkshire. Still, Lacey was forced to admit that she might have such an impression just because every mile took them farther and farther away from Beecham Manor.

It was as if even the slightest thought of the place conjured it again in her mind, complete in every loathsome detail from the stagnant fish pond to the chuckling gargoyles that stood guard on the roof. Made of uncompromisingly drab grey stone, the house stood like a prison for souls, but yet, when Lacey had first seen it—herself newly orphaned and adrift in the world at a tender fifteen—the manor had seemed to be a grand place, fully fit for royalty and much too good for the likes of her.

The family who inhabited Beecham Manor had thought so, too: proud Agnes Mary, dreaming of a London Season as only her due; bitter Mrs Stoker, always complaining at being stranded in the back of beyond; disgusting Mr Stoker, who spit when he talked and always had an eye for young women, whether they were supposed to be under his protection or not; and, lastly, young Chester, who fancied himself a Dandy of the First Water and second to the Prince Regent only by his own choice. No, it had been only the elder Mrs Stoker, the mother of the head of the house, who had welcomed the vicarage orphan when the rest of the world was all too ready to forget her existence.

Louisa Anne—nicknamed Lacey through some long-forgotten childish lisp—had presented a pretty question to the parish council. Her father, the recently deceased Reverend Barton Chyngford, had passed on at last, following a lengthy illness during which his daughter had nursed him devotedly, as she had her mother before losing her the previous year. So far as anyone in Potter's Ford knew, neither the Reverend nor his wife had had any kin save their daughter, and that posed a problem.

The child was just fifteen, too gently bred and well educated to become a servant or apprentice, yet too young to seek suitable employment. Times were hard, as they always were for the farmers and common folk, yet the good council had to make some provision for the orphan. Several offers had been received, including some of marriage from the single men of the district, but with a show of spirit altogether improper for a young female, the orphan had declared her preference for death in the gutter than for any of the alternatives put before her. This ingratitude raised the collective backs of the councilmen's good ladies, until it was learned just who had made these offers—drunkards and wastrels to a man—and then the lass was credited with a sensibility suitable for a member of the gentry.

Exactly how the elder Mrs Stoker heard about the child's plight was never certain, for to be sure the Stokers were an odd bunch and never really accepted into the life of Potter's Ford. Like any true English yeomen, the citizenry of Potter's Ford had a well-developed nose for the Quality; and despite its amount and prodigality, the Stoker money carried a definite scent of the shop; rumour had it that Mr Stoker had been a draper despite his constant claims that he was a member of the nobility. No one knew for sure, and after several embarrassing attempts to assume the rôle of squire, Mr Stoker and his family kept pretty much to themselves. Still, the elder Mrs Stoker's desire to take the orphan for a companion was more acceptable than any of the other alternatives, so at last Lacey was removed from the tiny vicarage that had been her home for the last dozen years to the cold grandeur of Beecham Manor.

Life at the manor had proved to be more pleasant than she had expected, for most of her time was spent with the elder Mrs Stoker and mercifully apart from the rest of the family. Crippled and nearly blind, Mrs Stoker treasured the only thing left her undistorted by age: her mind. She would have Lacey read to her by the hour—great dull stuff, Lacey thought at first, all about laws and statistics—and then the old lady would query the child about what she had just read, at last to be shocked by uncovering a mind as keen and piercing as her own.

No, that had been a wonderful time, reading and discussing and discovering with Mrs Stoker. Then, because it must, the last bastion against age began to waver and the frail old body became unable to hold death at bay.

The winter sun had been shining palely that day, giving the great bedchamber a glowing sense of light and space. Mrs Stoker always hated having the curtains drawn, despite the chill of undraped glass, declaring that the vistas God had provided were better for the soul than the heavy tweed of Lancashire. Already the old lady had been confined to her bed, and it twisted Lacey's heart to see her lying there so oddly tiny.

"There you are, child! Come quickly, we must talk." The vigorous old voice had faded to scarcely more than a whisper.

"Shouldn't you rest instead, ma'am? I'll read to you." Lacey sat on the side of the bed and took the old woman's hand. It felt more like a desiccated bird's claw than a human member.

"I know you would, Lacey, I know, but I haven't time to listen. I'm going to die soon. . . ." Here she had squeezed Lacey's hand in comfort as the young woman gasped. "And we must talk. There's your future to be considered. I haven't dared leave you anything in my will aside from a few pounds, because that family of mine would say you had beguiled me and take it all away. Damned greedy bunch, all of them. No, don't say anything polite, because you know it, too. Now, look in the bureau and bring me my jewel case."

There was an urgency in the soft voice, but when Lacey placed the chest in Mrs Stoker's lap, the old hands made a slow, loving trip over the worn leather, her fingertips familiar with every rent and scar. "This was my mother's— my father gave it to her before they married. It wasn't grand enough to interest Felicity, so I was allowed to retain it." Her snort was an indictment; she and Lacey shared the same unflattering opinion of the younger Mrs Stoker. "Anyway, I wrote this after the doctor's last visit. That man isn't such a fool as I used to think him. Or maybe if you just give him enough time, his diagnoses will prove correct. Here, my dear." She opened the case and took out a sealed envelope.

Lacey accepted the envelope with trembling hands. The old lady's businesslike approach convinced her of the seriousness of the moment more than any amount of tears or hand-wringing. "What's this, ma'am?"

"A letter of recommendation. It should guarantee that you have no problem obtaining a good situation. Now, to more immediate matters. Your wages are paid to the end of the quarter and my son has agreed that you should stay until that time whether I do or not. You've been very dear to me, and I don't want you to have to hurry into a situation just to have a roof over your head."

"That's very kind of you, Mrs Stoker. And of Mr Stoker," Lacey said tightly. She could just imagine how precipitately Mr Stoker would agree with such a plan, especially once his mother was past the point of interference. Already he had taken too uncomfortably close an interest in Lacey, including an encounter in the library from which she had managed to escape only by an undignified tussle.

"But, just in case you should choose otherwise, this is a little extra." Once again she reached deep into the case and pulled out a tattered purse of a style many years gone. "There are fifty pounds in there. I've left you that much more in my will, but at least I know you'll get these." For a moment her lips compressed as if against a bitter taste.

"Mrs Stoker—"

"Hush, child, don't cry on me or neither of us will stop. I merely want to see that you are safely provided for. I've never known not having the security of a family, but I can imagine nothing more horrible. Do you think I could rest easily, knowing you were unprotected?"

Despite the firm injunction, two tears rose and slid down Lacey's cheek. "You're so good to me, ma'am. . . . I just wish there was something I could do in return."

"There is." The old voice was surprisingly firm. "It's a new world out there, different from any I ever knew. At last women are starting to be accepted as thinking creatures. Keep going, Lacey. Don't stop thinking, reaching, learning . . . . You have a mind, my child. Use it."

The words, uttered with fervour and an ageless conviction, sank deep into Lacey's being, crystallising a feeling that had been developing for a long time under the old lady's tutelage. "I will," she answered, making the simple statement a vow.

"Thank you, my dear, for so very much. Now I have but one more thing to give you, and I hope very much that you will appreciate it. My Thomas gave it to me the first year we were married. It's not a very valuable piece in the way my dear daughter-in-law thinks, but I own none any more precious." For the last time, the aged hands dug in the box. "I want you to have it."

Mouth ungracefully agape, Lacey stared at the magnificence spread over her lap. Perhaps the younger Mrs Stoker would not find it interesting—she liked nothing less than diamonds and rubies and great quantities of them—but to Lacey the little necklace was the most beautiful thing she had ever seen. Her mother had owned no jewellery but her wedding ring and a tiny pearl brooch suitable for a very young girl, her father nothing but his watch; even modest jewels such as this were totally alien to a poor North Country vicarage.

"It's the most beautiful thing I've ever seen," Lacey breathed.

Indeed it was a pretty thing, a tight neckband made of small enamel flowers with a shimmering brilliant set in the heart of each. The years had not faded the colours, which covered the spectrum of pinks from the most delicate to a brilliant hue found only in tropical blossoms. Two medallions of pink porcelain in the style of Mr Wedgewood dangled in close proximity from the flower chain, their delicately sculptured male and female busts looking longingly at each other from the silver-gilt frames.

"They were called lovers' necklaces," murmured Mrs Stoker. "The gentleman gave one to the young lady of his choice. They were quite fashionable when I was young. Wear it in good health, my dear."

That was the last time Lacey saw Mrs Stoker, for the old lady had been correct in her prediction: she had died peacefully in her sleep not two days later. She had been correct in her other fears too; at the reading of the will, both Agnes Mary and her mother had sniffed when Lacey's bequest was enumerated, disapproval of such a munificent gift to an upper servant of such short standing very evident in their subsequent behaviour. Lacey could ignore their barbs with reasonable equanimity, but the attitude and behaviour of Mr Stoker was harder to bear. As his mother had predicted, he did not turn Lacey's legacy over to her. "There's no rush," he had said. "You need for nothing and we don't want to run the risk of your losing it. Time enough when you get a new post."

Easily said. Lacey had advertised for a new position, but

there had been hardly enough time for any reply, let alone a suitable one, yet she had soon started debating the wisdom of leaving Beecham Manor, new job or not. Without the elder Mrs Stoker's protection, ignored by the younger Mrs Stoker and her daughter, alternately overlooked and ridiculed by the younger Mr Stoker—who regarded women like his grandmother and her companion, those who aspired to intellectualism, as mutant freaks—Lacey found herself quite literally at the mercy of the elder Mr Stoker.

It was a mystery to her how a woman as literate and intelligent as her late employer could have given life to such a licentious clod as the one who then tried to dominate her life. She scarcely dared enter a room or turn a corner for fear of finding him awaiting her, bubbling over with leering glances and innuendo-filled talk. More than once, when he had her effectively cornered, his hands had passed over her bosom and waist, lingering with painful pressure on her breasts as if they were some sort of magical key to her compliance.

In the clever guise of kindly employer, he had already suggested that it was a shame she should have to think of leaving the area; wouldn't it be much more sensible for her to remove to a certain nicely appointed house not five miles from Potter's Ford, where she could continue in her employment of companion, albeit in a slightly different connotation?

Thank Heaven for the late Mrs Stoker's foresight in the cash gift of fifty pounds; had Lacey depended on the availability of her legacy, she would indeed have been in desperate straits for ready money, since all but a few shillings of her last quarter's wages had gone to replace her outgrown wardrobe. The tattered purse lay in Lacey's bureau, where she checked its safety daily, partly to ensure that it had not magically vanished in the night and partly as one might caress a talisman.

Fifty pounds was not a great deal of money as far as the world went, she knew, and in these hard times, when bread was dear, it would not last long unless she found other employment; however, after one final harrowing meeting with Mr Stoker in an upper hallway—when he had fumbled wildly with the buttons of her bodice, his mouth drooling just inches behinds his hands—Lacey began to think that starvation in some dank gutter was more appealing than staying another fortnight in Beecham Manor, and began to make plans for departure, position or no position.

It was then that the Miracle had occurred.

Mr Devenport was as unlikely-looking a candidate for a Heavenly messenger as could be imagined, with a long cadaverous face and yellowed teeth ill-concealed behind oddly thick lips, but to Lacey—after his mission was explained—he appeared an angel.

For Miss Chyngford, the late Mrs Stoker's companion and the vicarage orphan, to have a visitor all the way from London was startling enough; for her to prove an heiress and a member of an ancient and noble family was enough to send Mrs Stoker and her daughter into a fair spasm. By the time the solicitor had presented all the proofs, the drawing room of Beecham Manor had become a pandemonium, with Mr Stoker playing an unconvincing Paterfamilias, inwardly fearful that his anticipated joy would be removed from him; Mrs Stoker alternately cursing Fate that one so deserving as her Agnes Mary should be overlooked in favour of a mere companion for such good fortune, and exhorting the stunned Miss Chyngford not to forget the family which had taken her in during the time of her extremity; and a sardonically amused Chester unrepentantly laughing at his sister's tears.

Mr Devenport had expected an excess of emotion at his news, but not in such fearful quantities—and certainly not from every person *save* the one most involved. Had not Beecham Manor appeared such a genteel residence and the Stokers a family of unquestionable reputation—though somewhat overly emotional—the staid solicitor would have felt less satisfaction in the successful completion of his mission. Through years of employment with Ingham and Associates, Solicitors, Mr Devenport had taken a great deal of personal interest in poor Lady Chyngford's affairs and had dreaded to find someone totally unsuitable as an heir for the grand lady when he executed her orders.

Even though Miss Chyngford's response to the immediate removal from Beecham Manor was somewhat unseemly in its desire for swift completion (even considering the circumstances), he was pleased with her look and demeanour. To be sure, it was regrettable that anyone bearing the name Chyngford should have had to seek employment in the manner of lesser mortals, but to have served as an elderly lady's companion in a respectable household such as the Stokers' was no shame. Mr Devenport began to relax and think about the reward promised him for the swift completion of his task.

With a precipitancy that everyone save Lacey thought unseemly, Beecham Manor was left behind that very day. Even Mr Devenport had not expected a young lady of Quality to move so quickly, and the respectable female he had brought along to be young Miss Chyngford's companion and chaperone thought such haste indecent and ill-bred, but neither of these worthies could translate the look of desperate frustration writ on Mr Stoker's face as well as Lacey could.

Twice in the past week Lacey's employer had all but trapped her with his groping hands, and two nights previously he had actually tried to force open her bedroom door. No matter how heavily she was chaperoned, Beecham Manor was no safe place for her, but to explain might cast aspersions on her character. Better to be thought a greedy eccentric than a fallen woman.

There was no telling what else the hired chaperone thought of her, for save to complain about the weather or to order more and more food to fill her vast bulk—and to ingest it—she never opened her mouth. Mr Devenport, being unfortunately prone to travel sickness despite the excellently sprung coach, was scarcely more talkative, as he spent most of his time alternately pressing a handkerchief to his mouth and sniffing a vinaigrette; so it was that when Miss Lacey Chyngford finally arrived at Greathills—which she instinctively recognised as being of a much more refined style than Beecham Manor—she knew almost nothing save the raw facts about the family.

The great sweeping drive circled around a sculptured garden in front of the weathered stone house, bigger and grander than anything Lacey had ever seen. From the carriage she was escorted with due pomp up an impossibly long sweep of stairs and through a magnificent doorway into a hallway surely fine enough for the Prince Regent himself and seemingly populated with enough inhabitants for a small village. The young Miss Chyngford had no way of knowing that such display was hardly her grandmother's style and that the crowd was there solely to view the lost heiress; anyone who had the slightest business in the entrance hall at any time had arranged to be there during her arrival, for to be sure it was—as Mrs Timmons, the cook, said—as good as any romance.

Later Lacey would see and appreciate the old Oriental carpets spread like muted jewels over the floor, the perfect sweep of the rising stairway, the rich ebony furniture and pallid marble busts, but now all her wide eyes could focus on was the black Bath cloth stretched over the butler's stooped shoulders as he led her toward an ornate pair of doors.

"Her ladyship is in the green salon," he had intoned, approvingly taking Lacey's measure with a glance and bowing more deeply than was absolutely proper to a young lady. "This way, please."

There had been servants at Beecham Manor, but none so imposing as this man. Trying to emulate her gently mannered parents, Lacey stiffened her backbone, tried to hide the anger she was feeling, and fought the craven impulse to run when both the great carved doors swung inward.

"Miss Lacey Chyngford," the butler intoned.

From a chair of a particularly distressing shade of green, a figure rose—a delicate, aged lady in old-fashioned ruffles and high-piled white hair.

"You're here at last! Come in, my dear."

Later, Lady Chyngford would not be able to recall either Perkins's presence or the girl's attire—which Lady Dunfield was often at pains to remind her was hideous—for it was the child's face that claimed the old woman's attention.

There was little of Charlotte's conventional prettiness to be seen in those features, though to one who had loved her well, there was a certain resemblance. Perhaps the nose was a shade too long for beauty, the cheekbones a mite too pronounced to be declared incomparable, but it was a face that would be memorable. It would age well, Lady Chyngford knew, for the visage that looked toward her with remote interest was the mirror of her own, forty years ago. To be sure, that mane of chestnut-coloured hair was a legacy from Barton Chyngford, but the blue eyes were hers, though those of the elder Louisa Anne Chyngford had never held such a cool appraisal in her eighteenth year.

Lady Chyngford rose from her chair, fighting a sentimental urge to go gather the girl in her arms. *No, to play the prodigal would be all wrong now,* she thought, restraining herself at the last moment, to the undisguised relief of her children; time enough for emotionalism when they were a family again, when Charlotte's child was no longer a stranger in their midst.

Lacey's first impression of her grandmother was that an improbably large antique doll. She stepped into the room, scarcely aware that the big doors closed quietly behind her. The pompous pouter pigeon who aspired to be a peacock must be her uncle; the plump lady in the wildly unflattering dress snuffling inelegantly into a handkerchief must be her aunt. It was difficult to imagine either of these two being brother and sister to her own delicate, tasteful mother or to think of that creature of black lace and silk as being the mother of a woman who had made all their clothes, who had never had more than three dresses at a time, and who had uncomplainingly driven herself to her grave doing all the work in the house.

Lacey's full lips hardened.

"You're Charlotte's child," said the old lady eagerly. "I am your grandmother, and this is your Aunt Leonora and Uncle Cicero."

For a moment Lacey's eyes glittered with diamond-hard resolution, seeing not the shabby elegance of the salon but rather, the pathetic vicarage at Potter's Ford with its cold, bare rooms; the back-breaking old kitchen; the inadequate fireplaces, which, despite their tiny size, there was never sufficient coal to fill. Beneath her sorry blacks—donned for respect of the late Mrs Stoker—there was a turmoil of emotions, none of which her gentle and loving father would have approved; still, the Chyngfords had been warriors before they had become clergymen, and this long-dormant martial blood was slowly stirring in the frail vessel of Charlotte and Barton Chyngford's daughter.

"I am Lacey Chyngford," she said clearly, "and you are the ones who abandoned my mother."

The Viscount Jordan Piedmont hated toadies and grovellers of any station, but when they came from a family that was supposed to be of the nobility, such behaviour was especially odious. Why had he allowed himself to be persuaded to come here to Greathills? And the worst thing of it all: His predicament was all his own fault.

No, not quite that; in London his association with Sir Cicero Chyngford had been scant, barely enough to warrant exchanging nods until that day a fortnight ago when they had bid on the same horse at Tattersall's. That had naturally led to a discussion of the various beasts offered, and by the time the auction was over they had decided on a spot of supper at the George Inn; Sir Cicero had been a little fuzzy from the amount of punch consumed, as had

Lord Piedmont himself, but he had seemed a decent enough chap, and when he had mentioned having a great bay stallion in which his lordship might show an interest, it was only sensible to set a day to come to Greathills and see the beast.

The viscount had expected a pleasant visit with a congenial host; instead, he had found an obsequious social-climber who, under the guise of being his very best friend, hoped to use the cachet of the Piedmont title and connections as an entrée into all the best clubs in town. Too late, the young viscount had remembered the reputation of his host's late father, Sir Homer, who had borne the dubious title of the most notorious rake in London and the six surrounding counties.

And, Jordan told himself viciously, nothing in the civilised world could have induced him to come within miles of Greathills if he had known the Dunfield harpy would be here. He had never connected her with Sir Cicero, though in retrospect they seemed to be birds of a feather. All last Season she had pushed her totally uninteresting daughter at him with such dauntless persistence that despite his constant demurs several wagers had been lodged in the Betting Book at White's on the odds of Lady Dunfield's at last running him to earth. The fields of North America and their savage inhabitants—both red and white—had begun to look almost preferable by comparison.

Despite the rigours of the battlefield, a soldier's life had been pleasurable to Jordan, but the accidental death of his elder brother, followed by his father's passing, had made his succession to the title and attendant dignities necessary, an inheritance which fit ill with the demands and dangers of a coronetcy. He could not let all go to the despised cousin of his father who was next in line, so according to his late father's wishes his commission was sold and Jordan returned to London, where he thought he would probably die from boredom instead of an American bullet.

Or from Lady Dunfield's treacly manner, he reflected. There was no escaping her tonight; that was obvious. He was committed at least until the morning, but at first light he was leaving, no matter what. Even the allurements of the bay stallion were not enough to persuade him to remain at Greathills one moment more than necessary. In a way, it was a pity, for the house, though somewhat shabby, was nice enough and well suited for interesting riding, and the old lady to whom he had been briefly introduced by an oddly nervous Sir Cicero was so charming that it had been difficult to believe she was related to those two social disasters.

If he had arrived a few minutes later, he thought, he probably wouldn't have been introduced to the mysterious Lady Chyngford at all, for she had been on her way upstairs when he arrived, and Sir Cicero had seemed very reluctant to introduce her. Doubtless she was a bit dotty or a tippler whom the family was at pains to keep concealed; most families had at least one "upstairs lady."

Even now he had the rather craven feeling of hiding out, though to be sure it was not unusual for a guest to take a turn in the garden before dinner. It was a pleasing garden, with a small pool in the centre, and he would have enjoyed it even if it hadn't taken on the atmosphere of a refuge. Rather a come-down, he thought, from facing Yankee fire with oft-commended heroism to consciously avoiding the social company of two rather unpleasant people; behaviour hardly to be expected of a Piedmont, though to his credit, neither of his two nemeses suspected that he was having anything but a very pleasant time.

The garden was not empty. By the fading sunlight, he had an opportunity to study the girl sitting by the pool. She looked like an angel sitting there, the low sun turning her chestnut tresses into a nimbus of flame. Even clad in an ill-fitting black dress of dubious origin and lacking any of the artificial trappings of beauty, she far outstripped any of the females he had seen at Greathills—and most he had seen in London. The juxtaposition of such a beauty with such shabby clothing intrigued him. It would be hard to accept that a servant, even an upper one, would be allowed the freedom of the formal garden, but she could not be a member of the immediate family, not wearing clothes like that. The Chyngfords were all peacocks, and no one at all had a scrap of taste except perhaps the old lady, though hers appeared to have solidified some years before.

"The garden is lovely," he murmured conversationally, moving to a position where the light hit her full face.

She looked at him with eyes as blue as the pool. "It is indeed." Her voice was soft and cultured and very pleasant despite a slight slur of the North Country.

His lordship moved closer and refined his theory; a poor relation, perhaps, taken in as a companion for the old lady. A shame, for she was even more beautiful than he had thought and younger than her calm self-possession would seem to allow.

"My name is Piedmont," he said easily, and chose a seat on the pool coping, but only after carefully dusting the spot with his handkerchief.

"It is a pleasure, Mr Piedmont," replied the lovely apparition with an unconsious—and, to his lordship, somewhat amusing—democracy. "I am called Lacey," she added after a long moment. Although it was definitely not the thing even in Potter's Ford to use one's Christian name, especially without a formal introduction, Charlotte's child could see nothing wrong with speaking to someone within the confines of the family garden. Yet despite the pride she had always borne in the name, she would not summon up the courage to call herself Chyngford for the moment, not after that shattering scene earlier in the green salon.

"A lovely name for a lovely lady," replied his lordship with a little inclination of his head. "Do you live here?"

The slight figure in black stiffened as if he had said something objectionable, but her answer was softly noncommittal. "I do now. I have come here to learn to be a lady." Her tone made it sound a questionable occupation.

Jordan's eyebrows rose slightly, as did his interest. Usually a young woman's fondest dream was to have a chance to become a lady, yet here was this stunning but badly dressed child treating such an opportunity like a dose of nasty medicine.

"And will you have a Season? In Bath, perhaps, or one of the other spas?"

"Probably, though I believe Lady Chyngford"—impossible to say "Grandmother," as she had been asked—"has London in mind."

Such indifference about a London Season was a little hard to swallow, but his lordship could detect no artifice about the girl's melancholy face. Being at least eighteen or so, she was not quite a child, but despite her carriage and demeanour not quite a woman either; there was a reserve, a depth about her that intrigued him despite a longstanding resolve to avoid barely fledged girls. He smiled and, making light of the situation, asked humourously, "So you can land a nobleman, what?"—only to stop short at the furious blaze in the blue eyes.

"No," Lacey snapped, her mind full of images. Mr Stoker had claimed to be descended of noblemen, yet he had had no compunction about trying to force his attentions on a young lady under his protection. Sir Cicero, her mother's brother, even bore a title, yet had recommended she be sent away to the islands or the Americas as if she were some sort of embarrassment and, when she had hotly declined to be treated as a parcel, had challenged her ability to keep from disgracing the hallowed Chyngford name. Even the late and unlamented Sir Homer had banished his own daughter from her home and station to a life of unremitting poverty for daring to disagree with him. "I despise noblemen! They are odious and hateful."

Lord Piedmont recoiled a bit in shock at such vehemence. To one who had been used to having his station admired and envied, finding his kind held in antipathy was slightly unnerving. "That is a most unusual attitude, to say the least. Might I ask what brought about so decided an opinion?"

"Noblemen are supposed to be examples to the rest—good examples—but they take their position and misuse it with no thought at all for the feelings and desires of others," said Lacey with feeling.

"You seem to be most decided, Miss Lacey, and I own I should like to hear your reasoning further; however, I think that is the dinner gong just going, so may I escort you to the dining room where we can continue our conversation?"

She gave a strange, twisted smile. "I thank you for your kind invitation, Mr Piedmont, but I shall not be eating in the dining room tonight. There is some odiously important old man due whom Sir Cicero is anxious to impress, and I am deemed not mannered enough to join them."

"Probably well done of Sir Cicero," Jordan replied with a wry smile, never having heard what he suspected to be himself so unflatteringly described. "No, don't eat me! I just meant that in your current mood you would be just as inclined to dump the soup over the poor unfortunate's head or set about him with the roast joint."

The absurdity of the idea made Lacey laugh. "Yes, perhaps it is just as well. Good evening, Mr Piedmont. Perhaps we shall meet again." She rose.

She was taller than he had first thought, Jordan noticed, finding her to be barely half a head shorter than he. Idly, he wondered how she would do on the hunting field. A well-cut habit would become her wonderfully. Her figure, he noticed from long custom of such awareness, was excellent.

"We will most definitely meet again, Miss Lacey," he replied with surprising decisiveness, "though I doubt it shall be before you go to London . . . after you 'become a lady.' Might I be quite forward and ask a favour of you?"

Lacey regarded the handsome Mr Piedmont through cool eyes. He was unlike any man she had ever met. "Of course you may ask, but I cannot guarantee to grant it," she said, and could not resist returning his smile. He had a lovely smile, she thought, and something within her vibrated.

"When they teach you to be a lady, don't let them change you too much."

"Mr Piedmont," she replied with candour, "I don't think they will."

No, I don't think they'll be able to, Jordan thought, watching the girl depart, her figure and carriage elegant despite the cheap blacks. If she were properly gowned and coiffed, Miss Lacey—he had forgotten to find out if that were her first name or her last—would doubtless be a sensation, with those looks and such novel ideas.

After five years as one of the town's most eligible bachelors, both as Captain Piedmont and as Lord Piedmont, Jordan had seen almost every variety of young female from the drawing-room miss to a regrettably long string of lightskirts, but never had he encountered one such as this outspoken, chestnut-haired chit named Lacey. He would look forward to seeing her again in a few months' time, if the Chyngfords had not succeeded in turning her into a copy of every other mealy-mouth debutante in London.

Perhaps his visit to Greathills had not been such a dead loss after all, he thought, and walked slowly along the rose-lined path back to the house.

= 3 =

LACEY'S SUSPICIONS REGARDING the dinner arrangements
were correct; Perkins had brought her a tray sumptuously
loaded with enough delicacies to feed an entire family back
in Potter's Ford. There was mutton in a delicate sauce, rare
beef, lobster patties, green peas in cream, and a host of
other dishes which she was unable to identify even after her
time in the food-loving Stoker family.

She could not imagine the number of kitchen workers it
must have taken to produce such plentitude; her mind saw
instead the huge, inconvenient old kitchen at the vicarage
and her mother struggling to turn a stringy chicken into a
halfway tasty dish. Help at the vicarage had been both
unskilled and sporadic, and long before the time retained in
her daughter's conscious memory, Charlotte Chyngford
had preserved some semblance of a well-run larder by
taking over the chores of cooking herself. It had been a task
both difficult and challenging, for the parish was a poor
one. The Reverend Chyngford had always answered his
wife's complaints about the sparseness of their lives with
the observation that the parishioners were very good about
tithing, to which his wife usually replied that ten percent of
nothing was still nothing. Then, as likely as not, he would
take their dinner to some poor family who had nothing and
Charlotte would contrive a table of bread and milk.

With anguished eyes, Lacey looked around the bedroom,
knowing without question that it had been her mother's.
Watered-silk curtains and hangings of soft yellow, only

slightly faded from the inexorable passing of time, hung in luxurious abundance over the windows and bed. Like fabric, sprigged with tiny flowers, covered the delicate furniture, harmonising with the pale wood rubbed shiny with years of care. More candles than had been in the entire vicarage stood in graceful holders, ready to make the room as bright as midafternoon. There would be no need to huddle over a single poor candle, straining one's eyes over a piece of mending; impossible even to think of the humble task of mending in conjunction with this opulence.

Though she had fully explored her new surroundings before going out to see the gardens, Lacey now put down her fork—the elegant food tased bitter to her—and walked to the dressing room. Her feet moved easily over the thick gold-and-brown Oriental rugs and the shiny parquet floor; her casual fingertips skimmed over polished wood and soft upholstery. The appointments of Beecham Manor had not been dissimilar to those of Greathills, but they had aroused no such distasteful emotion.

The dressing room, though smaller in comparison to the lordly bedchamber, was in itself larger than the room used by Lacey at the vicarage, and even that had been icy in the winters. This room was yellow as well, an unspoken confirmation that this suite had belonged to Charlotte. Lacey well remembered her mother's fondness for that colour. Thought it was easy to connect this room with Charlottte, try as she would, Lacey could not picture her mother actually living here. How could she imagine her mother's preening in front of this multiplicity of mirrors when Charlotte had never lingered in front of a glass more than just long enough to be sure her cap was straight and no stray lock of hair had escaped? How could she conceive of her mother as idling away hours in dreams or gossip in that arrogant chamber when she had never seen her without some sort of work to hand save during Divine Services?

For a moment Lacey's youthful bitterness at having to wear ill-fitting clothes scavenged from the charity barrel or hand-made with much love but without much skill by her mother, at living in a cold and uncomfortable old barn of a house, at lacking the niceties so dear to a growing girl's greedy little heart, overcame her with a force surprising in its intensity. Why had her mother left this? How could her mother have given up such wonderful luxury for the hard life of an obscure North Country vicarage?

Immediately Lacey was ashamed of herself; normally she was neither envious nor acquisitive. She had felt neither reaction during her time with the Stokers, and to be sure their things were quite as expensive as these, albeit less elegant. But they had not been her heritage, a nagging little voice said; this had been Charlotte's. Lacey's mother had lived here in this room, among these people. . . .

And then Lacey understood. Of course she had known the skeleton facts of her parents' marriage and her subsequent lack of relations; as a child she had bemoaned not having the cousins and aunts and uncles which her playmates had in liberal supply, and her mother had told her of the opposition her family held to Barton Chyngford, which had led to their elopement. Somehow Lacey had assumed that the family which had so cruelly treated her mother had died out, for who would be so relentlessly cold and unforgiving to such a gentle creature as Charlotte Chyngford?

That was before she had met the Chyngfords of Greathills; of course, the man who had been her grandfather was dead now—that was why she was here—but if he had been anything like Sir Cicero . . . Odd to think that Sir Cicero and Lady Dunfield were her mother's brother and sister, for no people could be more different from her dear mother. There had been such love and happiness in the stark, poor vicarage of Potter's Ford; even now Lacey could close her eyes and see the trusting looks of deep and abiding love which had passed between her parents. Her father's last word on Earth had been "Charlotte . . . ," as if he were calling out to someone waiting for him a short distance away. Lacey had dreamed of loving and being loved by someone as her parents had loved each other. Love had been very important to them, yet here at Greathills love was plainly absent.

Lacey stood by the soaring windows looking out into the dark that flooded the garden, her eyes moist with slow tears. Charlotte Chyngford had sacrificed everything material to live her life and raise her child away from this cold, selfish family; now Fate had placed her daughter helpless and unprepared squarely in their clutches.

Well, vowed the daughter of Charlotte and Barton Chyngford with a surprising fierceness, they would soon find that she was no milk-and-water miss to be ordered around at their whim simply because she was a weak female. Nor would she make their lives easier by running away!

"Why would you run away?" asked a small voice. "You just got here."

With a start, Lacey turned around, realizing that she must have made her dramatic vow aloud; now she was talking to herself! "Who are you?" she asked.

The child, sensing no hostility in the atmosphere, stepped completely into the room and silently closed the door. She was a small thing, thin and dark with huge brown eyes. Hair that shone in the firelight with the bluish gloss of a blackbird's wing was plaited into a long tail, a thick vigorous growth which seemed somehow to suck all the vitality from this child.

"I am Miss Helvetia Chyngford," said the girl, in the tone of one who has been well drilled. "I live at Greathills and my father is Sir Cicero Chyngford. He is a great gentleman in London.

They certainly start teaching them young, Lacey thought, vaguely repelled by the haughty pride which emanated from even so young a Chyngford.

"Who are you? I saw you arrive in a hired coach this afternoon." The child's tone implied that such a conveyance was unacceptable for a visitor to Greathills. "This is one of the family bedrooms."

"Is it?"

"You haven't told me your name yet. Although you are my senior, it is rude for you to demand my name without giving me yours, especially as this is my house."

"And it is very rude for a child to importune her elders," replied Lacey in the schoolmistress voice she had used to the children of the church. "You seem young to be a landowner."

Obviously, Miss Helvetia Chyngford was unused to anything which crossed her wishes, for the dark eyes flashed—she might be a beauty when she grew up—but curiosity won out over temper. Visitors were apparently a rare occurrence at Greathills.

"Actually, it belongs to my father, Sir Cicero. But it will belong to me when I'm grown," Helvetia said with assurance, taking a seat on the spindly desk chair.

"Please sit down," Lacey offered with gentle irony. "I doubt that, as the estates are probably entailed, but you certainly have a right to know who I am. We would most likely be introduced properly tomorrow, but my name is Lacey Chyngford."

Dark eyes widened. "You're a relative? I thought I knew all my relatives . . . Grandmother, Aunt Leonora, Cousin Elizabeth. . . . There are lots of cousins on my mother's side, of course, but they aren't Chyngfords." Their inferiority was undoubted by the younger Miss Chyngford.

"I am your cousin as well. My mother was your father's and aunt's sister."

"I never heard of her." The young face contorted with suspicion.

"She's dead," Lacey said shortly. The child couldn't be more than eight or nine; there was no need airing the old tragedy for her benefit.

"Why did you come now? What do you want?"

Such cynicism from a child was slightly sickening. Greathills was an ugly place if it put such questions in the mind of a very young girl. "Lady Chyngford sent for me," she replied.

"And for the man? The one you were talking to in the garden?"

Apparently, there was little which the child did not see. The handsome Mr Piedmont must have intrigued a child who lived in such isolation with her grandmother, aunt, and female cousin, for a very fever of curiosity was visible on her thin features.

"I don't know. I never met him before. His name is Piedmont."

"Piedmont. I think he's here to see Cousin Elizabeth. He's the one Aunt Leonora is always saying was so nice to her in London last Season."

For absolutely no reason Lacey's throat constricted. It was a perfectly logical reason for his being here, and they had talked such a short time, but he had not seemed like a young man come to make a declaration. She could not imagine him paying court to her cousin Elizabeth, not if that as yet unknown young lady was anything like the other Chyngfords of Greathills.

"He's nice-looking, isn't he? I'll have beaux like that when I'm bigger. Father is rich and I'll be very sought after."

Somehow the child's smug complacence filled Lacey with anger; not at the girl, for she was surely too young to know any different than she was told, but at the adults who had filled her immature mind with such warped values.

"Probably, but who would want to be wooed for their money alone? It would make one into an object of trade—rather like a horse."

Obviously, such an heretical notion had never entered the young Miss Chyngford's mind, and just as obviously, it found little favour there. With dignity, she rose and walked to the door. "That is a silly idea." The door closed soundlessly behind her.

Lacey relaxed; she had not known how stiff she was. What an uncomfortable little girl, as different from the normal children of Potter's Ford as could be imagined. But

. . . was it the child's decidedly unchildlike behaviour or the information she had imparted? Despite their short association, Lacey for some reason did not like the picture of the handsome Mr Piedmont as her unknown cousin's swain. The possibility bothered her until she fell asleep.

Lord Piedmont was also finding his worst fears about dinner confirmed. The menu was excellent, though he had not worried about that, for anyone with a girth like Sir Cicero's was sure to set a good table, but the company was worse than he had dreamed. The intriguing Miss Lacey was not present, as she had predicted, but everyone else was, including the mysterious old Lady Chyngford. Five minutes in her company dispelled any idea of her being an upstairs lady; she was not only extremely interesting but charming as well.

"I do hope you won't object to dining *en famille*," Sir Cicero had boomed jovially, clapping Piedmont on the back with a heartiness that threatened the younger man's balance.

"It is so difficult to make a party of interesting people in the country, don't you agree?" gushed the Dunfield creature, taking the seat to Piedmont's right. She was clad in a creation of pink sarsanet and satin sprinkled with rosebuds which would have looked babyish on a debutante; on a plump matron of middle years it was indescribable. "So few persons of Quality reside this far away from town."

At least Lady Chyngford had the taste to be discomfited by this speech, Piedmont noticed, watching the wrinkles in her face rearrange themselves into a frown. She and Lacey seemed to be the most interesting people at Greathills, yet they said the least.

No, he was forced to amend that; that particular honour was due to Miss Elizabeth Dunfield, who sat in dreamy silence and never spoke unless prodded—sometimes urgently—by her mother.

The young Miss Dunfield was not displeasing to look at,

a fact for which Jordan was most grateful, since obvious care had been taken to seat her directly across from him. He well remembered her placid, rather bovine features, for her mother had been at great pains to see that Miss Elizabeth appeared in his line of vision wherever he happened to go last Season; avoiding her had become rather a game for him and his friends.

The child herself seemed innocuous enough and, away from her mother, might be an acceptable companion for someone whose tastes ran to sweet-faced schoolgirls with mousy hair and pallid conversation. He could not remember exactly, but it seemed all too likely that she played either the pianoforte or—Heaven forbid—the harp.

"Freedom from social obligations is one of the benefits of country living," Jordan said, and then regretted the remark. Although it had missed Lady Dunfield completely, taking such a low shot could only reflect badly on his social graces, and he had no wish to descend to her level.

"Where is your home, Lord Piedmont? You must forgive my ignorance; I have lived retired for many years," Lady Chyngford said smoothly. This young man was a gentleman, to be sure, but hardly the ardent suitor of Elizabeth which she had been led to expect. The old lady wanted to see all her grandchildren happy and knew in her heart that this strong man was not for her gentle, dreamy Elizabeth.

"I have several homes, Your Ladyship, but I maintain my seat at Foxton Chase in Devonshire. You should not remain immured here at Greathills and make London the poorer with your absence."

Sir Cicero harrumphed as Lady Dunfield twittered in wordless distress. "Your address is most polished, Lord Piedmont, but I fear it is wasted on her ladyship. She hasn't been to London in forty years."

Beneath the hideous giggles and coughs, Jordan discerned a very real nervousness in his host and hostess; there was a mystery at Greathills! Why should the idea of Lady Chyngford in London so disconcert them? Perhaps there was more to amuse him here than he had hoped. "A loss for the ton, I'm sure. You are cruel to deprive us of your company."

"My husband preferred that I should stay at Greathills," replied her ladyship serenely.

"But surely we shall see you in town when Miss Lacey has her Season . . . ," Jordan began, then stopped with a sense of being distinctly uncomfortable.

His innocent remark had indeed set the cat among the pigeons; had it not been so bewildering their reactions would have been humorous. Sir Cicero's loaded fork hovered between plate and mouth as if held there by magic, Miss Dunfield's face was totally drained of all colour, and, conversely, her mother's was flushed a dangerous red; only Lady Chyngford seemed unruffled.

"What do you know of her?" hissed Lady Dunfield.

Lord Piedmont was not used to such bald questions, and his expression showed as much, but his manner was both correct and courteous. "We met by accident in the garden just before dinner. I own I was surprised that she did not join us. I had assumed her one of the family."

As if controlled by the same string, both Lady Dunfield and Sir Cicero began to speak in somewhat disjointed babble, but it was to Lady Chyngford's soft voice that Jordan directed his attention.

"Lacey Chyngford is my granddaughter, Lord Piedmont. She has just come to live with me. Both her parents are dead, so Leonora is going to sponsor her Season."

Lady Dunfield's colour deepened to a shade so alarming that her daughter, with some concern, felt obliged to question the state of her parent's well-being and received only a terse order to be silent as a reward for her filial worry. Jordan could not resist a small twinge of all-too-human glee at her ladyship's discomfiture. All last Season she had made his life miserable by constantly shoving her daughter into his presence, a circumstance which he felt Miss Dunfield found as uncomfortable as he did. Now the situation was reversed; her high and mighty ladyship was finding out how it felt to be chivvied about by someone else, but it would be awfully hard on Miss Chyngford. . . .

Jordan decided then that if he happened to be in London he'd see what could be done about giving the child a good send-off; after all, sponsorship by the numerous and influential Piedmont family could only do Miss Lacey Chyngford good. From what he could tell, it didn't make a ha'penny's worth of difference to Miss Dunfield, for he had never discovered a love of Society in her during any of their conversations, but it would be poetic justice should the ward of an unwilling Lady Dunfield become a social success. A sense of happy mischief filled him, a feeling he had thought long dead on the battlefields of the American war.

In an unprecedented action, Sir Cicero threw himself into the breach, lowering his fork and trying to draw attention away from his irate sister. He'd have to have a talk with Leonora later, for if Piedmont had wanted her pasty-faced daughter, he'd have spoken up by now; and he, Sir Cicero, wasn't about to have his chances to get in the Four Horse Club—for which he was hoping Piedmont would sponsor him—ruined by his sister's stubbornness.

"Hear you're setting up a racing stable, Piedmont. Going to give Prinny a bit of a challenge, eh?"

With a sense of regret, Jordan realised that the fun was over and they must return to the socially acceptable forms. "With all due respect to His Highness, that would not be difficult. No, Sir Cicero, my aims are more personal. It is for that reason I'm interested in your bay stallion . . . to upgrade the quality of my string."

"You sound rather grim, Lord Piedmont. I do hope you are not one of those tiresome fanatics who eat, sleep, and breathe nothing but racing."

Piedmont smiled at the older lady. "Hardly, ma'am. I've never cared for it over the ordinary. This is more an affair of honour . . . for my father, " Jordan replied easily, never knowing how far he fell in Sir Cicero's estimation by uttering those words. Being devoted to the track—and the attendant wagering—Chyngford could not understand any man whose passion for the sport did not equal his own.

"You intrigue me. Please explain." Lady Chyngford smiled, giving an intimation of the lovely charmer she must have been in her youth and showing an unmistakable resemblance to her absent granddaughter.

"It is not a pretty story, ma'am. My father was in many ways an estimable and honourable man, but he had an unfortunate addiction to wagering, particularly on racing. He kept a fair stable, and over the years he developed what he took to be a friendly rivalry with the Duke of Lowood. While I was fighting in the Americas, my father became even more deeply involved in racing and wagering. He bet his entire stable to the duke and lost. Then, when the passion of the moment was gone, Lowood refused to sell back even one horse to my father. Said that now the question of his stable's supremacy would never be questioned."

"The bounder!" Sir Cicero exploded. He had often admired the Lowood horses, as well as having won a fair bundle on them, but such unmannerly behaviour was not sporting.

"Oh, I always knew he was a horrid man," squeaked Miss Dunfield, then froze to silence under the gimlet eye of her mother.

"I do not recall your telling me that you had the pleasure of the Duke of Lowood's acquaintance, Elizabeth." Her tone was deadly polite. Leonora cared little for the ethics of the Turf, but the duke was one of the wealthiest men in the kingdom and therefore of interest.

"We met at the Stonecipher rout, Mama. Lady Marjorie introduced us. He solicited my hand for a dance." She shivered in remembrance, then went on to answer her mother's unspoken question. "He is not a nice man, Mama. He is old and not well featured, but beyond that . . . there is something unpleasant about him!"

"The Duke of Lowood? Don't be ridiculous, child! Did he ask permission to call?"

The huntress prowls in search of bigger game, Jordan thought, and decided to go in defence of the obviously intimidated Miss Dunfield. "Are you acquainted with His Grace, ma'am?" he asked his hostess. "I've met him but rarely, yet it seems Miss Dunfield has described him most accurately."

Lady Chyngford shook her head slowly. "I was presented to Lowood during my first Season, but that was an elderly gentleman then. I am afraid I've never had the pleasure of meeting his successor. And do you seek revenge against His Grace for the insult against your father?"

"A harsh, but regrettably apt, phrasing, Your Ladyship. I suppose it is a form of revenge, but not of my own accord. After the incident, my father took up the challenge and started building back his stables again, at a ruinous cost. When his health failed, he made me promise to carry on . . . knowing that deathbed promises are doubly binding, especially when he knew my interest in racing is marginal at best. However, promises or no promises, I must go on with the plans to get any use of the funds so far expended."

"Well, the racing world will stand behind anyone who will take Lowood down a peg; never met him myself, but I hear he's a deuced hard man," Sir Cicero contributed, planting his feet firmly in the Piedmont camp. Perhaps it would be a good idea if Leonora's girl did marry the viscount; it would mean he'd have to see a lot more of his tiresome sister, but never let it be said that Sir Cicero Chyngford let personal antipathy stand in the way of acquiring even a small say-so in a top-notch racing stable!

— 4 —

Two PAIRS OF eerily identical blue eyes faced each other with wary caution, the tea tray between them forgotten. The two Louisa Anne Chyngfords were an odd mirror image of each other, as if some brilliant artist had used the same model to convey the extremes of youth and age.

The two ladies sat in the small pink-and-white morning room, the blacks of their mourning jarringly out of place in that happy little chamber. Beyond the open windows lay the rose garden, and the sweet scent from the flowers flooded the room in an almost tangible wave.

"Did you pass a comfortable night, Lacey?"

"Very much so. I thank you for giving me my mother's room, Your Ladyship."

"I thought you might enjoy it, but can you not bring yourself to call me Grandmother?"

Lacey heard the faint undertone of longing in the old lady's voice, but it was secondary to the bitter memories of her mother's hands, abused and gnarled with work, and her mother's face as she lay dying, an old, old woman of young years. "As that term is normally learned in childhood and I have never had occasion to use it, familiarising myself with it will take some time, Your Ladyship."

"Do not be impertinent with me, girl! I will not bear such conduct in my house. You will act like a lady."

"I believe I have never acted the part of anything else, madam. Let me remind you that you brought me here; it was not I who solicited *your* favour."

"You are a Chyngford. Your place is here at Greathills."

"That is outside of enough, madam!" Keeping her temper in line had always been a sore cross for the young Miss Chyngford, especially since the congregation of Potter's Ford had always been watching the vicar's daughter, looking for a pattern card of proper behaviour. Now all the old struggles appeared to have been for naught as Lacey stalked the room for all the world like some caged beast, fighting a wild urge to scream, to smash things . . . .

"Lacey—"

"My mother was a Chyngford; she was raised here, but she died in Potter's Ford worn out by work . . . yes, and by sorrow after her family—you high and mighty Chyngfords—cast her off like so much rubbish! I wonder you had the courage to look for me!"

There was more Lacey could have said, words which had been festering within her since she had first heard the story of her parents' elopement, but she was also compassionate enough to recognise the eloquent grief written across her grandmother's face.

"That was all decided a long, long time ago," her ladyship said woodenly, her heart calling down curses on the memory of Sir Homer, wishing him ill repose wherever he was. "Charlotte knew the consequences of her actions, but she went ahead."

"Consequences? Actions? You make it sound like a battle manoeuvre! My mother only wanted to marry the man she loved, a man of reputedly good family!"

Two pairs of blue eyes flashed.

"Your sarcasm is not needed, young woman!"

"And neither is your charity! Do you expect me to grovel in thanks for your taking me up? Yes, it is a wonderful chance for me and so very generous of you to give me what should have been my mother's. I will probably go to elegant banquets, though when I was young we often didn't have enough to eat; no doubt you plan to buy me beautiful gowns and boast of your charity, but my mother never had more than three dresses during my entire life! It's ghoulish, that's what it is!"

"Please don't." Lady Chyngford was indeed a lady; her request was polite and only slightly shaky, but Lacey saw the tightness about the old mouth, the iron control in the pale face, and desisted.

"My apologies, Your Ladyship. I did not mean to be so vulgarly outspoken. What I do mean to say is that since my mother was not welcome in this household, I neither expect nor need your sponsorship. I have been earning my own living and am perfectly capable to go on doing so," Lacey said quietly, feeling oddly empty. She had carried her burden of anger and bitterness so long that now it was discharged she felt hollow and somewhat ashamed of herself for indulging in such histrionics.

"It was your grandfather. He had planned a brilliant marriage for Charlotte. Sir Homer would never stand to have his will crossed." The aged voice was little more than a whisper.

Lacey resumed her seat, astonished at the misery written across the face of someone whom she had thought a monster. "So he just banished any mention of her, like a barbaric mediaeval king. And you just let him."

"Sir Homer was my husband," the old woman stated bitterly.

"Mama was your daughter!" The moment of sympathy was gone.

"I am fully aware of that, Lacey. To think of never seeing her again nearly killed me. She was the only one of the children like me. . . ."

There was no mistaking the pathos in the old voice, the bitter self-recrimination, the pain, and Lacey knew instinctively what her gentle parents would say. "Scripture tells us forgiveness is the highest form of charity, my dear," her father would intone, peering over the edge of his Bible. "To be sure, the poor creature has suffered enough, Lacey. Revenge always bears sour fruit," her mother would whisper, always loving, always kind.

A wisp of a handkerchief redolent of violet appeared before Lacey's tear-dimmed eyes.

"Why are you weeping, child?"

Lacey swabbed dutifully at her damp cheeks. "Because my parents were so very good and loving and I am so unlike them."

"And you cannot find it in your heart to forgive me?" After an embarrassed moment, Lady Chyngford withdrew her outstretched hand. Somehow she had never dreamed that Charlotte's child would be anything but delighted to have all that she could lavish on her; to find such sensibility and integrity of purpose in a younger version of herself was a distinct surprise.

"I find it difficult, ma'am" was Lacey's disturbingly honest reply. "All they did was love . . . each other, me, their parishoners, everyone. . . . What's wrong with that?"

Her ladyship sighed. Had she not, to her sorrow, asked Homer the exact same question, and repeated it to herself over and over again through the years?

"Lacey . . . my dear, listen to me. Your mother was raised to be a Chyngford. That means she had a great deal of wealth and privilege, but in return for that, she, like the rest of our class, was expected to bear certain responsibilities. An excellent marriage had been arranged for her with a most acceptable young man. The match would have entailed a most advantageous financial settlement as well as bringing a considerable amount of land into the family. Charlotte rebelled and in eloping brought both embarrassment and disgrace to her family."

"But she didn't love that other man and she loved my father. Doesn't love count for anything?"

Seeing the echo of Charlotte's rebellion flaring in the face of Charlotte's daughter, Lady Chyngford despaired. "Not among our class, Lacey. We would never had forced a match with anyone whom Charlotte found distasteful, but even that is not as rare as one would like to think. Love, to people like us, is supposed to come after marriage."

Something in her grandmother's voice made Lacey look up with interest. The old lady's face was still pale, but her eyes were focussed into some far past which only she could see, suffusing the sagging features with an indescribable sadness. "What have you known of love?" Lacey asked softly.

"I? Would you be surprised to know that I was once loved? Beautifully, extravagantly, wonderfully loved? Don't shake your head; of course you are. I'm a hard old woman, but once I was as young and fresh as you." Louisa Anne, Lady Chyngford, looked back over the years and sighed. "That was so long ago."

"What happened?" prompted Louisa Anne, Miss Chyngford. "Please tell me."

"I was sixteen then . . . two years younger than you are now."

"And you were in love," said Lacey, vaguely surprised that her grandmother should know her age so exactly.

"Yes. I was in love." The memory of brief happiness touched her face and for a moment magically erased the lines of age and bitterness. "His name was Alastair Crewes. We met at a hunt meet. He was the best rider I had ever seen. That's what first drew me to him, for there were a dozen men there more handsome than he, but there was something about him. . . . We fell in love."

A smile of singular beauty touched the faded lips. She was talking almost to herself now, as if she were alone, examining the old memories like souvenirs.

How wonderful that short summer had been! They had enjoyed each other's company, planning their future and the wonderful life they would have. Being the son of a second son, Alastair was not heir to a large fortune, but there was an estate on which they could have lived in comfort and sufficient income for a style of living which, though modest, would not have been embarrassing. Young Louisa Anne Hampstead had never dreamed that her life should not follow a plan so happily laid out, for to anyone initiated in the ways of Fashion her chosen love was of acceptable fortune and impeccable birth, two of the major criteria for parental acceptance.

Unhappily, in the Hampstead parental eye the modest charms of Mr Crewes did not measure against the superior ones of Sir Homer Chyngford. So when Alastair left to see about setting his estate in order before speaking formally to Mr Hampstead, that worthy informed his daughter that Sir Homer was going to pay his addresses and that she would accept. No correspondence was allowed between the two lovers, and before the end of summer Louisa Anne Hampstead had become Lady Chyngford.

Lacey listened to the story with rapt attention, her tender heart touched. "Well? And what happened?"

"Your grandfather and I contrived a civil enough life." Her ladyship's cutting tone warned Lacey not to tread further in that particular direction.

"But what about your Mr Crewes? What did he say about all this?"

"I don't know. I never saw nor heard from him since that summer day he left to make his home ready for me. He's probably been dead these many long years. . . ." Lady Chyngford sighed. "I've often wondered how different my life would have been had we been allowed to marry."

"And you just let them sell you off to the highest bidder, like a piece of livestock, with no consideration for your feelings!"

"It was my duty," the old lady murmured, and in doing so summed up an entire philosophy. "Helvie was right. She could not wait to see me this morning and tell me about all the strange things you said. From what she told me, it sounds as if you delivered a moralising lecture last night. I do hope you are not one of those vulgar bluestockings with notions of independence."

"I did talk to Helvie when she came to my room. I found her ideas hideous. She has an arrogance that is most unsuitable in a child of her age and a manner that is an insult in a person of any age, plus a notion of herself as an article of barter! That is nothing more than a form of slavery, for as Miss Wollstonecraft says—" Lacey stopped as her grandmother gave an exclamation of horror.

"That creature! You have not read anything by that unnatural female or her accursed family, have you?"

"As a matter of fact, I have. Mrs Stoker—my late employer—had me read *A Vindication of the Rights of Women* to her several times. I thought it to be quite a sensible work on the whole. Perhaps it is too far ahead of its time to be entirely possible now, but there is so much to be done! I tell you—"

"Please do nothing of the kind! I have no desire to hear anything about that brazen female, nor about that Godless atheist her widower is sheltering."

"Shelley's rejection is more of empty organized ritual than of a monotheistic deity, ma'am. If one reads *Queen Mab* with a nonsectarian—"

Lady Chyngford froze the words on her granddaughter's lips with one imperial glance. "I have no desire to read anything by anyone of that immoral crowd, and while you are in my house and under my protection, you will forget that you ever have. Between the two of us, we can make a happy life for you, but you must work with me. I find your ideals and thoughts highly unsuitable in a young lady of your station, and I pray that as you learn more of life you will agree with me and forget such silly fancies. Do you understand?"

The law was thus laid down, and Lacey did understand.

During the five months following that conversation, an understanding grew between the two Louisa Annes, much to the dismay of the rest of the family. An air of uneasy civility prevailed over Greathills, though had there been such a thing as a casual visitor, the family would have appeared to be one of the utmost amiability. No quarrel ruffled their serene lives, everyone worked diligently at being cheerful and agreeable, but under all was an invisible tension.

Lacey had been looking forward to making the acquaintance of her cousin Elizabeth, but that estimable young lady regarded her with a chill courtesy sharply edged with suspicion so that what might have been a dear friendship withered to a mutual tolerance. Any sort of intimate relationship with either Aunt Leonora or Uncle Cicero was out of the question, so Lacey, long accustomed by a solitary childhood to keeping her own counsel, settled into an unaccustomed life of leisure and luxury.

Only in conversation with her grandmother did she approach anything like companionship, and as the time passed it became natural—to the old woman's delight and her relatives' distaste—for Lacey to call her grandmother by that same intimate and desired appellation.

Helvie proved herself to be not only a precocious child but one desperately in need of the counsel and companionship of children her own age. Acting on her own limited experience with the children in Potter's Ford, Lacey deduced the cause for Helvie's self-absorption and arranged for her to meet other acceptable children from the neighborhood, to a form of success. Lacey still felt that the child would have been more benefitted by a wider circle of acquaintance, including some of the farmers' children, but neither Sir Cicero nor Lady Chyngford would contenance such a revolutionary action, so Lacey was forced to be content with what little changes she had wrought.

Now change was the order of the day, for it was autumn, almost time for the Season to begin, and the oddly assorted group had removed to London. Leave-taking had been harder than Lacey expected; she had grown very fond of her grandmother and even of little Helvie, yet despite her impassioned entreaties they could not be lured to town.

Helvie was due to start lessons with her new governess, and the distractions of London life would not be good for her; perhaps a visit after the Christmas holidays . . . As for herself, Grandmother Chyngford merely shrugged and said, "I have been away too long. There is nothing for me there."

Looking back on that sad farewell from the security of her London bedroom, Lacey felt her eyes moisten slightly. All her life she had wanted nothing more than someone to love and be loved by, only to have all the people she loved most snatched cruelly away by Death, leaving her alone each time. Her dear mother and father had left her behind, even as had dear Mrs Stoker; thus had it been a severe trial for Lacey to leave her now beloved grandmother for fear that she, like the others, would vanish without warning.

Not that she had much time to brood, she reflected; from the moment they had set foot in London and put up the knocker, life had been a dizzying round of dress fittings, shopping expeditions, and morning calls on people who had looked her over as if she were a prize calf, then retreated behind their fans for a quick consultation in hurried whispers. Lady Dunfield had organized their assault on London Society with a singleness of purpose that was almost frightening as well as admirable; no general planning a battle campaign could have done better.

Before leaving Greathills, her ladyship had written a score of letters to her most intimate friends regarding her plans; to ensure their enthusiastic cooperation, she wrote about having the honour—with only a slightly wry twist to her mouth as she did so—of bringing out her niece. As the entire circle of her acquaintance knew that her only niece was Miss Helvetia Chyngford, who was just nine years old, Leonora cannily added an enticing bit about the girl's having been lost for a number of years and gave a soupçon of a hint that there was a dark scandal involved which she was obliged to keep secret but of course would have no qualms about telling her most trusted correspondent.

As her ladyship had intended, the bait worked like a charm, conjuring up a fair social calendar for them before the family even reached London.

London was almost beyond Lacey's comprehension; to a girl from a quiet vicarage in a small town off the main roads, the city was like something from a dream. Finely painted carriages drove through streets filled with waste and offal, pulled by horses who were better fed and cared for than the people on the sidewalks; prosperous-looking burghers in staid brown suits walked past ladies in dresses so delicate as to be indecent and beggars in filthy rags, all without any noticing the other.

The noise was an affront to Lacey's country-bred ears, for it seemed that everyone was involved in yelling—screaming abuse or cajoling their animals through the crush or selling a variety of wares from hand-held baskets—until the very air seemed to shake from such clamour. Carriages clattered over cobblestones, horses neighed, dogs barked, doors slammed. . . . Lacey wondered how anyone in this city could think, let alone converse. Later she was to find the small square where they lived tolerably quiet, but even so it was a far cry from the somnolent peace of the country.

Still, the ton was a fascinating place and Lacey had never lost her curiosity about it. On the day of their arrival, she had dropped the carriage's curtains only at her aunt's peevish command to stop gawking like a green goose. Aunt Leonora thought it ill-bred to show such blatant curiosity. And Heaven knew what sort of undesirable person might look at them! She had relented later, allowing the curtains to remain open on their subsequent journeys about town, since their routes took them through areas in which they wished to be seen, avoiding the poor slums where they might be forced to look upon the attendant ills of poverty.·

Even the square on which they lived fascinated Lacey; whenever possible, she would stand staring out the window, usually while her aunt and cousin chattered of places and people unknown to her. Built less than a century before, Harvey Square had not changed since. White-fronted town houses lined the four streets, looking for all the world like frosted cakes; there were twenty of them in all, and all faced on a tiny green jewel of a park in the square's centre.

By observation Lacey had learned a great deal about their neighbours; Number Sixteen was very popular socially, for rarely a day went by that at least half a dozen carriages didn't stop there. Number Five had a small baby still in arms, and the nurse carried it into the park every afternoon for an airing. Number Eleven surely belonged to a bachelor, for there were loud parties held there almost nightly, and on two occasions Lacey had been pulled from sleep by the noise. On occasion Lacey had dared to sit in the park for half an hour or so and take pleasure from the proximity of growing things, until her aunt had forbidden it as being dreadfully déclassé.

It would have been nice to be in the country today, Lacey thought, to be walking a hedgerow and smelling the incomparable perfume of the autumn wildflowers: She found herself more unsure than ever about this idea of a London Season. The more she learned about Society, the more it seemed she didn't belong.

"Lacey! Lacey, I vow you're asleep just like a horse—standing up and with your eyes open!"

"I'm sorry, Elizabeth. I was thinking."

Elizabeth shook her cap of curls. "I don't know about you. Who would want to think when they're in London? Anyway, Mama sent me to fetch you. The dresses from Berthe's have come! They're all in Mama's room and we're to come try them on, and guess what? We have been invited to a ball tonight!"

"A ball? A real ball?" Despite any misgivings she might have felt, Miss Lacey Chyngford would have required a stronger character than she possessed not to be excited at the prospect of her first London ball.

"Yes . . . at the Stanton-Hoggs'. Mama says it is frightfully late for an invitation, but Mrs Stanton-Hogg sent the most civil letter apologising for its tardiness, saying she had no idea we were in town."

In her excitement over such a treat, Elizabeth forgot herself enough to link arms with her cousin, and in this companionable attitude escorted her down the hall. Her hair had been cut almost shockingly short in a cluster of curls the day before when Monsieur Antoine had condescended to come to the Chyngford establishment. He was the most celebrated hairdresser in London, and despite the days of waiting it took to have him, Lady Dunfield would have no other. He had immediately shorn Elizabeth most shockingly—over that young lady's protest—saying that nothing but the 'Nosegay' would do for her. After the last tress had fallen and Elizabeth's tears had dried, all had been compelled to admit that Monsieur Antoine's inspiration had been genius. For Lacey he did nothing so spectacular, declaring to Lady Dunfield's displeasure that some things were too perfect to be tampered with, instead merely trimming to give Lacey a delicate, almost old-fashioned look.

"I thought your mother wrote her friends that we were coming in," said Lacey to her cousin.

"She did. I only know of twice that Mrs Stanton-Hogg has been presented to Mama, and they've never been close. Mrs Stanton-Hogg is fabulously wealthy and closely connected with all sorts of the right people, but for all that, she is only a 'Mrs.' I think she married beneath her," confided Elizabeth with the peculiar naiveté that equated a title with happiness, "for Mama says she is a close connection of the Piedmonts."

=5=

SIR CICERO, HAVING been deprived while at Greathills of his gaming and other, more questionable modes of entertainment, had come to town some weeks before the women, ostensibly to oversee the opening of the town house. Family was all well and good in its place, but when the family consisted of nothing but bickering petticoats, it behooved a man to get back to his proper circle.

Chyngford's not inconsiderable ego had been flattered to no end that not long after his return Lord Piedmont on two occasions had sought his company, being most complimentary both times about the bay stallion which he had purchased, and commending Sir Cicero's knowledge of horseflesh. Sir Cicero had almost reconciled himself to having his sister and her daughter about him the rest of his life, but now there seemed to be definite interest on Piedmont's part; each time they had met, he had asked to the health of Chyngford's pretty niece and her cousin, and when they might be expected in town.

Now that the family was actually in residence, though, Sir Cicero was beginning to have second thoughts about the advisability of such an intimate relationship with them. Leonora was becoming damned bossy and cross all the time; Elizabeth was constantly aquiver with excitement until she resembled a most unnatural greyhound. The thought of having a first-class Season after that fiasco last year had gone to her rather empty head, so that she prattled incessantly of dresses and parties and titled gentlemen

dancing attendance. The year before, the Dunfield excheq-
uer had only extended to a paltry type of a showing; and
being at the moment somewhat embarrassed in the pocket,
Sir Cicero had been unable to help, which he probably
would have, despite what his sister had thought. At the
moment only his new niece Lacey escaped the baronet's
immediate displeasure, a circumstance which was probably
due to the fact that she was quiet and stayed out of his way.
A pretty enough little thing she was turning out to be,
despite her radical ways. Handled carefully, she might
even do the family proud.

"Cicero Chyngford, you have not heard a word I said!"

The comment was somewhat superfluous, as both parties knew quite well that Sir Cicero never listened to his
sister with more than half an ear at most. Still, one of the
few words he had caught was "importantly," so with an
effort to be pleasant, the baronet leaned forward, recklessly
imperilling his balance on the spindly-legged chair, and
with a mighty effort focussed his attention.

"Sorry, Leonora. What was it?"

"I was telling you about the Stanton-Hogg ball and how
important it is that you escort us!" Lady Dunfield's flushed
face clashed against the livid purple of her gown. She had
loved it at Berthe's, but, being unable at the time to afford
that lady's exorbitant prices, had tried to have it duplicated
by a less skilled modiste; the result—especially when
placed in the orange-and-white drawing room of the town
house—was indescribable.

"I'm sorry, but tonight's the night I've pledged Harry
Parkhurst a game of dice at Boodle's. Seems damned—
pardon—short shrift for a ball invitation. Is she trying to
diddle us?"

Her ladyship stared upwards to the carved ceiling and
waited for control; really, of all the creatures on Earth, she
was the most beleaguered! With her abilities and ambi-
tions, to have been shackled with an eccentric mother, a
do-less brother, and a husband who had been less than

worthless—he had died during one of his penniless turns— was almost more than a Christian body could stand.

"That is what I've been trying to explain, Cicero! Mrs Stanton-Hogg is a lady of excellent qualities, but we have never been more than acquaintances. However, she is a first cousin of Lord Piedmont, and I had it from Clarissa Hovington this morning that we were asked to the ball at his especial request!"

"Deuced nice of him, I should say, but I see him at the club. No need to break my date with Parkhurst—"

Without a blush Leonora uttered an oath more suited to the stables than to a lady's lips. "I declare you are the dullest man alive! The viscount had his cousin invite us. Remember how you told me he always asked about your pretty niece and when she was coming to town? It's Elizabeth he wants to see, and I think you are a most unnatural uncle for not wanting to be there!"

"Think he's after your Lizzie, huh?" Sir Cicero leaned forward, a new gleam invading his piggy eyes; if he fostered the romance, perhaps he could get a part of the stables as a marriage settlement. . . . Of course, he was only the girl's uncle, but since her father was dead and he himself was an acknowledged Patron of the Turf, surely something could be arranged! "So quickly?"

"Don't call her by that vulgar name. Only servants are called Lizzie," snapped Leonora. The new fashion of informally diminutising names found no favour with her.

"Elizabeth, then. He did seem to take kindly to her at Greathills . . . was most charitable about her playing the pianoforte. Even complimented her!"

"She was out of practice," Leonora snapped automatically, ignoring the undisputed fact that no matter how much Elizabeth practiced, her ability would not rise to the professional heights her mother demanded.

"Lizzie . . . Elizabeth, a viscountess. Surely sounds all right to me. I never thought you'd pull it off, old girl. Tell you what: I'll send a note around to Parkhurst. He's a bachelor, but surely he'll understand the sacrifices a man must make for his family!"

It may well be imagined that a young lady of fashion on the brink of her first London Season would be excited; it may be equally imagined that a young lady raised in a poor North Country vicarage in such a situation would be terrified. Miss Lacey Chyngford, despite indubitable courage concerning things she knew and understood, was only human and therefore vulnerable to alarm. That very night she would actually appear among Society at its most exclusive, its most glittering, a wholly more overpowering undertaking than merely drinking tea with one group of silly ladies after another. That night would be a test, for that exalted group called the ton could decide which course one's life might take. If they approved, you were accepted as one of them and, as the naughty rhyme said, "could do no wrong"; if they disapproved of a debutante, she might as well plan to emigrate to the other side of the world.

"Lacey, you appear pale. Are you quite well?" Leonora's voice came from the bottom of the stairs. Though the words were friendly enough, the tone was cold. Her niece looked all too well for Lady Dunfield's comfort.

Smoothing her long white kid gloves as if an untoward wrinkle would ruin her forever, Miss Chyngford stood at the top of the stairs. The hallway lights picked up the brilliant chestnut of her hair and set it glowing with deep, rich colour. By contrast she was pale, but it was an interesting pallor, seeming to grow out of the white dress that clung to her statuesque figure.

"I am fine, Aunt; merely a little nervous."

What a pity debutantes could wear only white, Lacey thought. Her figure was ghostlike in the stairwell mirrors as she descended. She had always preferred pure colours, such as blue and yellow, to complement her hair and skin. Elizabeth was so fortunate to be in her second Season and therefore privileged to wear colours, though the shrimp pink she had on tonight was an unfortunate choice.

Being a modest girl, Lacey could not compare herself favourably with her cousin, a fact that was all to Elizabeth's good, for Lacey looked a fairy princess. Her dress had been designed by Madame Berthe herself, a flattering confection of silk so delicate it almost seemed transparent, caught under the breasts by a ribband studded with diamonds and silver-thread embroidery. Lady Dunfield had thought it dreadfully plain, but Lacey was grateful that her grandmother had made it quite clear that Lacey alone would have the final say on her own wardrobe, within certain easy limitations, the primary of which was that Madame Berthe would personally approve every item of clothing purchased for Miss Chyngford.

That ultimatum had caused a memorable family row, after which Leonora retired to her room for two days with hysterics that Elizabeth feared would turn into brain fever; but Lady Chyngford, knowing her daughter, held her ground . . . and her pocketbook.

When at last the agreement had been reached, Lady Dunfield said nothing, which was just as well with the rest of her family. It was well known to all save her ladyship that Leonora's taste was notorious—as evidenced by her choice for the evening: a garnet-red gown and a cloth-of-gold turban studded with sapphires. At least, Lacey thought philosophically, she hadn't begun damping her dresses as the French ladies did.

Lady Dunfield waited until they were in the carriage to make her attack. "I thought you were going to wear Mother's little diamonds tonight, Lacey; I had them sent up to your room earlier."

Automatically, Lacey's fingers went up to the two Wedgewood silhouettes of the lovers' necklace. She had chosen it hoping that it would act as a talisman, giving her some of old Mrs Stoker's courage. "I know, ma'am. I had Bailey take them back to the safe. I prefer to wear this one."

Sir Cicero harrumphed briefly in the dark. The girl must be demented, preferring cheap enamel and china to diamonds. One could only hope that Piedmont wouldn't notice and shy away from Elizabeth just because her cousin was a bit coddled in the noggin.

"I did not ask you what you preferred, Lacey. I told you to wear the diamonds. Elizabeth did not disdain to wear what I chose for her, I hope you notice."

Lacey had indeed noticed the magnificent coral *paure* which decorated and almost overwhelmed her cousin's person. It was a perfect colour match for her dress, but unfortunately, whenever Elizabeth blushed—which was often—dress, beads, and skin ran together to create a monochrome whole.

"You will remove it at once," said Leonora to her niece.

"But Mama," Elizabeth wailed, "we haven't time to go back to the house, and then Lacey will be without a necklet!"

"Be quiet, Elizabeth."

Lady Dunfield had indeed seen the bauble when Lacey first appeared like a princess at the top of the stairs and she had purposely waited until this moment to demand that it be removed. It was indeed too late to return to the house, which meant that Lacey would go without jewels to the party, a solecism roughly equal to going only half-dressed. After such a gaffe, no one could possibly take her seriously—after all, she was just a poor relation jumped up from nowhere. When news of the ton's rejection reached Lady Chyngford at Greathills, she would have to acknowledge her mistake and will her funds to Elizabeth. Lady Dunfield's smile was wolfish.

"With all due respect, dear Aunt, I will wear my necklace. It is very dear to me."

"And very old-fashioned! I vow Mother wore one like that when she was a girl. Do you wish to become a quiz?" Her ladyship let loose a determinedly girlish trill of laughter which instantly put the others' teeth on edge.

"Some things in the old fashion are worth keeping," Lacey replied sweetly. At that moment Mrs Stoker's gift was more than an ornament to Miss Chyngford; it had passed into the realm of a symbol. Had it been a savage fetish of feathers and bone, she would have fought for the freedom to wear it.

Leonora shrugged; she had tried to do her duty as a chaperone. If the girl was a headstrong fool determined on ruining herself, it was not a fault of hers, and she said so emphatically.

Lacey's aunt's exhortation went almost unnoticed, for the Stanton-Hogg house was approaching, and what ill-tempered lecture could hope to compete with a scene of crowding carriages and *flambeaux* runners, of elegantly dressed guests and shabby street-side watchers?

Lacey had never seen such a spectacle; everything seemed to take on a magical glow under the runners' torches. Indeed, it was a scene taken straight from the old fairy tales. As she watched the guests mount the red-carpeted stairs, a sizeable lump seemed to grow in Lacey's throat. As soon as their carriage worked its way to the door, they would be going in the same way; she would be socialising on an equal basis with all those figures of fantasy.

Elizabeth all but hung out the window, showing off her perusal of the Court News by naming off all the partygoers in the tones of an excited child.

"There's the Lane-Harrises—he's ever so good-looking— and Lord Bromford and the Thorleys and that elegant Mrs Valelyn, and there's Lord Petersham!" Her voice dropped with awe.

As the excellencies of that gentleman had often arisen in Elizabeth's chatter, Lacey leaned even farther forward in her curiosity. "Which one? That funny-looking man with the padded shoulders? You must be roasting me!"

"He is only the foremost dandy in London," Elizabeth replied condescendingly. "Everyone thinks he is the veriest Pink of the Ton. I've heard it isn't unusual for him to be seen in three or four complete outfits in one day and each in the same shade of brown."

"That's ridiculous!" her cousin cried, fully expecting a fight, but Elizabeth had already followed another thought, and turned to her mother with a lively face.

"Mama! Do you think he will bring Miss Foote tonight?" Lady Dunfield harrumphed with affronted dignity. "An actress? He'd best not try to bring that woman to a party like this! The ton would never forgive him!"

Slowly, the carriage inched forward. It seemed rather silly to Lacey for them to wait such a long time, until the carriage drew abreast of the red-carpet walkway, but even though they were so near, she wisely refrained from suggesting they walk. To arrive by carriage made an impressive entrance, and Aunt Leonora would never hear of another kind.

"Uncle Cicero, how did the Stanton-Hoggs get to be so important?" asked Elizabeth. "He isn't even a knight."

"They're nobodies who just happen to have a lot of money—"

"Now, Leonora, don't you start muttering! Both Stanton-Hogg and his wife—she was a Farquahar, I believe—came from excellent families . . . both totally unexceptional. Only trouble was, both were poor as church mice. Diana went to their wedding and said it was the paltriest thing she'd ever seen—only five removes at the reception and sour champagne, as if a woman could have a palate for such a thing. She died not long after, poor dear." Sir Cicero gave a sigh. He had been sincerely, if not deeply, attached to his late wife and gave her every compliment, even if now he could barely remember her features. "Anyway, they hadn't been married long when some blackguard uncle of his who'd been sent away years before died rich as a nabob and made the boy his heir!"

"Well," Elizabeth said doubtfully, "that made it all right, but how horrible it must have been to marry a man knowing you'd have to wait for the money."

"That's the rich part," Sir Cicero replied, and chuckled at

his own pun. "No one knew that he was going to get it. Quite a nine-days' wonder it made in town, too, for everyone thought the old man had died long since."

"And now they're lording it over everyone," Leonora muttered bitterly. "They've got enough money to."

Elizabeth was still puzzled. "But if he was poor and didn't even have any sort of an inheritance or a title, why did her parents allow her to marry him in the first place?"

Having bitten her lips and clenched her hands until everything was numb, Lacey could stay silent no more. "Because she loved him, you goose!"

Doubtless there would have been some sharp remonstrance from her aunt if not from her cousin—and Lacey was fully prepared to enjoin in a spirited battle—but the carriage had pulled to a showy stop in front of the red carpet and the footmen were reaching up to hand them down. Due to a miscalculation on Lady Dunfield's part, Lacey was the closest to the carriage door; her ladyship had planned for Elizabeth to alight first, in all her glory, outshining her upstart cousin, but somehow things had not worked out as her ladyship had planned, so that to exit first, Elizabeth would have had to clamber most ungracefully over her cousin.

So it was that Lacey dismounted first, putting her foot on the tiny step as if she had been alighting from expensive carriages all her life. She could hear the slight murmur of approval that passed through the assembled crowd of streetwatchers lining the red carpet and could not help but wonder what those people thought, they who stood and watched the Quality going to amuse themselves. Times were difficult, jobs were scarce and bread ever scarcer, yet here the ton went to parties in garments the price of any single one of which would have fed a family for a year. What did those people think who so approved of the way she looked?

Lacey did not know how ethereal she looked in her white

dress, standing under the flaring *torchères*, their light flashing dazzlingly from the diamonds and embroidery on her bodice. It was enough to turn a man's head.

The sounds of a small altercation caused Lacey to turn around; Elizabeth's shoe heel was caught in the hem of her skirt, trapping her in a most ungraceful position in the doorway and causing quite a noticeable delay in the procession of arriving carriages. No footman would think of touching a lady's ankle in such a situation, and the carriage rocked as Lady Dunfield rearranged her position to attend to the emergency, all the while apostrophising her daughter as a graceless, unnatural girl in a low voice which nevertheless carried very well.

Lacey's full attention never reached the small domestic drama, for it was caught and held by an almost spectral face, gloomily framed by a carriage window. The carriage had been brought to a sudden stop, for the horses were prancing in their traces, but it was not that which brought a gasp from the crowd, not the dried and sunken face which stared whitely out.

Even as green a newcomer as Lacey could recognise the strawberry leaves of a ducal crest, though not the arms of the family. The crowd seemed to approve—it seemed a duke was always approved—but Lacey stood as if frozen. Only she could be sure that the unknown cadaverous face had been staring directly at her with a surprised expression which very much resembled a gasp of horror.

—6—

JORDAN, VISCOUNT PIEDMONT, was in his cousin's bad looks. Venetia Stanton-Hogg was devoted to her Jordy and had been since childhood, but at the time he was really too much. She had seen his point when he had asked her to invite the Duke of Lowood to her gathering—after all, it was only the stuffiest of hostesses or those with pretty young daughters who refused to receive him, and Jordan's plea not to make the unpleasantness over the stables into a full-blown feud was sensible—but she had been appalled at his insistence on the inclusion of the Chyngford ménage in her party.

"Really, Jordy!" she had expostulated when he had pressed his argument. "You can't mean it! Sir Cicero is a notorious gamester—and a bit on the shady side from what I hear—and as for that Dunfield creature . . . she's laughed at all over town for being such a social-climber. Don't you remember how she pushed that plain daughter of hers at you all year . . ." Venetia's voice faded as quickly as her complexion as the dreaded thought came. "Jordan! You aren't possibly thinking . . ."

Jordan laughed heartily. "You should see your face, Vinnie! It's as white as your lace. No, you needn't worry about my succumbing to the dubious charms of the Dunfield chit, but I will admit there is a girl there who intrigues me."

Immediately attentive, Venetia leaned forward. Jordy had always been very much in the petticoat line, but usually he had been the pursued rather than the pursuer; his exerting himself enough to request that she invite a girl was interesting, but for him to insist on her inclusion despite the obvious disadvantage of her family was unheard of.

Venetia begged for details. "After all, Jordy, if I am going to invite these people to my house, I should know why. I've got to be able to tell Bernard something, for to be sure he will be livid. He hates Lady Dunfield since that unpleasantness at the deLieven rout."

"Especially since the dear princess isn't as picky about her guest lists as you are," teased Piedmont, his eyes alight. He was more than fond of his cousin and her husband, both as childhood playmates and as adult friends. They had shared many adventures and much affection through their lives, at times the only affection he had known; if he had not felt so, he could not have insisted so blithely on an invitation for the Chyngford contingent.

"I'll tell you, Vinnie. Do you remember that trip I made to Greathills last spring about that big bay stallion?"

"Indeed I do. Bernard said you were driving into the lion's mouth."

"It wasn't quite that bad; just almost. Anyway, before dinner—which was excellent, by the way—I took a turn in the garden, and there sat this exquisite child named Lacey—"

"Lacey! What a lovely name!"

"Yes, I agree, but don't interupt. She had on the most awful mourning dress, and at first I thought she was some sort of servant, but then she said that she had come to learn to be a lady and that Lady Chyngford—the old lady I told you about—had a London Season planned for her. Didn't sound like she was too enthused about it, and said she doesn't like noblemen."

Jordy paused there as if for a suitable comment, but Venetia wore a look of amazement. "How extraordinary! I thought that Lady Chyngford had died years ago."

"I had heard that, too. But she is quite alive. Another mystery."

"How *very* extraordinary. Well, and what did this exquisite Lacey say about you?"

Lord Piedmont smiled as if at some extremely funny joke. "She didn't. After I said my name was Piedmont, she said, 'Hello, Mr Piedmont,' as nicely as you please."

Venetia's jaw dropped. It was inconceivable to her that any female in the entire country over the age of twelve should not know her cousin's title and honours, for it seemed that each one of them wanted to marry him. Although she had held her breath over a few, until now he had never evinced more than a casual interest in the many hearts thrown at his face.

"She's roasting you!"

"I doubt it. She looks as if a lie would choke her, but there is something odd going on there, for she didn't join us for dinner that night, and when I mentioned having met her, a cloak of silence descended on all her relatives. I tell you, for a minute I thought I'd seen a family ghost or something."

"Well, don't stop there, goose! Tell me what happened!"

"Nothing. Lady Chyngford then said very graciously that Lacey was her granddaughter and had just come to live at Greathills, and that was it. Until I left the next morning—as quickly as I could, believe me—it was very obvious that the child's name was not to be mentioned."

Vinnie's fine white brow wrinkled in thought, making a serious face which looked incongruous under a tousled mop of guinea-gold curls. "How odd! I have heard of only two children in that family . . . the Dunfield one and poor Diana Wentworth's child. It's at least seven years since Diana died, so that girl must be about nine now."

"I'd say, and a total brat too."

"Poor darling, did they foist her on you, too? How sad Diana would be that her daughter turned out like that. She was always such an exquisite creature. Jordan . . . do you think . . . ? I know the Chyngfords are a rackety bunch, but surely they wouldn't be sponsoring the girl into Society if she were illegitimate? Not even *they* would do something so vulgar!"

"I don't think so . . . not that I would put much past Sir Cicero or that Dunfield woman if it would benefit them, but Lady Chyngford struck me as a totally different sort. Heaven only knows how the rest of her family turned out as they did, but I know she wouldn't have anything to do with a havey-cavey deal. Besides, I'd lay a guinea to a goose that neither Chyngford nor Lady Dunfield was enthusiastic about the project."

Vinnie laughed. She was an exquisite creature, dainty and delicate against Piedmont's muscular bulk. "Trust you to land in the middle of such a mysterious imbroglio, Jordy! Very well, I'll invite them all, but I wish you could find your mysteries among more congenial people. Bernard will be furious. Now, tell me about this mysterious young lady of yours."

"She is . . ." Jordan paused, a half-smile which alarmed his cousin no end creeping over his face, "unusual."

Now, the day after that rather unsatisfactory conversation had taken place, Venetia was having definite second thoughts. No guest at her glittering party could have divined that their hostess was upset; her golden curls lay in careful disarray, exquisitely threaded with pearls to match the pearl embroidery on her sea-green gown. Though she had been lauded during her Season as a Pocket Venus, she thought herself lamentably short, a questionable defect which did not stop her from being adored by Society despite the fact that to enjoy watching the dazzling array of her guests she was obliged to stand a few risers up the staircase.

Jordan and Bernard both looked well tonight, she thought with affection. She was indeed the luckiest woman in the world to have the two best-looking men in the room—if not in London—standing with her. Bernard was as usual quite conservative, having chosen to wear cream satin knee breeches, a waistcoat embroidered in three shades of yellow, and a jacket of gold brocade. Secretly, Venetia preferred such opulence to the scarecrow black and snowy linen of the new fashion Jordy preferred, but she had not the heart to refuse him her door, even though he did wear full-length trousers for evening.

She had been unable to pry any more information from him about his mysterious girl and so was all the more interested when her butler at last announced in sonorous tones that the Chyngford party had arrived. There was the Dunfield woman and her daughter in front, the daughter attired in a salmon hue all wrong for her ruddy skin and the mother in a gown of garnet colour which would give a jeweller a headache. Beside Venetia, Bernard tensed, rehearsing the peal he would ring over her head later in the evening for joining in another of her cousin's wild schemes, even as he was listening politely to Lady Dunfield's effusions.

"Miss Lacey Chyngford."

Venetia gasped at the vision before her. Jordan had said she was unusual, but he had never said she was such an Amazonian beauty! Fully a head taller than Mrs Stanton-Hogg, crowned with a reddish-brown swirl of hair, the mysterious Miss Lacey Chyngford was a beauty.

No, thought Vinnie a moment later; pretty, but no beauty. There was too much strength in that chiselled face and too much intelligence obvious in those startling blue eyes for her to be called beautiful, but it seemed that Vinnie was the only one who noticed. Bernard was practically gibbering a welcome to this otherworldly creature on his wife's left even as Lady Dunfield was gushing over poor Jordy to her right.

"It is so kind of your dear cousin to invite us to her ball," her ladyship simpered. "Dear Elizabeth was all atwitter from the moment we got the invitation, for we had no idea dear Mrs Stanton-Hogg knew we had returned to town. We have been looking forward so much to seeing you again!"

Elizabeth had the sensibility to blush, erasing all distinction between her dress and jewels. Lord Piedmont ground his teeth and could not restrain taking a small glance at Lacey, who was talking composedly with a bewildered-looking Bernard.

Lady Dunfield saw and correctly interpreted his lordship's glance as one of interest, then mentally cursed her mother for loading her with such a problem before turning to bat scanty eyelashes at her prey. "I do apologise that we must inflict our cousin on you, but Elizabeth is so kind-hearted she couldn't bear to see the poor child left at home."

Hearing the last part of this ingenuous speech, Venetia decided to intervene, as she knew Jordy's temper could take only so much before exploding.

"And we are so glad you did, for to be sure Miss Chyngford is a lovely girl. Jordan, my dear, won't you please introduce me? Pray don't let us keep you from the party, Lady Dunfield. I do so want you to enjoy yourself. Sir Cicero, you will find the card room down the left there, past the curtains."

Thus dismissed, however graciously, Lady Dunfield had no choice but to go on and spent a good portion of the next quarter-hour berating her daughter and brother for not thinking of a way to detach Lacey from their hostess's party.

"That abominable woman," Jordan hissed through gritted teeth. "Thanks for the rescue."

"Think nothing of it. It's better than having murder done on my staircase. Now, introduce me!"

"Do you really want to meet her yourself, or are you worried about that stricken-calf expression on Bernard's face?" Piedmont teased, then raised his voice to an audible level. "My dear cousin, allow me to present Miss Lacey Chyngford of Greathills. Miss Chyngford, my cousin, Mrs Stanton-Hogg. I hope I do not presume upon our faint acquaintance at your home . . ."

Lacey looked with awe at the vision before her. She had forgotten how handsome the man in the garden had been.

The new Brummell evening suit found favour with her, and she thought it might have been designed to flatter Mr Piedmont's excellent figure. His exquisite cousin resembled him to a great degree, though her hair was lighter and her frame so small and dainty.

During her childhood in Potter's Ford, Lacey had dreamed of a handsome prince like those in the fairy stories; but she had never thought that the man of her dreams would actually appear before her. Having been by dint of circumstance a practical person, Lacey could scarcely credit that such a thing might happen, but being a woman, she was intensely grateful.

The two women said their *devoirs* as properly as could be wished, but Vinnie was amused to notice that although the Chyngford child was being introduced to her, the great blue eyes kept returning to Jordy's face. One of Vinnie's fears had been that when her unpredictable cousin did become interested in a woman, it would be with an undesirable adventuress; at least she could put that fear to rest, for the mysterious Miss Lacey Chyngford was prettily mannered and quite respectable—save for her rather shabby relations, and there was nothing truly unacceptable about them. Thoroughly pleased, Venetia decided the match would be a good one if it should come about and put herself out to be charming.

"Enough, Vinnie! If you stand here chattering all night, the poor girl will never get to dance. I believe the next dance is a waltz, Miss Chyngford. Might I have the honour?" Jordan bowed low, his dull-gold curls glinting in the candlelight. Never had he expected a small curiosity about a strange girl in an odious house to turn out so well. Nor had he thought she would turn out to be such a beauty, either. She had been attractive enough at Greathills, but here, dressed like some sort of dream . . . If he didn't move fast, he would never get a dance with her at all, for already the young men were gathering, ready to pounce as soon as he quit the field.

At that moment Lacey was so bedazzled by her handsome cavalier she would have followed him anywhere. He was without doubt the best-looking man she had ever seen, and that he paid her so much kind attention was unbelievable. The fact that Aunt Leonora claimed him to be courting Elizabeth faded from her mind. Whatever it cost to be in his arms even for one waltz was well worth it.

"Jordy, have you lost your mind?" Venetia asked sharply. "Miss Chyngford is new to town and has not yet been approved to waltz. If she does so before getting the approval of the patronesses, she'll never get into Almack's. You know that as well as I."

His cousin's words brought Jordan up short. He had forgotten just how young and inexperienced this girl was, and oddly felt all the more protective for it. Ordinarily, green girls just bored him.

"My apologies, Miss Chyngford. I have indeed forgotten that restriction. Please know that I meant you no harm or disrespect."

Lacey could have wept to see her dreams wilting so quickly; still, she should have expected it, for she was nothing but a country girl from a vicarage. Why should a dazzling specimen of manhood such as Mr Piedmont give her more than common courtesy?

"I know, but I doubt I shall ever see Almack's in any event. They're quite exclusive and I shouldn't fit in."

"That's ridiculous, Miss Chyngford. Almack's is not all that difficult; I'm sure Vinnie has already set about getting you vouchers, " Jordan said, to his cousin's total amazement. "In the meantime, since we mere mortals do not dare offend the lady patronesses, might I ask the favour of sitting out this dance with you?"

"I would be honoured, sir," replied a smiling Lacey, threading her arm through his.

With a skill that bespoke a thousand social encounters, Piedmont steered them past the envious crowd to a seat discreetly screened by a large potted fern. Hidden from the prying eyes of the ballroom with just enough privacy to be interesting yet just enough exposure to satisfy the censorious eyes of the chaperones, the tiny couch was barely big enough for two. Lacey had never been in such close proximity to a man—especially one as handsome and virile as Mr Piedmont—and prayed she would not blush.

"It seems you were a most successful pupil in learning to be a lady, Miss Chyngford. Every eye in the room is on you tonight."

"You flatter me, sir," replied Lacey demurely, inwardly breathing a small thanks for the lessons in polite deportment among Society which her grandmother had drummed into her unwilling head.

"Not at all. Did you know you are something of a mystery? We are not accustomed to having a goddess spring full-blown into our midst. Did you rise fully formed from sea-foam?"

To be so flatteringly compared with Aphrodite brought the dreaded flush to Lacey's cheeks, making her look more attractive than she realised. It also shook her delicate composure sufficiently that she forgot the handsome Mr Piedmont was a gentleman of Fashion, a rare and delicate breed in need of special handling, and spoke to him as directly as she would have to a friend.

"The furthest thing from that, I'm afraid. I was raised in the vicarage in Potter's Ford in Yorkshire. A small, poor farming community is as removed from the romantic Greek coast of legends as I can imagine."

Jordan hid his surprise well. He had been prepared for almost anything save the thought of this delectable creature's growing to young womanhood among the coarse farm folk of the North. "Your father was a clergyman, then?"

"Yes. He held the same parish for years. He loved the Church."

"That," drawled a fashionably affected voice, "is doubtless the reason you look like an angel. Don't be selfish, Piedmont; introduce me!"

"We were trying to have a private conversation, Melsham," Jordan protested, but without much hope.

Avery Melsham, Esq., was notorious for being precisely wherever he was not wanted. The pet of a few superannuated dowagers, he lived precariously on a diet of scandal and gossip. No one would admit to liking the man, but conversely, everyone was terrified of offending him for fear of feeling his sharp tongue slashing at their reputation, and most felt it quite justified that the pamphleteers pictured him as a very well-dressed snake.

"I see that, but according to the rules of etiquette, exclusivity of a partner lasts only the length of a dance, and methinks that the music has ceased to assault mine ears. Decadent stuff, waltzes, don't you agree? Well, since your charming companion has declined to honour me with an introduction, I must prevail on sheer bravado and present myself to you . . . Miss Chyngford, is it not? My name is Melsham, Avery Melsham, and you are quite the loveliest thing to grace this dull town in many a day."

Slightly overcome as much by the spate of words as by the splendiferous creature before her, Lacey could only stare. Mr Melsham, Esq., was tall and painfully thin with a shock of corn-yellow hair which hung in loose hanks to his shoulders. He wore an old-style brocade jacket, knee breeches in shades of dark blue, and a cherry-striped waistcoat, none of which was overly clean, a fact which he had attempted to disguise with a curtain of flowery scent.

"It is a pleasure, sir," she murmured.

"And you are a clergyman's daughter. How unusual it is to have such lovely sanctity in our midst. Tell me, are you going to spend your days lecturing us about the decadence of our ways and the necessity of taking charity baskets to the poor? Ah, how lovely! The beauteous vicar's daughter—clad in virginal white, of course, with her attendant retinue of admiring acolytes—calling at some poor cottage to leave a basket of the necessities of life, such as lobster patties and *pâté de la maison* . . ."

Had she been more accustomed to the outrageous characters who hung around the fringes of Society, Lacey could have laughed off this creature's absurdities with the disdain they deserved. Instead her mind filled with memories of her father trudging through snow to visit a parishioner sick with malnutrition, of her mother doing without so that a poorer family might eat enough to stave off starvation one more day, of herself clad in twice-turned homespun sitting a death vigil with an old woman too weak to die, and the Chyngford temper—never very far from the surface, even in the clergy branch of the family—bubbled into life.

"Hardly, sir. It would be my fondest wish that no charity basket ever be delivered again."

He smiled, showing sharp and yellowing teeth, while Piedmont sought a method of extracting Lacey from Melsham's clutches without raising a scandal. That society leech loved to cause scandals. Of all things, to run into that damned gossip-monger on her first night out!

"What a hard-hearted beauty you are! How like our late lamented cousins in France to sit and watch the peasants starve while we dawdle over breakfast hoping to catch the last one popping off! Such divine detachment!"

Lacey's fists clenched, the delicate white kid stretching taut over her knuckles. This creature was nauseating! "You misunderstand me, sir," she said crisply, the words flying like ice slivers. "Anyone of intelligence knows that the poor do not want charity nor bounty baskets laid at their door."

Ferret-eyes gleamed in Melsham's thin face. "I fear you must count your poor servant in the vast majority who know nothing of the kind, my dear. I always thought that the poor were nothing but one vast outstretched hand always ready to gobble up as much as they could. What do they need, since everything is given to them?"

"They need employment. Bread is unreasonably high, most other things out of reach of a slim purse. The economy must be rearranged so that it is more equitable to all instead of being a private plaything of the heartless nobles and landowners. Mrs Stoker said that revolution was like a bomb, destroying the good as well as the bad, and that the Corn Riots in 1811 showed we are well on the way to a revolution in England unless something is done now!" Lacey's voice echoed the fervour it had had during her spirited debates with her late employer, during which they had never dreamed that the use of one's mind made a girl unfeminine.

Both gentlemen's eyes were round with disbelief, and Lacey's heart sank with the realization of the awful thing she had done as Melsham intoned with relish, "My, my, what a little radical bluestocking we have in our midst! I'm surprised you deign to join our degenerate little gathering, let along hobnob so cosily with one of the enemy!"

Thoroughly bewildered, Lacey turned to Piedmont. "What does he mean, Mr Piedmont?"

The damp snicker Melsham used for a laugh slipped from between his thin lips. "Mr Piedmont? You mean you haven't told her? Jordan, my dear boy, is that playing fair with our beauteous little firebrand?"

Lacey tried to salvage whatever shards were left of her fragile dignity. "I don't understand. Would you please explain?"

"Oh, my dear Miss Chyngford, it is too choice! No one will believe that you have been sitting here vilifying both landowners and the nobility to one of the prime examples of both! Perhaps I should do the introductions, don't you think? Miss Chyngford, I should like to present Jordan, Viscount Piedmont, one of the largest landowners in the country."

"Viscount?" Lacey asked weakly.

Suddenly a lot of the conversations between her aunt and cousin made sense; Lacey had thought there were two men, not just one. The subject had not been much discussed in her presence, for both ladies did not seek her company nor offer confidences, but she was stupid not to have figured it out before.

Jordan saw the questioning look in Lacey's eyes. For the first time since his scrubby schoolboy days, he felt somehow in the wrong, a curious sort of sensation he would do anything to change. Had he stopped to analyse his feelings, he would have been surprised, but for now the humiliation of being made a fool of by such an unspeakable creature as Avery Melsham crystallised into ill-concealed anger. No matter what loss he felt in the cooling of Miss Chyngford's gaze, he would not apologise for being what he was, even if such an heretical idea had occurred to him.

For her part, Lacey's assaulted emotions wavered between an odd sense of betrayal and intense anger. She was not used to being made fun of, and the thought of this man, handsome though he was, laughing at her for her naiveté made her furious. Doubtless it would be a joke among the whole rotten bunch of them, those inbred arrogant fashionables whom her grandmother so wanted her to join. Mr Piedmont—no, curse it, His Lordship the Viscount Piedmont—might have appeared handsome and personable, but he was cut from the same cloth as her grandfather and uncle and Mr Stoker. Liars, all of them! The famous Chyngford temper began to rise again; if she stayed, she would have no control.

"It appears I was misinformed. I apologise for not having known your true status, Your Lordship." Lacey's words were unexceptionable save that they were delivered in a voice which could have cut glass. She rose with a graceful movement and extended her hand. "Mr Melsham, would you please escort me back to my aunt?"

Delighted to have been the sower of so much delicious discord, the reports of which would probably keep him in dinner invitations for at least a night or two, Melsham proclaimed his delight to perform such a small service for the lovely Miss Chyngford and led her out into the ballroom just as Mrs Stanton-Hogg's butler stepped forward to announce a late arrival.

"His Grace the Duke of Lowood."

=7=

LADY DUNFIELD, ALONG with everyone else, had watched the beauteous Miss Chyngford and the handsome Lord Piedmont cross the room, her beady eyes taking in the knowing smiles and little nods which followed them like a rippling wave. Unless something happened soon, there would be talk of An Interest; such an unpleasant eventuality must be squelched before it was begun, her ladyship decided.

"Do you see that?" she hissed in an undertone, and emphasized her point by applying an ungentle slap with her fan to Elizabeth's arm. "She is stealing your beau from under your very nose, and you do nothing about it!"

Having been well indoctrinated by her mother, Miss Elizabeth Dunfield had no love for her cousin, but her eyesight was excellent. "Lacey is very pretty, Mama," she replied in a small voice.

"Pretty is as pretty does, and making a public spectacle of herself is not pretty," said her ladyship piously. She had the good fortune to possess a memory flexible enough to overlook completely her own determined and public pursuit of the same quarry for Elizabeth. Now, lacking other relief for her maternal frustrations, she proceeded to lecture that girl on the necessity of entangling the viscount's heartstrings.

"After all, my pet, you don't want to be left dependent and scrabbling as I was. Piedmont has land and money and the good sense not to lose either."

"But I don't love him, Mama, and he doesn't love me." Lady Dunfield reacted to this heresy a great deal better than her mother had, merely making a mental note to forbid the reading of any more vulgar romantic novels. "Love is important in a marriage, my dear, but it comes after the wedding, not before," she murmured, remembering her own passion for the late unlamented Sir George Dunfield after discovering he was a considerable landowner and quite warm in the pocket. That unfortunate aberration of the heart had lasted until some six weeks after the wedding, when she had discovered to her sorrow that his reputation as a solid citizen was rapidly being replaced by that of a reckless gambler bent on running through his patrimony—and then his wife's dowry—as quickly as humanly possible. It was only fair that Elizabeth should have the guidance of her mother's counsel, since such wisdom had been so painfully bought. "Love is a pitfall, a trap for the unwary. Romantic love wears off soon enough. Your dowry is small, but it is the best I could save from the wreck your father made of things. You must do better for your children, see the things that last, Elizabeth. Money. Property. A title. Those will last long after any sort of emotional flush is gone."

Had the dance in progress not been a rather noisy and complicated reel, Lady Dunfield's impassioned oration might have drawn some attention. As it was, the collective gaze of the party was distracted from the finishing bars of the music to two separate and easily more interesting events. The mysterious Miss Chyngford, having gone into the greenery-shaded alcove with Lord Piedmont, was now coming out with that notorious gossip Avery Melsham, while at the front entrance the viscount's decided enemy on the Turf was being announced.

Her ladyship herself was quite pleased to see the change of partners for her niece, though Elizabeth, to give her credit, was not. "Mama! Look! Lacey is with that horrid Avery Melsham. Shouldn't we go claim her?"

"Certainly not. She is perfectly all right here in the Stanton-Hogg home, and Mr Melsham is received everywhere." *And serves the hussy right*, she added inwardly.

"Why, Miss Dunfield! What a pleasure to see you again . . . and your lovely mother too, of course."

At the sound of a masculine voice, Leonora changed her focus of attention from the satisfying situation of her niece to the young man who was standing before them. It took a moment for her to recognise the pink, smooth cheeks and spaniel eyes, but that moment was long enough for Elizabeth's tidal flush of colour to rise and ebb unheeded.

"It's so nice to see you again, Mr Litchfield. I did not expect to see you in London this Season. Mama, surely you remember Mr Litchfield, who was so obliging to us last year?"

Indeed, Lady Dunfield did remember with scant charity the round-faced young man who had spent most of the previous Season sniffing around Elizabeth and getting mightily in her way. A distressingly earnest person, Mr Litchfield was one of the younger offspring of an ancient family with excellent breeding and little capital; on coming of age, he had used family influence and set about to earn his fortune in the Foreign Office. To Leonora's dismay, he had hung around Elizabeth all last Season, regaling her with tales of life in foreign parts, despite several unsubtle hints from her mother that his presence was superfluous.

His round cheeks resembled nothing so much as juicy apples. "I am on furlough pending reassignment. I had hoped to see you again before leaving. . . . I'm off for Florence by the end of the week."

Lady Dunfield's rather chilly demeanour softened, and her countenance split into a blazing smile. Florence! It was a perfect solution—and he was even of good family, which was more than that upstart hussy deserved! "Of course I remember you, Mr Litchfield! What a pleasure it is to see you again!"

Such affability after a Season of frosty stares almost

overwhelmed the imperturbable Milton Litchfield. No august foreign dignitary, no gimlet-eyed diplomat had ever had the power to make him quiver in his boots as did Lady Dunfield, but several years in the Diplomatic Service had taught him that no one changed directions suddenly without wanting something, so he smiled blandly and waited.

Lady Dunfield did want something, but to set her machinations in motion, she desired for once the presence of her niece and swept the ballroom with her eyes. Drat the girl, could she never be where she was wanted?

"Elizabeth, where is your cousin? I should like her to have the pleasure of Mr Litchfield's acquaintance."

"There, Mama," the dutiful girl replied in a painfully colourless tone. She knew her mother very well. "Mr Melsham is presenting her to the Duke of Lowood."

At first Lowood had decided not to attend the Stanton-Hogg rout. It was bound to be a much too proper style of entertainment for his tastes, and a man at his age deserved a little interesting diversion; however, he did know that Piedmont was behind his invitation. It might be interesting to see what sort of a stratagem that young pup had in mind, thinking to cozen him into a alien mellowness by some social flummery. He had finally decided to make an appearance and then depart for other, more salubrious pastimes.

That was before he saw her standing in the glare of the *torchères* like some sort of otherworldly visitant, an old-fashioned miniature come to life, even to jewellery and hairstyle. Even the necklace was identical to the one he remembered.

She had seen him, too, and had puzzled at his reaction, but by the time his composure had been recaptured, the vision had been joined by a party of lumpish mortals and swept into the building. There was no question of Lowood's determination to attend the party, and as his carriage inched forward into position by the red carpet, he opened the ornate gold locket dangling from his watch chain. Under the flaring torchlight, the painted ivory portrait was difficult for his old eyes to see, but that did not matter. The beautiful face of his dear, dead darling was graven in his sight and in his heart forever.

The hands holding the locket were creased and old; years of indulgent living, of drink and gaming and wenching, had taken their toll on him. *She* had appeared magically untouched—if she existed at all in this world of flesh and not just in his lonely heart; how would she recognise him in this wrinkled and aged shell?

"His Grace the Duke of Lowood."

No matter the provocation, Lowood was not one to discard the social graces if it pleased his purpose to use them. Recently two young ladies of Fashion had turned him down in an offer of marriage because of his disregard for social mores in his private life; this had been a severe shock to His Grace, who, having decided on the necessity of setting up his nursery at last, and having hopes of succeeding despite the belatedness of his decision, thought his title and fortune would allow him to purchase any young chit who happened to take his fancy. He scraped through his hostess's greeting with the minimum of propriety and within a moment had spotted his quarry—who thankfully appeared to be of flesh and blood—being escorted by that damned womanish sponger Melsham. Somehow it was not even a surprise to find that her name was Chyngford; he felt he had known it all along.

Ever anxious to curry favour with one of such lofty estate as the Duke of Lowood, Mr Melsham was more than delighted to introduce his lovely companion. He did note with slight interest that she went pale on seeing His Grace, but considering that Lowood was hardly well favoured, not to mention being quite advanced in age, any young lady of such a beautiful aspect as Miss Chyngford might well recoil even if she hadn't heard of his chequered reputation. It took a great deal of Mr Melsham's carefully cultured manners not to show a bit of pique when Lowood dismissed him like a lackey; but even if the duke were not wealthy and important, it would never do to cross him.

Lacey looked after the retreating back of her late escort with a sense of unease. She had recognised the duke's face as the one glimpsed so briefly in a carriage window and had also recognised the name of the bogeyman of several of Elizabeth's tales of High Society. Elizabeth did not like this man, and neither, Lacey was certain, would she. She wished Melsham had stayed, scant improvement though he was, for even in the crowded Stanton-Hogg ballroom she felt uneasy, being to all intents and purposes alone with the man.

"That was not kind," she said. Duke he may be, but he would never intimidate Lacey Chyngford!

"I am seldom kind to people I wish to be rid of," His Grace replied, not unpleasantly surprised at the unexpected show of spirit. His beloved would never have dreamed of speaking so to anyone, soft and gentle creature that she had been. Now that he was close, there were differences as well as similarities; the resemblance was there—yes, so strongly that it wrenched at his heart, an organ he had long since thought dried and dead—but this face, however beautiful, had more strength than his dear one had ever possessed. She was so different and yet so much the same that he felt almost dizzy, as if the images of the past and the present superimposed themselves one over the other. "I wished to be alone with you . . . as alone as possible under these circumstances."

That, Lacey thought fervently, was an eventuality to be devoutly avoided! Even his glance made her feel unclean, and if he touched her with those thin dry claws, she felt sure she would scream.

"You are very lovely, you know. It's so nice to find a girl who appreciates the old styles," he murmured, and Lacey resolved that the very next day she would have her hair redone in the most modern fashion, "I haven't seen one of those lovers' necklaces in years," he added. "They used to be quite stylish."

"So I have been told. This was a gift from a very dear friend of mine in the North. Have you ever travelled there?" It was a slight but definite signal any gentleman should recognise that a change of conversation was desired.

Unfortunately, the Duke of Lowood was not a gentleman, for he continued on with a frightening concentration of purpose. "No, but I surely would have if I had known you were there; that is your home, is it not? I detect a distinct hint of a burr—quite charming, I assure you—in your speech."

So much for all the elocution lessons Grandmother had forced on her, Lacey mused. "Yes, I lived there for many years. I've only come south recently."

"I wasn't aware that any branch of the Chyngford family lived in that area. . . . Might I ask your father's name? I have a slight acquaintance with your family, you see."

"We lived very quietly," Lacey replied with just a hint of irony. "My father was the Reverend Barton Chyngford. He was raised not far from London, though. Perhaps you knew his father, the Reverend Laurence Chyngford?"

A shadow passed over the duke's face. It was the wrong branch of the family; he had met Laurence Chyngford, of course—prosy old minister that he was—but it was not the side of the family in which he was interested. Still, in a way, it was a sort of poetic justice, he thought, and murmured conventionally, "We met a time or two. He was indeed a gentleman." His eyes strayed again to the necklace; it seemed to draw his eyes like a magnet. How many years had it been?

Lacey felt his gaze and wished she had never worn the silly thing, but even as she wished, she knew through some inner sense that it would have made no difference. This man would have sought her out no matter what. And where, oh where, was Aunt Leonora?

"That becomes you. Would you believe that once I gave a necklace like that to a young lady?"

"You did? And what became of her?" Lacey asked more from a desire to make polite conversation than from any real interest. Why didn't someone ask her to dance? The entire party must have seen her predicament by now!

"She married another and died not long after." His voice was harsh even to his own ears. All the years had not mitigated the pain.

Lacey heard the anguish in his voice and for the first time regarded her unwelcome companion as a fellow human being capable of pain and loss, instead of an ugly old man with a foul reputation. Doubtless her natural compassion would have betrayed her had not a white knight ridden to the rescue in the unexpected guise of Sir Cicero Chyngford.

"Lacey, m'girl! Where have you been hiding? Your aunt has sent me to find you; she has been looking for you."

It was curious that Aunt Leonora should be unable to see her when apparently everyone else in the ballroom could, but Lacey was in no mood to find fault. She scraped through the necessities of an introduction between her uncle and His Grace, and made a civil farewell, then fled with all due decorum to the solid protection of her aunt, who belatedly seemed to have recalled her duties as chaperone. Innocent as Lacey was, she would never have done her aunt the disservice of suspecting that she had rescued her from the odious Duke of Lowood only as insurance that if anyone were going to catch a title, it should be Elizabeth!

Later Lacey was to remember the rest of her first ton party in fragments; she was somehow even more out of favour than usual with her aunt and cousin, especially the former, who shunted her into the company of a rather prosaic Mr Litchfield for the supper dance and the following meal, the taste of which she never noticed. She did notice that Lord Piedmont was enjoying the company of a doll-faced beauty named Eustacie Featherstonehaugh; the girl's flattering fragility was just the sort of quality a man like the viscount would look for in a woman. She would believe anything he said! After supper there was more dancing and more partners than she could ever remember, and over all there was Elizabeth's disapproval and Aunt Leonora's chilling stare.

When at last it came time to go home, Lacey said a devoutly insincere thank you to her host and hostess, bid a frostily civil farewell to the viscount, and was more than grateful to lean back her aching head in the privacy of the coach. Her rest was short-lived, unfortunately, for no sooner had the carriage pulled away from the lights of the Stanton-Hogg house than Sir Cicero leaned over and patted her knee in a most paternal and unprecedented fashion.

"I'll say you made a splash tonight, Lacey. Snagging a duke on the first time out. Lowood's a warm man, they say."

"I find him odious," Lacey replied with feeling.

"At least you are not completely immune to sensibility, I am glad to see," huffed Leonora out of the dark. She was determined that no vicarage upstart should think of capturing a higher title than her own well-brought-up daughter. "It was a point of question after your forward behaviour tonight. . . . To think that I should live to see a niece of mine throwing herself at every title in the room! Such conduct is a blot on the entire family!"

There was more in the same vein, but Lacey was too tired both inside and out to pay much attention. When they finally reached Chyngford House, she bade them all a civil good night and trudged upstairs to the sleepy ministrations of the parlourmaid who had been decided good enough to "do" for her.

At last alone, Lacey stretched out in bed and tried to think of some way out of this insupportable mess. All the people to whom she could have turned in her distress—her parents, Mrs Stoker—were dead. To return to the Stoker household would be unthinkable even if she were sure of a welcome there. She could not go home to Greathills; her grandmother was the one who had put her in this situation in the first place.

Odd that she should think of Greathills as home, Lacey thought mistily. Home had always been the draughty old vicarage which had been made warm with love. Twin tears bubbled in the sleepy blue eyes, and the redoubtable Miss Chyngford berated herself for such weakness. She was strong; she had made her own way before at the Stokers' and she could again in another household.

Acceptable employment for a gentlewoman was limited, but surely someone would hire her as a lady's companion or perhaps a governess; she had a reasonably complete education, though it was more suited for a boy than a girl. The Reverend Barton Chyngford had had a passion for Biblical languages and had taught them to his surprisingly adept daughter, a fact which Lacey's grandmother had begged her to conceal.

Struggling against the covers, Lacey thought over her assets. She had never received the fifty-pound legacy due her, but thanks to Mrs Stoker's foresight she had another fifty pounds, that in gold, still untouched and safe in the shabby purse beneath her chemises; such a sum would be enough for a start, and she would never, ever have to see any of these people again, especially that odious Lord Piedmont!

With a total misattribution of her unstable emotionalism to fatigue, Lacey at last cried herself into an uneasy sleep.

Lady Dunfield was in a fearful temper, even though it was barely past breakfasttime. The entire household knew it and tried to be as quiet as possible, but each jangling of the bell to announce the arrival of yet another bouquet set her ladyship off afresh.

Miss Lacey Chyngford had apparently made a spectacular debut into the world of Fashion, for to her cousin's embarrassment and her aunt's fury it was her name which predominated to an alarming degree on the dozens of posies beleaguering the house. Being of an easygoing temperament by nature, Miss Elizabeth would have been satisfied by the number of flowers sent her—especially by a small but stunning offering of red tulips and ivy in a dainty gilt holder—but in the light of the plunder her cousin was reaping, it would have taken a stronger person than Elizabeth not to be affronted.

Being female, Lacey could not help but take pleasure in her offerings—from a small posy of common violets sent by a highborn but impoverished poet to an almost vulgarly opulent display of blood-red roses bearing the Duke of Lowood's card—but her aunt's behaviour had efficiently erased that enthusiasm during breakfast. Leonora had never been renowned for her sweetness of temper; before the covers had been cleared from the morning meal, she had spread her ill-humour with equal venom among the family members until Sir Cicero had risen, announcing that he was spending the day at his club, and Elizabeth had been driven to leaving the room in tears. Only Lacey, her thoughts consumed with alternatives for her future, paid scant heed to her aunt's ranting, even though most of it was directed at her.

Such indifference by the object of her displeasure only further incensed her ladyship. She was on at least a third repetition of condemnation of Lacey's conduct the previous evening when the butler stepped into the breakfast room— he told Cook later he'd as lief have stepped into a den of hungry lions—carrying a note on a silver salver.

"Well, Quilling, what is it? Another bunch of flowers?"

The butler, a lugubrious soul at best, assumed an expression more suitable for a man about to be hung. "No, madam. Some callers have arrived, and I took the liberty of putting them in the morning room. They sent this note."

"Early for morning callers. Doubtless they wish to commiserate with me for being saddled with such a disrespectful hoyden! Well, don't just stand there, man, give me the note!"

Quilling gave a discreet cough. "Excuse me, Your Ladyship, but the note is for Miss Chyngford."

All too aware of her aunt's furious eyes, Lacey took the note from the salver and, as she read, knew her world had gone from bad to worse.

"Well, miss? Am I allowed to know the identity of your friends? I am only your chaperone and this is only your uncle's house!" Leonora's voice fairly dripped with venom.

Lacey looked up with apologetic eyes. "It's my former employers. . . . It's the Stokers."

= 8 =

"JUST A LITTLE more sugar, if you please." Mrs Stoker smiled as she extended her cup. She had always had a sweet tooth, as her figure evidenced. "Thank you. As I was saying, I told Mr Stoker we simply could not come to London and not call to see how our dear Lacey was doing."

Lady Dunfield replied with a frozen smile.

"After all, she was like one of our family for over two years. Dear Mother-in-Law was so fond of her. . . . We could not help being interested to hear of all our Lacey's adventures since her stroke of good fortune," Mrs Stoker went on, smirking.

Lacey sat silently watching her former tormentors and wondering why she had ever thought them so formidable. Mrs Stoker was nothing but a gossipy country squire's wife and her husband a lecher not too unlike the Duke of Lowood. Agnes Mary was a rather plain young woman in an ill-styled dress, not a viper-tongued young lady of Fashion. Her eyes devoured Lacey's simple but expensively exquisite morning dress through a veil of envy. Chester . . . Here Lacey paused. She did not remember his stare being so solemn nor so firmly fixed on her.

"It is most kind of you to show such an interest in our niece," Lady Dunfield murmured regally when it became apparent that no one else was going to speak. She regarded the entire family with scant charity, having accurately typed them as minor country gentry out to benefit from the fact that they had once had a Chyngford in their employ.

Very minor gentry, her ladyship added inwardly, for one could always tell by the clothes. The men were sartorially acceptable in a bucolic sort of way, but the girl's dress was one that should have shamed a London ladies' maid, and the mother's . . . Lady Dunfield scathingly compared Mrs Stoker's dull grey silk with her own stunning creation of cherry-striped muslin.

Mr Stoker laughed genially. Lacey thought the laugh oily, and wondered afresh at the contradictions of the human race; that as intelligent and great a lady as the late Mrs Stoker could have birthed such an individual.

"No," he was saying, "Lacey was an important part of our household, and overjoyed as we were for her stroke of luck, we regret her leaving our happy circle. It left a great gap in our home, I can tell you, losing her so quickly after Mother died. Mother was so fond of her."

Swallowing hard, Lacey looked away, seeking distractions to occupy her mind and tongue so that she would not say out loud the unflattering things which she was thinking. For a brief moment her gaze locked with Chester's—he was apparently studying her intently, much to Miss Chyngford's distaste. She looked away quickly, her eyes falling on a red-eyed, morose Elizabeth. Aside from a mumbled greeting, she had not spoken since Lacey, bade to find her so that she might aid in receiving the morning callers, had located her in the library, weeping and loath to give over reading about the Italian countryside—for which Mr Litchfield would so soon be leaving—in order to face unwelcome strangers.

"It seems our Lacey is still as shy as ever," drawled Chester in a surprisingly rich voice.

Enough was enough! Lacey could not stand this sticky morass of spurious sentimentality any longer. "As I recall, you never took enough notice of me to know if I were shy or not," she said sweetly.

Lady Dunfield bristled. Lacey knew her aunt's danger signals well enough by now. She remembered her grandmother's caution that a waspish tongue and toucheous temper was out of place in a true young lady of Fashion, so with a bland smile fixed firmly in place, she turned to Agnes Mary and made determined conversation about the few mutual acquaintances they possessed in Potter's Ford.

The time for a polite call to end had long since come and gone, yet the Stokers showed no sign of leaving. Never overly ample, the topics for small talk between an ill-assorted set of relative strangers soon ran out; the conversations became more and more desultory until Lady Dunfield decided that, etiquette or no etiquette, she would soon have to bring the encounter to a speedy close herself.

As far as Lacey was concerned, such a move was long overdue. Chester's unwinking surveillance had some time ago begun to irritate her nerves to such a high degree that she avoided speaking to him and was far from pleased when covert glances his way only proved the unwavering quality of his gaze.

"Stap me if I haven't gone and forgotten one of the main reasons for coming," ejaculated Mr Stoker with an extremely theatrical gesture. "First of all, we wanted to see how our dear Lacey was getting on in the world, of course, but that's not all. After you left in such an understandable hurry"—here his voice took on a slightly wounded tone— "we realized that you had left something behind. We didn't dare send it on after you, and decided to wait until we saw you again. Here you are, my dear."

With ceremony worthy of a coronation, he laid a finely worked leather purse in her lap. "Your legacy from my dear mother."

"Thank you," Lacey murmured around a fair-sized lump in her throat. The memory of her aged friend was very poignant.

"There's no need getting sentimental," Lady Dunfield said later, when the Stoker tribe had at last taken their leave. "It could have been sent to you at Greathills by bank draught or here by messenger. What stratagems some people won't try to associate with their betters! I can't say I think much of them."

Her ladyship would have been greatly surprised to know that the Stokers—safely bound back to the unfashionable part of Wimpole Street in their heavy old carriage—thought much the same way about her.

Agnes Mary sniffed. "So that's her ladyship Dunfield. Well, I can certainly see why 'our precious Lacey' never said anything about her grand relations. Did you see her dress?"

Mrs Stoker nodded vehemently, her sense of fitness still offended by the memory of the cherry stripes. "No one of her colouring should ever wear that shade. For that matter, no one of her age should wear a dress like that at all!" Her mouth, never overly generous, clamped into a tight line of righteous disapproval.

"And the daughter—did you ever see such a spiritless lump? She just sat there looking like a great green frog in that bunchy dress!" Agnes Mary made a moue of exaggerated distaste, but when she spoke again her voice was heavy with undisguised jealousy. "I see Miss Lacey at least has some taste. That morning dress must have cost more than the whole of my clothing allowance."

"You'd think they would have at least mentioned sending a card of invitation to some of their entertainments. You know they're going to give several." Mrs Stoker was fretful over the fact that a former dependent should have advantages her own precious child lacked. If only Agnes Mary and that Chyngford girl had been friends!

Agnes Mary was caustic. "Dear Miss Lacey has become too high and mighty in the world to bother with the likes of us. We were good enough to save her from starvation when her father died and left her destitute, but not good enough for her now."

Without raising his head from its contemplative position on his chest, Chester produced an uncanny imitation of a miaouing cat. "You should hear yourselves! Ladies, ladies!"

"Don't be vulgar," remonstrated Mrs Stoker, but she was drowned out by her sister's "Well, at least we said something there, while you were close-mouthed as an oyster! I didn't see her falling all over herself to bring you into the conversation, for all that she's supposed to be so crazy about you!"

"That's true, boy. She didn't act like you were her long-lost love. I do hope you weren't bamming us, because I'm counting on you." Mr Stoker cleared his throat and began once more the litany with which he had hounded his family for weeks. "It's been a bad year, and with corn prices so unreasonable and the war lingering on and the market so bad . . . Unless we get an infusion of new capital . . . Are you sure she'll marry you?"

Chester smiled with an easiness he did not altogether feel. "Of course. Didn't you see her looking at me when she thought no one was looking, especially that aunt of hers? Before, she didn't want to let her lack of fortune hinder me, but now . . . Everyone knows the Chyngfords are filthy rich. Her uncle is one of the most notorious gamesters in town. Her dowry will probably be plenty."

"She did seem to miss Potter's Ford—Heaven only knows why," sighed Chester's mother. Like the rest of the family, she was skeptical of Lacey Chyngford's supposed attachment to her son, but any means was acceptable to prevent the seemingly unavoidable penury which was fast approaching due to her husband's bad investments.

"Yes, it was her home most of her life; doubtless she misses it. And," Mr Stoker added, his eyes glowing with the other unholy benefits of having Miss Chyngford in their family beyond the mere monetary, "what better way for her to return home than as the wife of the heir to Beecham Manor?"

His head slumped once more to hide his worried eyes;

Chester fell silent. He had begun this fiction of an unrequited passion on Lacey's part primarily to annoy his father, whose desires toward the young Miss Chyngford were not as secret as that gentleman would have wanted them to be. It was only recently, when money had become so scarce, that the thought of the Chyngford fortune had come to mind—and everyone thought Miss Lacey did owe them something for the way they had taken her in during her time of need. Chester had never been one to sacrifice himself for the needs of his family, but when certain secret debts of his own became pressing, the thought of marrying part of the Chyngford fortune had occurred to him.

Marriage to the lovely Lacey would not be unpleasant; she was physically attractive, though not as voluptuous as he preferred. She would be excellent as both a good companion to his mother and future *châtelaine* of Beecham Manor, assuming they should contrive to keep it. Since Potter's Ford had been Lacey's home from girlhood, she would not object to staying there—especially as Lady of the Manor—while he sought the more exciting pleasures of London; besides, his father would be there to console her in her loneliness after he had tired of her. And then there was always the Chyngford fortune and the Chyngford connexions, both of which would doubtless be made available to dear Lacey's husband. No, marrying the chit would solve a number of problems if only she could be persuaded to cooperate!

At least Chyngford House looked respectable enough, Venetia Stanton-Hogg was pleased to discover. True, it was small for a truly elegant town home, and the little square on which it stood, though neat and quiet, was too obscure to be of the first stare of Fashion; the shutters and woodwork had been freshly painted, though, as if the entire place had been brushed up for the Season.

With deft grace, she stepped down from the high-perch phaeton without aid and smiled to her tiger Timmy, who had already gone to the horses' heads. "They're fresh, but not skittish; just hold them, please, and I'll be back in a moment."

Timmy nodded, never failing to be touched by the miracle of her. Ever since she had rescued him from the living hell of a climbingboy's life, he had regarded Mrs Stanton-Hogg more in the light of a divine being whom he was lucky enough to serve than as a mere mortal mistress at the moment clad in a driving outfit of a most flattering primrose.

Unaware of the saintly devotion her kindness had inspired, young Mrs Stanton-Hogg mounted the steps of Chyngford House with mischief in her heart. She had been unable to ascertain just what had gone wrong with Jordan during the party; before it started and at the first of the festivities, he had been as happy as she could ever remember in the viscount—an almost half-remembered kind of gaiety that belonged to the recklessness of childhood.

After the gala was over and he had been helping them shoo the last stragglers on their way, he had been a perfect grouch, no better than a bear with a sore head, which was an unusual state of affairs for her usually even-tempered Jordy.

Then, when she had asked a most civil question about the lovely Miss Chyngford, he had almost bitten her head off. She had known better than to ask him for an explanation, and since her dear Bernard had refused to help ferret out answers to assuage her curiosity—"It's Jordan's problem, dear. If he wanted you to know, he'd tell you about it."—Vinnie had determined plans of her own. Men!

Having sent over a note earlier in the afternoon regarding hopes of taking the Misses Chyngford and Dunfield driving, Vinnie knew she would be expected, but her welcome was beyond her wildest dreams. The Friday-faced butler behaved as if she were a Royal, ushering her into a salon shockingly decorated according to a blessedly abortive

"Spanish" style briefly popular some dozen years past. Here Lady Dunfield waited in state, casting herself as the perfect picture of a Society matron.

"My dear Mrs Stanton-Hogg! What a delight to have you honour my girl . . . girls in this manner. Pray sit down. Might I offer you some refreshment? Tea? Ratafia? Negus?"

Stunned and a little overwhelmed by the unhappy juxtaposition of a cherry-striped dress against an orange-and-white salon, Mrs Stanton-Hogg declined the offer with thanks, saying her horses mustn't be kept standing; she had only meant to collect the girls and go.

"Elizabeth is probably ready by now," gushed her ladyship in a daze of happiness. Such unprecedented favour by Piedmont's beloved cousin could only mean that he was getting more interested and that the family meant to look Elizabeth over well before he fixed his interest. "I'll just inform her that you're ready to leave."

Herself a veteran of the social wars, Vinnie scented a manipulation. "And Miss Chyngford?"

"Oh, I am so sorry, but my niece is unable to come this afternoon. She is desolated to pass up such a treat but hopes that you and Elizabeth have a pleasant time."

In a pig's eye, Vinnie thought vulgarly. *I'd wager a monkey that the girl was never told of my invitation! You just want to keep the Chyngford girl out of anything to do with Jordy's family so you can push that plain daughter of yours down his throat! Not while I'm around, you won't!*

Mrs Stanton-Hogg raised her chin in an imperious gesture which added the impressive illusion of many inches to her height; it was a trick learned from her grandmother, a woman who was both insufferably proud and shorter than Vinnie herself.

"I'm sorry, Lady Dunfield, but it appears there has been a misunderstanding. My invitation was to both girls. I am surprised that you did not extend me the courtesy of sending word that one of them was otherwise engaged. Perhaps we had better postpone this until a time when both girls are free?"

Her ladyship studied the suddenly haughty features of her guest and knew that her ruse had not worked. Curse the girl, was Lacey going to foul up every one of Elizabeth's chances? That young miss needed to be taken care of and quickly, but since Mr Litchfield had proved unenthusiastic, no new idea had penetrated the curtain of her ladyship's anger.

"Very well," she said at last, with a slight attempt at graciousness. "I suppose she can be spared this afternoon if you really wish it." Her ladyship shrugged, making it sound as if the girl's company were something distasteful.

Vinnie smiled regally. "I don't want to keep the horses standing. Why don't I drive them around the square and the girls can just come out when they're ready?"

There was just time for Vinnie to make two circuits of the small square and for her to decide that she really did thoroughly dislike Lady Dunfield before the girls joined her. A careful driver, especially in the notoriously unstable high-perch style of phaeton, Vinnie limited her conversation to greetings until the tricky traffic of the streets had been negotiated and they were safe on the uncrowded trails of the park.

"Well, are you girls both recovered from last night? I remember my first Season and how I never could get used to staying up half the night," their hostess said, laughing.

Her humour unimproved since the morning, especially as her mother had given her a highly coloured version of the reason Lacey was present in the phaeton with them, Elizabeth replied sulkily, "This is my second Season."

If you don't mind your behaviour, my dear, it may be your last, Vinnie thought with sudden displeasure, then realised charitably that no better could be expected from the daughter of such a mother.

"Even in my second Season I found it difficult to keep up

the pace. Thank Heaven I'm married now, for I've always been the most shockingly indolent creature. And what about you, Miss Chyngford? You haven't said a word since we started out."

Not only had Lacey not said a word, but she had no intention of saying anything unless spoken to directly. She had known of Mrs Stanton-Hogg's invitation since the furor over its arrival but had not known that it was intended for herself as well as Elizabeth until receiving Aunt Leonora's white-lipped orders to get dressed. Her ears ringing with a harangue regarding the viscount's suit of Elizabeth, a strangely subdued Miss Chyngford had descended to the carriage. Only she knew that her lips were sealed by anger, not obedience. How dare Aunt Leonora intimate that she might be interested in his lordship—as if the daughter of Barton and Charlotte Chyngford would have any truck with a man who lied to her—or, even worse, that she might be so vulgar as to be "on the catch" for any man, let alone her cousin's beau?

Mrs Stanton-Hogg was looking at her, obviously expecting an answer, so Lacey replied in a colourless voice, "I fear I have nothing to say."

Vinnie gritted her teeth and went on. "Surely that is an unusual statement from a young girl new to the Haut Ton? Ah, perhaps I understand. . . . I noticed that last night you were cornered by both Lowood and Melsham; I'm afraid their attentions are part of the penalty one pays for being young and pretty, but I'm so sorry you had to encounter them on your first evening, and at my party too. Oh, look! What a coincidence!" she cooed with palpable falsehood. "There's Jordy, and he's all alone. . . ."

Jordan Piedmont knew his cousin well enough to know when she had some cork-brained scheme or another going, but loved her enough so that he usually went along with such schemes. He had been mildly curious when her note had all but insisted that she meet him in the park this afternoon, and now that he saw her phaeton crammed with young ladies, he felt the first faint stirrings of anger. Miss Chyngford had made it clear that she did not wish any part of his company, and he thought that Vinnie understood he had no desire to see Miss Dunfield. Good Lord; of all people, Vinnie should have known that!

"Jordy! How delightful to see you," cried Vinnie, smiling broadly, as if it had been weeks instead of hours since parting from him.

"And you, my dear Venetia," Jordan replied, knowing full well how his cousin disliked her Christian name. "Ladies." He sketched an impersonal bow to her passengers and was interested to observe that while both young ladies maintained dignified poses, Miss Dunfield went ghastly pale while Miss Chyngford blushed painfully.

"How wonderful it is that we met, for now you can take up Miss Chyngford and show her the park while I have a comfortable cose with my dear Miss Dunfield. I vow it has been an age since we've had a chance for a talk!"

Since the two ladies had scarce exchanged more than commonplaces, it was not a good excuse, but Vinnie Stanton-Hogg was quite accustomed to making outrageous demands and getting them. Blithely, she overruled any and all objections until the transfer of Miss Chyngford to his lordship's phaeton—a tricky maneuver in itself, which would have been much more difficult had not Mr Litchfield suddenly appeared from nowhere to offer his assistance—was accomplished; and without any clear knowledge of how she had been persuaded into such a situation, Lacey drove away in the sole company of Jordan, Lord Piedmont.

"Thank you so much, Mr Litchfield," Vinnie cooed. "How kind of you to be here just when you are needed."

"It was my pleasure to be of assistance, Mrs Stanton-Hogg," he replied, square fingers nervously mistreating his hat brim. "I had been hoping to see a friend here in the park today. . . ." He might have been speaking to Mrs Stanton-Hogg, but his eyes never left Miss Dunfield, and the play of colour from white to red and back over again upon the younger woman's face was not lost on Vinnie.

So that's the way the wind lies, she thought and, never averse to a bit of matchmaking, smiled.

"I believe you are with the Foreign Office, Mr Litchfield."

"Yes, ma'am. In fact, I'm due to leave for Florence at the end of the week."

Miss Dunfield took a singular interest in a finger of her glove, worrying it until the thread gave way.

"Don't you find it lonely in those foreign cities? Since you don't have a family, I mean?"

"It is very lonely," he replied with feeling.

"Well, Vinnie said with surprising briskness, "I feel it is our duty to do what we can for you gallant gentlemen who are trying to put Europe back together. It's a dangerous business, with the fighting so recently over. My dear Miss Dunfield, why don't you walk for a while with Mr Litchfield? We can have our little chat anytime, and Mr Litchfield is to be gone so soon. . . . I'll make a circuit of the park and meet you here in three-quarters of an hour or so."

With the same gentle ruthlessness she had used on Jordy and Miss Chyngford, Vinnie detached Miss Dunfield from the phaeton and deposited her beside Mr Litchfield, taking note of their glowing looks at each other before driving away at a smart pace. Bernard had told her time and time again not to meddle in other people's affairs, but it seemed a shame not to when all it took to arrange things properly was a little resolution!

=9=

OVER HER SHOULDER, Lacey could see the figures of her cousin and Mr Litchfield leave Mrs Stanton-Hogg's phaeton; that made yet another thing about this day over which her aunt could be unhappy. Not only was she, Lacey, paired with the man earmarked for Elizabeth, but Elizabeth had been left with the man Aunt Leonora had decided on as perfect for Lacey herself. It was definitely an uncomfortable situation, for Lacey had convinced herself that she had no desire to talk to Lord Piedmont under any circumstances, let alone one of such enforced intimacy. The seats of the high-perch phaetons were indeed small, and the viscount was a big man.

Despite all good intentions, Lacey sneaked a look at him under the cover of her lashes. Without a doubt he was the best-looking man she had ever seen. His shoulders, encased in dark blue superfine cut by a master's hand, were broad and shapely; his muscular legs were sharply defined by buff-coloured trousers and boots polished to a dazzling gloss. No wonder he was so odiously proud; he'd have reason to be even if he lacked both title and wealth.

"Good afternoon, Miss Chyngford," Jordan said politely, hoping to make her say something. She had maintained a stiff silence since entering the phaeton, a fact which his lordship, despite wide experience with the female sex, found somewhat disconcerting. Jordan Piedmont, had no intention of being put out by the stubborn silence of a green girl from a North Country vicarage, no matter how delicious she looked or how much she stirred him. Jordan put himself out to be charming. "You look quite well today. That outfit becomes you."

It was true, he thought. The girl looked very pretty in her tailored driving outfit of pale yellow trimmed with ecru. The hem was daringly short, according to the new fashion, showing almost the whole of her ankles—and very neat ankles they were, too, Jordan noted. A stylishly huge muff dyed to match the ecru trim lay in and all but covered her lap. With the late-afternoon sunshine glinting around her in a golden nimbus, Miss Chyngford was almost ethereally beautiful, as the straggling crowd of the Fashionable World attested by their stares.

"Thank you," she said softly. Then, surprisingly, "I fear I owe you an apology, my lord."

"An apology? For what?"

"For failing to call you by your correct title. It was very *farouche* of me not to have ascertained your proper styling."

A slight frown of annoyance crossed Jordan's brow. Trust the chit to make her apology sound like a criticism! "It makes no matter. I didn't realise you didn't know."

How odious that he should be so self-assured as to think it general knowledge he possessed a title, Lacey thought. He and Elizabeth were well made for each other, since they were both so obsessed on the subject!

"I only wish Melsham hadn't twigged onto it. He'll make it into an amusing *on-dit*; it's probably all over town by now. I only hope it won't make you too uncomfortable."

Lacey looked at him in surprise. "Why should you care? If it's uncomfortable for me, I mean?" she stammered hastily, all but deafened by the thud of her quickened heartbeats as Jordan turned on the full charm of his smile.

"Because people will gossip and point and tease and in general make a public figure of you until some other incident claims their attention."

"You are jesting, I hope?"

"Hardly." Piedmont was somewhat taken aback by the

open incredulity in her lovely face. She was such an innocent. . . . How could he ever have thought she was not a beauty? She was quite the most beautiful girl he had ever seen.

"But that people should be so inconsequential . . . so petty! They have all the advantages of music and learning and—"

"And prefer to dawdle away their time with scandal and gossip. It's human nature."

"They have so much and do so little with it," Lacey murmured. "Shallow—"

"Thank you, Miss Chyngford. Am I included in that unflattering denunciation?"

Lacey ignored the question. "You must admit that it is true. What do they know of real life, of hunger and misery and poverty?"

"Nothing," Jordan said, glancing at her. "To them it doesn't exist."

"Let them eat cake." Her young voice was bitter.

"May I speak frankly, Miss Chyngford?"

A faint ghost of humour flitted over Lacey's face. "I am in no position to stop you, my lord. I cannot imagine your not doing anything you wish to do."

Jordan frowned. "Such a reply is unworthy of you. I merely wished to say that you have a chance for a London Season among the Haut Ton. Most girls would give their eyes for such an opportunity, yet you seem indifferent, if not downright hostile! I cannot understand."

"My family was . . . estranged from the main branch of the Chyngfords, so I grew up in a different atmosphere." Lacey, for some unexplained reason having decided on giving him her confidence, chose her words carefully. "A Season was my grandmother's idea. I like fun as much as the next person, I suppose, but the pursuit of it to the exclusion of other endeavor seems somewhat unhealthy."

His lordship hid his surprise well. Amid the hustle and clamour of the Season, he had often felt that way, but thought it a solitary aberration; to hear it now from this green girl was astounding.

"What do you know of life, Miss Chyngford? What has happened to make you so different from your peers?"

At the intense note in his voice, Lacey studied his lordship's face for any sign of mockery and, finding none, began to speak of the harshness of life in Potter's Ford, of the unreasonable rents and overpriced bread, of indifferent landlords and unscrupulous managers. She tried to keep personal details from her narrative, but her tone told Piedmont a great deal, not only about her past but about the low esteem in which she held him and his kind.

And with good reason, thought Jordan after she spoke haltingly of the bad year when the cattle froze on their feet and the poorest people ate earth to keep the pangs of hunger down.

"Do you think there will be a revolution, like the one in France?"

"I pray not, Your Lordship. I hope that good English farming folk know that such a radical course can only end in their own ultimate loss—one cannot say that the French are any better off now after their own uprising and that mad corporal who tore all of Europe apart, can one?"

"Two decades of bloodshed and upheaval are not an enviable legacy."

"Yet it is a final resort, and I fear for the consequences if there is not some sort of understanding reached. No sensible person wishes for violence, but if there is no alternative and people are desperate enough—"

"You frighten me. What a pity you could not make your case before the House of Lords," Jordan said sincerely, then unthinkingly chuckled at the absurd thought of a woman in that august body of government. "Imagine a woman in Lords."

"And just what is so funny about that? Why shouldn't a woman sit in Parliament? Or be Prime Minister, for that matter?"

Jordan so forgot himself that he turned to stare at her in amazement. The horses, having not been exercised in some time, were still devilish fresh and quick to sense a negligence in the hands that held their reins. It was an exciting few moments and an excellent display of superb horsemanship before they were returned to a sedate trot. Miss Chyngford breathed sincere admiration, untinged by fear, but his lordship, his mind still stunned, paid no heed.

"Women? In Parliament? They'd turn it into some damned ladies' aid society and exchange needlework patterns! Women have no place in government!"

The ghost of Mrs Stoker rose in outrage behind Lacey. "What about Queen Elizabeth?" Miss Chyngford asked sweetly, her mouth speaking for both. "England had her greatest period of expansion during her reign."

"She reigned for a very long time, remember, and probably had very good advisors."

"And you probably believe that women shouldn't be educated or have any say in their lives. Did you know that a married woman in England is little better, legally, than a slave? Mary Wollstonecraft says—"

"That unnatural creature!" ejaculated the viscount in unconscious echo of Lady Chyngford. "No wonder you have such damned blue ideas. Whoever let you read such radical trash?"

They had almost completed the circuit of the park, for ahead were Miss Dunfield and Mr Litchfield cosily arm in arm, and Mrs Stanton-Hogg's phaeton was visible bowling along just past the Yew Walk. Lacey was livid and stared woodenly ahead.

"Since the idea of a thinking female is so abhorrent to you, I find it wonderful you can bear to speak to me. I shall not burden you with my company any longer if you will have the goodness to set me down."

"I took you up from my cousin's company," his lordship said through gritted teeth. "I shall return you there."

"Like a parcel?" Miss Chyngford rejoined sweetly.

Before he could think of an adequate reply, they were beside the rest of their party and Miss Chyngford was being aided down by the ever-correct Mr Litchfield. Piedmont returned her glacial *devoirs* in kind and sped smartly away with a glance at his cousin that boded ill for her the next time they should meet!

White-faced with conflicting emotions, Lacey accepted Mr Litchfield's help in mounting Mrs Stanton-Hogg's phaeton, where, once settled, she sat staring straight ahead. That worthy lady, having taken one look at her guest's set face, developed an overwhelming interest in arranging the reins just so.

What went wrong? Vinnie wondered. *I thought they'd straighten out whatever it was; instead they both look like doing murder!*

Bernard would be so upset with her.

The gallant Mr Litchfield was boosting Miss Dunfield into the phaeton with a great deal more care than he had expended on Miss Chyngford. His hand clasped hers fervently.

"Thank you for this afternoon, Miss Dunfield."

"It was my pleasure, Mr Litchfield," Elizabeth replied in a particularly throaty voice. "I wish you good fortune in your assignment."

"I don't leave until Friday. Might I take the liberty of calling on you and your family?"

Miss Dunfield turned an alarmingly pale hue. "No, you mustn't. . . ."

"Remember my bouquet," he whispered, and gave her hand a final squeeze. Then he was walking briskly away without even the courtesy of bidding the other ladies goodbye.

As if I could forget, Elizabeth thought, and surreptitiously dabbed away a tear. Red tulips and ivy were an unusual combination, but in the language of flowers . . . Unfortunately, declarations of love and marriage were not enough to satisfy her mother.

For once Lady Dunfield's foresight had failed; despite all her efforts, no invitations for that evening had materialised, leaving the Chyngford party dependent on themselves for amusement. It was a gloomy evening. Right after dinner Sir Cicero had announced his intention of decamping to Boodle's. He did not feel it necessary to raise Leonora's hackles by telling her it was to keep a gaming engagement with the Duke of Lowood. She was so set on landing Piedmont for that pudding-faced daughter of hers that she was like to grow hysterical if she found her brother being cultivated by the viscount's rival.

After Sir Cicero went upstairs to change into an outfit suitable for accompanying a duke, the evening became even more depressing. By unspoken mutual assent, the young misses had said nothing of the more unorthodox aspects of their outing in the park and had somewhat satisfied Lady Dunfield with a tepid recital of their limited social chitchat. In a fit of melancholy, which her mother attributed to Miss Chyngford's unwelcome presence that afternoon, Elizabeth huddled in a chair near the fire, eyes staring at the flames until they watered from the heat.

Lacey was in a state no better. Glad of a lack of desire for communication on her aunt's part, she sat listlessly turning the pages of a book, not seeing a word. Her mind was too full of Lord Piedmont to assimilate any of Elizabeth's Italian Baedecker.

It was astonishing how much that gentleman did occupy her thoughts since his thinking seemed to be so antithetical to her ideals, but what young lady—no matter her principles—could fail to be stirred by a male of such perfection? Not only were his looks enough to turn heads and create dreams wherever he went, but under that fashionable exterior Lacey sensed an intelligent, amenable man whom her parents would have liked. Even Mrs Stoker would have found him amusing, once she got past that stupid prejudice of his against intelligent women.

With a sigh, Lacey turned yet another page to stare sightlessly at a singularly bad sketch of the Roman Forum.

The worst thing was Aunt Leonora's assurance that the viscount was just on the verge of offering for Elizabeth at any minute. If her aunt could bring it about—which Lacey doubted—they would probably make a very happy couple, Lacey thought morosely. Elizabeth certainly never had a serious thought in her head, which would support the viscount's conception of womanhood. As for him . . . how could Elizabeth not be happy, being his wife?

Perhaps, Lacey thought sadly, she should take her hundred pounds and disappear to some place where she could live quietly and find work, but even as the thought came it died. Despite her strong words that afternoon, she could not leave town now, though she mistakenly thought it was the lure of the Season which held her.

The announcement of a visitor lightened the atmosphere until it proved to be Mr Litchfield. Perhaps he was not excessively adept in social situations, but Milton Litchfield was not lacking in courage.

"Mr Litchfield!" exclaimed Lady Dunfield in not-altogether-pleased surprise. His failure to respond immediately to her machinations concerning Lacey had left her ladyship somewhat cool toward him.

"Good evening, Your Ladyship . . . Miss Chyngford . . . Miss Dunfield. How fortunate I am to find you at home this evening. I trust I do not intrude. . . . It's just that I return to Florence on Friday and could not go without paying a final visit to your charming family," he said with but the slightest pause for breath.

Lady Dunfield's smile spread as her hopes once again came to flower. "How delightful! Lacey, my dear, here is Mr Litchfield to see you."

Seeing the rapid change of colour in her cousin's all-too-transparent face, Lacey sincerely doubted that assertion but decided against saying so. "How pleasant to see you again, Mr Litchfield. Don't you think it nice of Mr Litchfield to want to see us again before leaving the country, Elizabeth?"

"Very nice," she replied through stiff lips.

"Dear Lacey was saying just today how much she envied your journey to Italy," Lady Dunfield gushed after seating that worthy and their guest in suitably close proximity. "It has always been one of her favourite countries."

"Have you been to Italy, Miss Chyngford?"

"No, I've only read about it. Elizabeth was kind enough to lend me her own book on the country."

"Baedecker," he murmured, turning the well-worn volume in his hands. "It is a good one."

An uncomfortable silence fell, broken only when her lady chirruped with sudden inspiration, "Perhaps Mr Litchfield would care for some music. Lacey, my dear, would you play?"

"I'm sorry, Aunt Leonora, but I fear I cannot play. As the vicarage possessed no pianoforte, I never learned, but perhaps Elizabeth would favour us with a selection or two?"

Mr Litchfield's face brightened. "Please, Miss Dunfield? That would please me greatly."

As one in a dream, Elizabeth moved to the piano. At Greathills it had been one of Lacey's dearest joys to listen to her cousin practising, even though Miss Dunfield's enthusiasm for music unquestionably exceeded her gift. This evening, however, she outdid herself in a surprisingly passionate selection of Italian songs. Lady Dunfield's eyebrows lifted higher and higher as the emotionalism of the music swelled, until with a final, thrilling major chord Elizabeth finished.

"Bravo, my girl, bravo!" thundered Sir Cicero from the doorway. He was resplendent in old-style knee breeches and brocade coat of blue and silver.

"Uncle Cicero, we thought you'd gone."

"And I should have, Lacey, but when I heard Elizabeth playing, I just couldn't leave until I had heard it all."

It was only a small untruth, for often he had complained of being tone-deaf, but the sight of that shy foreign officer chap sitting by Lacey had given him an idea—which is, as everyone knows, a dangerous thing. He knew of his sister's half-baked plan to match this chap off with Lacey and saw a chance to put Leonora in his debt.

With a request which was scarcely less than a command, he pulled the confused young man out of the house, barely giving him time for an acceptable farewell to the ladies; there was, after all, Sir Cicero's appointment with the duke, and he had no desire to be any later than he already was.

Once safely in the street, he turned to the bewildered Mr Litchfield with a smile. "Sorry to be so high-handed about that, but our time is limited and we need to talk man to man. You're sweet on my niece, aren't you?"

"Yes, sir," Milton Litchfield said sadly.

"Thought so. She's a good girl . . . headstrong at times, but just the sort of wife a man in foreign parts needs. Have you asked her to marry you yet?"

Startled, the younger man tried to study Sir Cicero's face in the shadowy light of the *torchères*. "I know I should have spoken to you first, sir—"

"Hang it all, man; we're friends, I hope! I'm not calling you to account. Did she refuse you?" he asked jovially.

"Yes, sir."

Foolish chit, thought her uncle somewhat uncharitably. *That vicarage girl is harder to get rid of than a dun!*

"Well, I suppose that means you'll just have to ask her again. I know she likes you. . . ."

"Do you really think so?" The note of hope in Litchfield's voice was pathetic.

"Of course I do; trouble is, she's just a silly romantic girl who doesn't know what's good for her. You need to be strong . . . convincing. . . . Don't ask her—Dear Heaven, man, don't ever ask a woman what she wants, because they don't really know. They're like children; you need to be firm but tender. Don't ask her; tell her."

It was a conversation that stayed in Mr Litchfield's mind long after Sir Cicero's discovery of the lateness of the hour and after the two, not knowing they had reached a perfect misunderstanding, had parted. Indeed, the young man made somewhat of a spectacle of himself by rehearsing firm but tender speeches to the evening air as he walked slowly home.

═10═

IT WAS A busy evening. Even as Lacey was apologising to her cousin for having asked her to play when she was obviously pale from a headache and Sir Cicero was parting from an astonished Milton Litchfield, His Grace the Duke of Lowood was shocking the staff and habitués of Boodle's with his unprecedented affability. Long known as a deep player with the blunt to back it up, His Grace was always welcomed in a game for his brass, but not his gall. Cursed with a volatile temper and a disagreeable disposition, Lowood was not personally popular.

The regulars at Boodle's, therefore, were to a man astounded by the duke's congenial smile—though it was somewhat grotesque, as if rusted from long disuse. His Grace spoke cordially to the assembled group and, slipping a sizeable gratuity to the astonished butler, bespoke a fine dinner for all his friends.

"I say, Lowood," drawled Lord Petersham in the affected lisp which was much copied by aspirant dandies, "are you trying to seduce us?"

A nervous titter ran around the room. The duke's behaviour was indeed questionable, but Lord Petersham was the only one sufficiently wealthy to count himself safe from financial reprisals should his curiosity prove uncomfortable to the duke.

"Seduction is not my line, my lord, as I think Lady Mickleham proved. No, I wish merely to have you gentlemen join me at supper and provide an evening of excellent gaming. Will you be my guests?"

It was an unprecedented moment. To be asked to be Lowood's guest was incredible enough, but to hear him refer so calmly to the disastrous affair of Winterthorpe's daughter, who had jilted him for an army officer just before an official announcement was to have been made of their betrothal, was incredible. For some weeks after that unfortunate experience, Lowood had been the laughingstock of the ton, a state of affairs which he did not accept with good grace, and before long several of the rasher young bucks learned to their sorrow that, despite his years, Lowood was a formidable opponent on the field of honour.

Lord Petersham flicked an invisible bit of snuff from his exquisite lace. "I for one accept, my dear fellow, if for no reason than to see what you're up to."

"Up to?" His Grace's face was an improbable study of innocence. "I merely wish to provide a good evening's gaming for myself and my friends. . . ."

Emboldened by Petersham's success, young Canfield, who was known to love a good game whether or not he could afford it, smiled lazily. "And we thank you, good sir. Since there is no time but the present, shall we begin?" he raised his hands in a languid manner to call for fresh cards and dice.

"Wait," His Grace said, and his smile took on a slightly bitter twist. How easy it all was and how right he had been that everyone could be bought; the only question was price. For Petersham, it was curiosity; for Canfield, high play and a good dinner; for Chyngford . . . What price would the Chyngfords demand? "There is one more to come. I should not like to begin without Sir Cicero."

Petersham's eyes narrowed. "Chyngford? From what I've heard, he's fairly well in the basket."

"Is this to be a low-stakes game? If Chyngford's pockets are to let, he'll not want to play for any interesting wagers," Canfield whined. The spectre of pennilessness followed his heels too closely for him to relish a possible win from someone unable to pay.

"I assure you gentlemen that there is nothing for you to worry about. Any debts incurred by our dear Sir Cicero will be made good," His Grace said, and his smile broadened. This time he planned to be prepared, no matter what the future might hold.

Jordan, Lord Piedmont, was also considering the future that evening. Since he had succeeded to the title, he had been reminded regularly by his superannuated Great-Aunt Harriette of his duty to marry and set up a nursery. Of late the old lady had become more blunt in her letters about her desire to see her grand-nephew wed and the family line preserved before she died, stating flatly that she wasn't getting any younger and neither was he.

Great-Aunt Harriette's latest espistle, received that very afternoon, had been particularly strong, threatening to leave her entire fortune to her six cats instead of to him unless the nursery at Foxton Chase were on its way to being filled soon. Of course, Jordan would never have thought of marrying just to suit his great-aunt's whim, for he knew that the possible loss of her fortune was no threat at all to the future of Foxton Chase; however, he also knew how big a threat she thought it was.

The family was sacred to Great-Aunt Harriette, so even the mere threat that she might leave her personal fortune to any other than the head of the Piedmonts was itself an indication of how strongly the old lady felt. She had never married, devoting herself to the service of her parents and, finally, to the whole of the Piedmont tribe. It was she who had raised Jordan and his brother after the early death of their mother, and it was because of her that he found duty and family responsibility more familiar than love.

It was out of a sense of duty, then, that he went to the ball at the Swedish Embassy that evening instead of dining with a few cronies, as planned, and having a quiet game later. Coming right on the heels of his disastrous drive with that impertinent Chyngford chit, Great-Aunt Harriette's letter was decidedly unwelcome, but still thought-provoking. She had written long and lovingly of the glorious history of the Piedmont family and of Foxton Chase, and of how the futures of both were dependent on his bestirring himself to find a wife.

Great-Aunt Harriette's letter spurred him to action; damned if he wouldn't go to the Swedish ball that night, look over the new debutantes, and find a nice group of young ladies who had proper thoughts of marriage and home and other normal ideas, unlike the very blue Miss Chyngford.

Although it had been several years since the Frenchman Bernadotte had been adopted as Crown Prince to succeed the mad Vasa king, the reforms he was making in the archaic Swedish government had yet to sift down to the layer of social protocol. Any affair at the Swedish Embassy was sure to be laden with antique pomp and circumstance to rival any ruling of Almack's Rooms, which were thought by many to be the ultimate delineation of gentility; the Swedish guest list was pared to the most distinguished of the Haut Ton and, though it usually made for a very dull party, invitations were extremely prized. It would be an ideal place for him to go look over the current crop of young and eligible girls.

Wearing the old-style knee breeches as required, Lord Piedmont made a striking entrance into the ballroom. He had chosen a suit of creamy brocade, accentuated by great spills of exquisite lace, and a waistcoat shot with golden thread; his legs in their silken cream hose needed no artificial aids, and the buckles of his pale shoes were fashioned of gold. All this, combined with his lightly tanned, handsome face and crown of dark gold curls, made it seem as if the great god Apollo himself had come to grace the party. Within minutes all the young, and some of the not so young, ladies made obvious note of his entrance so that instead of Lord Piedmont's looking for suitable companions, they were looking for him.

"An ice!" Tiny, delicate hands reached for the proffered treat. "How kind of you, my lord. I vow I am perishing in this heat!"

Jordan smiled at such flagrant fibbing, for Phoebe Remington looked nothing but delicious. She was a delicate creature almost as tiny as her cousin Vinnie, though where that worthy lady was all pale pink and gold in colouring, Miss Remington was cream and roses with heavy black hair. She did not show to advantage in the white required of a debutante, but even in such adverse circumstances she was undoubtedly an Incomparable and would have been thought so even if her father were not fabulously wealthy nor her mother a daughter of one of the royal dukes.

It had taken the better part of the evening for Jordan to select Miss Remington for his attentions and a good deal more time for him to detach her from her retinue of admirers, but he had done it. Now they sat on one of the discreetly placed *fauteuils* reserved for courting couples, where they could at least feel alone with no social stigma attached for lack of an immediate chaperone.

"Would you care for a taste?" Miss Remington asked, very politely extending the cup and showing her dimples. Her eyes were a sparkling hazel, like new wine.

"Thank you, I have punch." Easily, Jordan lowered himself beside her, absurdly afraid that his bulk might somehow injure one of such adorable frailty merely by his proximity. She was such a delicate thing, just as high as his heart. It was a relief to be able just to sit with her, for while dancing it was difficult to see anything save the top of her head.

"This is not at all what I'm used to," Miss Remington said after a judicious taste. "It isn't sweet enough."

"Shall I get you some more? Or something else?"

She debated a moment. "No, because this is probably all

they have, and it would be impolite to give insult by implying that they don't know how to make a good ice even if they don't. Mama says we have to be tolerant with foreigners because they aren't all lucky enough to know our ways."

"How are you enjoying your Season?"

"I don't know," she said ingenuously, looking with wide eyes. "I mean, it's just begun and so I don't know. I expect it will be marvellous, with lots of parties and beaux and a great number of men asking for my hand. I'm really very eligible, you know," she confided in an offhand way to a suddenly very uncomfortable Jordan. "Papa has said that there will be lots of fortune hunters around just after my money, so that I must marry someone of equal or greater status and fortune to be sure that we are not taken advantage of."

"Do you plan to marry your first Season?"

"But of course!" Again the dimples played. "It would be too humiliating to be obliged to come back twice, you know. But I don't have to worry about that, for I shall marry quickly." With the insouciance of a cat preening, she brushed back a stray lock of hair and in doing so made a picture designed to be appreciated.

"Is this your first trip to London?" Jordan asked, pulling deeply at his punch and wishing for something stronger. It was all too suggestive of discussing a business transaction to appeal to him; Heaven only knew he didn't believe in all the rampant romaticism so prevalent in the current fashion, but surely not even proper Great-Aunt Harriette would expect him to make a match purely along the lines of a purchase!

"Yes, and despite the lovely time I am having, I tell you I will think twice about making the trip down here again! It was dreadful! They threw stones at me!"

"Stones?" Observing Miss Remington's inflated sense of self-importance, Piedmont wondered idly whether or not some carriage had sent a shower of pebbles against hers, but her next words gained his full attention.

"Yes. We were driving through this dirty little town and the square was so full of people that we could not pass, so of course Papa sent the outriders on ahead to clear the way quickly, because we didn't want to slacken speed. Those dirty louts not only made us stop—and our horses all sweaty—but they threatened my papa when he demanded that they move!" Her kittenish voice was almost shrill with remembered indignation.

Such immediate confirmation of that annoying Miss Chyngford's fears was unnerving to Piedmont; were they really in danger of a revolution? "What were they saying?"

Miss Remington shrugged exquisite shoulders. "I paid no attention to such rabble. I was wearing my very best travelling outfit—in case we should see anyone of worth on the road—anyway, it's made of blue superfine and cost a great deal and looks so beautiful, so I was taking no chances that those people should get it dirty with their muddy rocks just because they were jealous because I had such pretty things. Right after we got to London, Papa complained to the Marquess of Sarnell, for that awful place was not two miles from his principal seat."

"I see," Jordan murmured. Another of Miss Chyngford's predictions had been proven. The Marquess of Sarnell was notorious for being both a dissolute spendthrift and a damnable stingy manager of his estates. There had been an article some time ago in the *Times* lamenting the disrespectful burning of some of the marquess's hayricks. "Do you think there is going to be a revolution?"

"I should hope not! After we are just now able to travel abroad again and at last get French silks without having to make the risk of shopping for smuggled goods! My mama ordered six new silk dresses for me . . ."

The little voice drawled on, enumerating the various colours of her gowns; the skill and outrageous prices of Madame Berthe, the fashionable modiste; the abundance of flowers she had received the morning after her first ball . . . Despite his best intentions, Piedmont's mind began to drift;

not, as one would suppose, to the growing unrest among the hungry poor, but to what Miss Chyngford would say about it.

". . . then Mama wanted to lace it with blue ribbands, but Madame Berthe said . . ."

Doubtless Miss Chyngford would be in sympathy with the rioting "rabble," whose violent emotions had likely been not jealousy for "pretty things" but anger at the cost of bread and fear of retribution for their actions.

Knowing Sarnell's temper, Jordan almost felt sorry for the malefactors and wondered how bad their situation was that they should resort to such desperate action.

". . . then when Lady Jersey met me, she was so kind as to say she remembered my mama as her bosom bow during their Season and it would be a lucky man who would marry me . . ."

If indeed there were internal trouble brewing, it was only proper that he do something about it. He was a member of Lords; he had made his maiden speech the year he had succeeded to the title and scarcely anything since. Perhaps he should start working actively to try to defuse this potential domestic bomb as soon as Parliament sat again.

". . . so when my mama and I made out our list of the desirable qualities for a potential husband, Mama said he must be of the highest ton and Papa said his fortune must be commensurate with mine, but I said that by no means would I accept him unless he were quite handsome. . . ."

For a moment Jordan's somewhat glassy eyes saw not the prettiest girl in the room opposite him but Miss Chyngford as she had been that afternoon, her hair a glowing flame lit by the sun, her attitude that of a warrior princess lecturing him on his shortcomings—

"I vow Your Lordship has not heard one word I've said!" The kittenish voice was gone now, replaced with a tone that carried a grating edge.

"You were saying something about a list your parents made out," muttered Jordan. He was embarrassed at having been caught in so flagrant a violation of courtesy; such behaviour was disgraceful, especially from who was a viscount of the Piedmont line.

Her luscious little mouth turned downward with displeasure. "That was such a long time ago. You do not care one bit what I was saying. . . ."

The effect of her lowered lashes and trembling lip was everything she could have wanted. He all but leaped forward, proffering his own handkerchief to stanch the incipient tears.

"Please accept my apologies, Miss Remington. My only excuse is that the horrid story of your attack was still on my mind. You might have been hurt."

This statement, uttered with proper fervour, seemed to mollify the young lady somewhat, and she smiled bravely at him in the manner of a true heroine, saying that if he had been her protector, those nasty thugs would never have come near.

Then the conversation developed into the sweet kind of mutually complimentary nonsense typical between a pretty young lady and a handsome young gentleman, and was of no interest to anyone save themselves.

Sweets, however, have a way of leaving a bad taste in the mouth, and Lord Piedmont was finding this true on the following morning. With the ease of a welcomed member of the family, he paid an early call on his cousin to seek counsel, only to be told that she was asleep and had left orders not to be disturbed for any reason. Jordan then turned his attention to Mr Stanton-Hogg, who was not only an earlier riser but an amenable fellow who had no objection to a serious talk while he sipped his morning chocolate.

"And so you have captured the heart of the rich and

beauteous Miss Remington," intoned Bernard, somehow managing to look sober and judicial while perched in the big bed and still wearing his nightcap.

Jordan stared. "How the devil did you know about her? You weren't even there last night."

"Don't underestimate the way information travels, Jordy. I wager most of the ton already knows about Miss Remington's definite favour to you last night, and those who don't know by tonight are distinctly beyond the pale. I got the news from Davidson, who came to the Duvalier party directly from the Swedish affair."

"Interesting. Makes you wonder how any secrets are kept at all in this town." Jordan took a drink of chocolate, then put the cup aside. His cousin's household favoured a cinnamon-flavoured blend that was not to his palate.

"Very few are. They merely become limited circulation gossip. Now, tell me about Miss Remington. Is she as beautiful as they say?" Bernard asked, carefully watching his guest for a reaction. He was fond of his wife's cousin, and the unprecedented behaviour Jordy was exhibiting indicated there might be a deeper involvement beyond the usual flirtation. If this were true, Bernard hoped that Jordy might find the happiness which he and Vinnie shared.

"She is very beautiful in a sugar-doll sort of way" was Jordan's surprisingly offhand reply, uttered in so casual a tone that Bernard began to rethink his speculations.

"Did she give you leave to call on her?"

Jordan nodded languidly. "Decidedly. It was all but an order."

Repressing an urge to shake his cousin-in-law for being so vague, Bernard decided that he had read the situation wrongly. Something was definitely afoot, for never had Jordy seemed so downcast and bemused, but apparently the very desirable Miss Remington was not the cause.

"I see," he said slowly, not really seeing at all. "The most popular heiress in London, a true Incomparable, has to order you to call on her. Are you going to?"

"I don't know," Jordan replied, and in doing so almost made his cousin-in-law fall from bed. "She bores me."

"She what?"

"We talked for quite a while, nothing important, just the puffery stuff one always nonsenses around with . . . . Do you know, she told me she and her parents had made up a list of the qualities her suitors must have. Did you ever hear of such a thing?"

"It's unusual of her to mention it, but I believe such lists aren't uncommon. Vinnie's folks made one."

Now it was Jordan's turn to stare. He had always thought his aunt and uncle to be the epitome of English gentility, not some sort of clerkish listmaker.

"Luckily for me, she tore it up in their faces and married me despite my lack of fortune, though I do believe that alone was their sole objection to me."

"But a list. . . ," Jordan said in distaste.

"We were lucky, with Uncle Edgar leaving me his fortune, but one can't rely on luck. If Vinnie and I should ever be blessed with a daughter, I should fight to the death to see her happily settled in life commensurate with her upbringing." Bernard finished his chocolate while Jordan digested this in silence. "You must have fit the qualifications or she wouldn't have asked you to call. Does it bother you so much that her parents want the best possible match for her?"

"Lord, no! She's a decent enough girl, though I do have a sincere hope her future husband will be deaf; he'd have to be to keep from going mad living with such a curst gabble-box."

"Jordan Piedmont, whatever is the matter? Miss Remington is unlikely to be much different from any of the other young ladies of Society with whom you've been amusing yourself these past years. What happened?"

"You're right, Bernard." Jordan unfolded himself from the depths of the brown leather chair and began to pace the room. It was both annoying and gratifying that his companion could see so clearly his own confusion. "It's not Miss Remington . . . though she is both pretty and a prattle-box. It's me. All the time we were together, she babbled on about nothing. On the way to London her father's carriage was pelted with stones by some farmers, and she thought it was only because they were jealous of her fine clothes and things. When I tried to talk to her about the incident, to get some solid information, she just chattered away about nothing! It was pleasant, but it was like talking to a child!"

Bernard camouflaged a sudden snort of laughter into a cough. "Well, my dear cousin Jordy, you are privileged to find out something that many men never discover until after they are married. When you are wed to a lady, you must spend a certain amount of time in conversation with her."

"Don't make fun of me," Jordy replied with ill grace. "A man wants a woman to make his home and bear his children and do credit to his name. I don't want a bunch of learned chatter when I come home. If I did, I'd find a bluestocking like that bad-mannered Miss Chyngford."

Suddenly Bernard understood, though he was not sure he approved of the connexion. He slid from the big bed and, after pulling the bell to summon his valet, shrugged on his silken robe.

"Well, that's a decision every man has to make, but by feeling so, you do a great disservice to your cousin Venetia. She is not only my beloved wife but my most trusted confidante and partner in all I do."

"Vinnie?" asked Jordan, unable to combine the images of his flighty cousin and the paragon so lovingly depicted by her husband.

"I know such an arrangement is heresy to the mores of Society, and becoming more so—more's the pity—but we are happy with our partnership and if you settle for less than the most you can get you are not half the man I think you are."

— 11 —

ALTHOUGH IT WAS long past dawn, it was still the earliest Lacey had been up and about since going to Greathills. The ton would be in their beds for hours yet, but the city was long awake. Pushcart vendors and women carrying baskets and pails each extolled their wares in the ageless chants, industrious maids scrubbed steps and polished brass, unidentifiable people on unidentifiable errands scurried through the streets looking somehow furtive no matter the innocence of their mission, and here and there a chair or coach gently bore homeward some late reveller who was more likely than not oblivious to the panorama.

Lacey loved it. The life of the city, the hustle and hurry of so much motion in such a relatively small area, fascinated her. Until now she had been caught in the genteel boredom of a walk in the park or shopping in the best areas under close chaperonage, an onerous state of affairs to a girl used to the relative freedom of the country.

She looked down at her dress and hoped she wouldn't be too conspicuous. The ill-fitting blacks she had worn to Greathills would have been better, but those had been burnt almost immediately at the disdainful orders of her grandmother. Lacey had chosen the simplest of her new clothes, a morning dress of soft pink muslin that should have clashed with her hair but somehow didn't, over which she had thrown her plainest cloak of dark blue wool fastened with black braid frogs.

"Will I do, Effie?"

A queer combination of fear and worship filled her companion's eyes. "Ye look like a queen, Miss Chyngford, sure and swear ye do." She hesitated, then tentatively offered to give away her hope in order to ensure the safety of her idol. "Miss Chyngford . . . ye don't have to come with me, honest. It be an ugly neighbourhood, not what ye be used to at all."

Lacey looked down into the pinched little face. Ever since she had found the little maid the evening before, sobbing her heart out for an ailing mother even as she tended to Miss Chyngford's evening fire, Lacey had felt a great sense of shame for allowing the hedonistic life of Greathills and Chyngford House to keep her from living up to her parents' ideals.

The maid, scarcely more than a child, had been terrified to be caught by one of the gentry. Tasks were supposed to be done when the family was not there, as if by invisible genies. To be found working was a cause for shame; to be surprised in any sort of personal emotion was grounds for dismissal without a character, which was little better than a death sentence.

Had it been Lady Dunfield or her daughter who had found her, Effie knew she would have been let go immediately. Miss Chyngford was different, however, and before she knew it, Effie had been tearfully spilling out the whole sad story of her ill mother, the unheated room and poor food; then the young miss was acting like some good princess in a fairy story, telling her that she herself would visit her mother on the morrow. . . . It was like a dream.

In the morning light, though, Effie was having second thoughts. Seven Dials was a notorious area, populated mainly by prostitutes and criminals, totally unfit for a lady. Even Effie, now that she was carrying a large basket of food suitable for an invalid, which Miss Chyngford had charmed from the cook, wasn't sure she could negotiate the area without someone trying to steal her bounty, though she was careful not to mention that to Miss Chyngford.

With exquisite courtesy Lacey listened to the tweeny's protests, then overrode them. She was the daughter of a country vicar whose whole life had been given to the work of the Lord, to helping those less fortunate than he; could she disregard such a heritage?

It would be less than honest to say that Lacey enjoyed her outing; for one thing, it had been a while since she had rambled so carefree over the Yorkshire distances, and she was ill-conditioned for the long walk from Chyngford House to Seven Dials. Additionally, the dainty kid slippers considered the proper footgear for a young lady were decidedly uncomfortable for long strolls on cobblestones; Lacey longed for her well-worn country boots.

What was most disturbing, however, was the filth. Poverty was no stranger to her, but the condition of the London poor was an unpleasant revelation. In most of the poor homes in Potter's Ford, there might be hardly any food for the evening meal, but the cottage and its grounds would be as neat as the inhabitants could make it.

Here Lacey's eyes were assaulted by a narrow street awash in filth, by old buildings leaning at uncertain angles seemingly untended since the day they had been built, by cracked and dirty stoops barely visible under their pitiful loads of human refuse.

That was the worst, for she could never have imagined that people might degenerate into little more than heaps of tattered clothing sprawled over steps and kerbs, watching passersby with dull and empty eyes. Greasy caps sat on greasier hair, and in dirty laps lay naked toddlers, bony and motionless. The air was thick with the pungent aroma of cheap gin and unwashed bodies, rising in waves to assail the nose and stomach.

At Chyngford House Lacey had felt her costume to be innocuous, even plain, but in Seven Dials it stood out as would have the Regent's purple robe of state. There was animosity in those blank stares, and Lacey could feel a small *frisson* of fear dancing up her spine. At Potter's Ford the poor had been indifferent and ungrateful at times, unwilling to appreciate the effort put forth on their behalf, but she and her parents had walked the parish from one end to the other with no fear whatsoever; here—

"Here we be, miss. Mind yer step." Effie led the way into a building that tilted just a bit more than its neighbours, almost as if it had stirred slightly in sleep. The stairs, lit only by the uncertain light from the door, led upward at a steep and crazy angle. Piles of rubbish lay like flotsam in the corners and the smell was incredible. Lacey pulled her skirts in close.

Effie's mother's room was like an island of sanity in a world gone mad. Spartanly bare, it had only a bed and a wooden chair, but save for a light gilding of dust it was clean. Once more on ground she could understand, Lacey softly offered a gracious greeting to the gaunt woman on the bed even as Effie was blurting out the tale of the visitor.

Both through habit and compassion, sickroom duties came easily to Lacey. She chattered with Mrs Feeny while unloading the hamper of goodies and learned that the older woman had been a seamstress until her health broke and the shop refused to keep her on. She and Effie managed to eke a bare living from the girl's meagre wages and Mrs Feeny's even more scanty savings, but those were almost gone. Tears rose in Mrs Feeny's rheumy eyes and her fingers picked aimlessly at the coverlet as she recited her tale of woe with no self-pity or whining. Lacey took note of the very real fear lurking in the woman's eyes as she explained with a pathetic dignity that no shop would take her unless she were strong enough to work a full fifteen hours, six days a week; it made no difference that she did the finest embroidery in London.

Often, back in Potter's Ford, Lacey had heard similarly distressing tales of misfortune and had longed to be able to do something to alleviate such suffering; now—thanks to the generosity of old Mrs Stoker and her grandmother—she could. Before she left the Feeny establishment a few minutes later, it was arranged that she should have a consignment of handkerchief linen sent to Mrs Feeny to be hemmed and monogrammed in a reasonable amount of time, one that would not put a strain on the woman's health. It would not be a permanent solution, but the Feeny women would be safe from immediate destitution.

Lacey left the decrepit house with the blessings of the two women in her ears, tempered by young Effie's reluctance to allow her mistress to return to Chyngford House alone through the unsavoury district. Laughing, Lacey lightly told of her childhood with solitary walks through deserted country and waist-high snowdrifts, and forbade Effie to leave her mother until noon. She herself would say that the girl had been sent on an errand; overriding Effie's protests, Lacey declared her ability to find her way home safely.

Once on the street Lacey's determination wavered; the countryside, however hazardous, had a certain sort of cleanliness—invigorating mentally and physically—which was conspicuously absent in this London slum. She had no fear about retracing her path, for being country-bred she had taken care to watch for markers—though where in the countryside she would have made notice of different trees and oddly shaped rocks, in London she had to remember street names and broken windows—but the waiting crowd seemed thicker, uglier. . . . The air of angry resentment seemed almost palpable, with dark mutterings ruffling the fringes of the crowd. Almost without volition, Lacey quickened her step. The sooner she was off this street with its shabby ocean of human dereliction, the better off she would be.

Turn left at the next corner; then two more streets, a right turn, and she would be on the big thoroughfare that led into the south side of the park; once there she would be less than five minutes from home. Lacey began to count the steps, anything to keep her mind occupied and away from dwelling on the crowd, which was growing bigger and uglier and following right on her heels.

Lacey squared her shoulders, knowing that the soonest

way to encourage attack from a maddened beast was to show fear. She turned the corner smartly and tried to hide her distress when the muttering mob followed right behind her. Their numbers were growing now, as was their courage. She could catch sentences now, disjointedly muttered through many throats.

"Damned swell, prissing around down here like she owned it . . ."

"Look at her . . . no better than a drab under those fancy clothes . . ."

"That cloak be new . . . and that dress . . ." The voice was a woman's, with a thin edge of envy beneath the anger. "My bairns go hungry, but that tart wears new clothes!"

The pathetic anguish in that voice touched Lacey's heart; she would be less than her father's daughter if she did not try to help. With only the slightest hesitation, she turned to face the crowd. She was totally unprepared for their number or their raggedness or the burning hostility in their stony faces.

"Who said their children were hungry?" Remembering her father's ways, Lacey smiled and spoke gently. "We must not let children go hungry."

The creature who stepped forward resembled an animated rag heap more than any form of human being Lacey had ever seen. Straggly hair hung in thin whisps from a cap which had not been laundered in living memory, around a face that was almost as dirty. Even from Lacey's distance the woman's stench was stronger than her voice, and her voice was certainly loud enough.

" 'We must not let children go hungry.' " Her tone was bitterly mocking. The mob was circling now, like a pack of scavengers. Lacey's retreat was cut off, and she realized her mistake. Now she was committed.

A ratlike fellow in the ruin of what had once been elegant evening dress gave a shrill laugh. "And why should the little buggers be any different from the rest of us?"

Lacey wet suddenly dry lips, hoping they would not see

her fear. "I know you have problems, but I want you to know you're not alone! There are men in Parliament who are trying to change things so that you will all have jobs—"

The putrid air around her erupted into a cacophonous babble of shrieks and catcalls which approximated for laughter. "Jobs!" the dirty woman howled, and then spat on the pavement. "The fine lady thinks we want jobs. She thinks we want to work. . . ."

A bull of a man stepped forward. His size alone would have made him impressive, but Lacey would remember him forever because half of his face was missing. At one time he must have been very handsome. "Work? What's that?"

The entire crowd laughed as if he had made the most amusing jest. They were moving in now, so close that the stench of their clothes and their cheap liquor blended in with and overpowered that of the open sewer.

"There is much satisfaction to be found in work," the proper Miss Chyngford babbled, trying to fight an unconventional argument with conventional rhetoric. "If you had some training, to teach you a trade of your choice—"

The incredible laughter came again, chilling Lacey's bones as they had never been in the direst of North Country winters. She would have backed away from their inhuman eyes, but there was nowhere to go; a dirty hand reached out to finger the wool of her cloak.

"Training!" shrieked the ratlike little man. "We be trained already, my fine miss, in the kind of work we likes best." A knife flashed in his grubby paw. "I'll wager she's got golden guineas in that pretty little bag."

Lacey grabbed convulsively at the tiny lace reticule dangling from her wrist; it was purely an instinctive gesture, for it contained naught but a few shillings and coppers wrapped in a clean handkerchief.

"Eh, Zacky, ye take care now! That cloak's mine. I care naught for the rest, but I has taken a sort of fancy for a warm cloak."

"You don't understand!" Lacey cried. "I want to help you—"

The woman laughed raucously, showing a mouthful of rotted stumps. She was no more than half a dozen years older than Lacey, but she acted toward the clean child of Society as she would have toward an unfledged babe. "We help ourselves, yer fine ladyship—"

A scream split the air, and for a moment Lacey could not be sure it had not come from her own throat, paralyzed though it seemed to be. Then there were other screams, and the crowd began to scatter like chickens in a rainstorm, shuffling through the offal and sewage before the great beast charging through their midst. Lacey felt herself being lifted from the pavement by an iron-hard arm. There was a wild sensation of movement, and Lacey gave herself up to the swirling lightheadedness until the world stabilized into a firm shoulder clad in immaculate superfine.

"You little fool," snapped Jordan, Viscount Piedmont.

Lacey did not even question his presence. For a moment she debated the relative merits of her two predicaments and decided at last that to be rescued by that odious prig was preferable to being mauled by an unwashed mob, but it did seem to be an unfair jest of the gods that of all the men in London to witness her humiliation, it should be he!

Jordan slowed the horse; the mob was far behind them, and they were still in an area where no one of their world would see them. With no small effort, he pulled her limp form into a more comfortable position on the saddle bow. She was most dreadfully pale, which was only to be expected, but seemed not to have been molested. He hadn't seen any of those filthy creatures lay hands on her, but it was a relief to find her unhurt. He had waited to ride in, hoping to teach her a lesson about treating such riffraff as one would gentlefolk, and then found to his horror he had almost waited too late. The thought that she might have been injured frightened him more than any threatening savage the American wilderness might produce.

"What the devil were you doing in there? Seven Dials is a cesspit, unfit for decent women. Doubtless you were in there trying to civilise those beasts. . . ."

"I tried to tell them that they could be helped." Lacey's eyes were closed. It was easier to keep them that way so she wouldn't have to look at his wrathful face, she decided, and by doing so alarmed him no end. "They weren't interested."

"Don't you realise you could have been killed?" Concern made his voice rough. Lacey could feel the thudding of his heart through his coat. "That kind of scum would just as soon kill you for that cloak as look at you. They're criminals, not your good and pious poor of Yorkshire, or wherever it is you come from. What were you doing there?"

"Visiting a sick woman." Lacey's eyes flashed open. "Where did you come from? What were you doing there? Or is that something a gentleman does that a gentlewoman is not supposed to mention?" She was irrationally angry at the thought of his being in some unknown woman's arms, though her emotion had not yet crystallised into thought.

"You ill-bred guttersnipe! How dare you ask such a thing! How could you know. . . ?"

Lacey squirmed against his confining arm, her anger rising fast. How dare he treat her like an ignorant child! "Parsons are told many things," she replied with dignity, "and vicarage walls are not thick. There are things one cannot help knowing," she added, hoping a lofty tone would conceal a vast ignorance of exact information.

"But it is shameless of you to admit it!" Really, the child was impossible, Jordan thought. Next she would be working in a mission to restore fallen women.

The viscount's being right did not endear him to Lacey. She could just imagine how her grandmother or her aunt would react to such an admission. "You are avoiding my question, Your Lordship. I am most grateful for your rescue"—it was a difficult admission, though one that must be made—"but I would still like to know how you knew—"

"You are a nosy child," snapped Jordan, embarrassed. "I was going for a ride in the park after an early visit to my cousin's house when I saw you going towards that notorious district with no one but a scrawny maidservant for company. I decided to wait until I saw that you were safely out."

Lacey teetered between gratitude and indignation; to her surprise, unqualified gratitude won. "I am glad you did. I went to visit a sick woman and take her some food. She is a respectable woman and I didn't expect . . ." In belated release, she started to sob and shudder with the memory of cold eyes and grasping hands and the sharp twinkle of a knife.

This sign of feminine weakness completely unmanned Jordan. His annoyance with this hoydenish creature vanished in a wave of protectiveness, and in a manoeuvre of no small undertaking, he fished a handkerchief from his pocket.

"Don't cry, Miss Chyngford, please. . . . Everything is all right. You are safe now. Lacey, please . . ."

Distressed by his tone, the urgency of which aroused a corresponding echo in her, Lacey bit back the sobs and dried her face. With a sudden clarity, she knew there would be a lifetime ahead for tears. "I'm all right."

"We must decide what to do with you. I think I should take you home. . . . After such a shock, you need rest and care—"

Lacey could just see her aunt's reaction if she were to be brought back at such a distressingly early hour by Elizabeth's beau. "No! I can manage by myself."

"Your aunt did not know of this expedition?"

Damn the man! Did he have to be so perceptive? That would only increase the need for her to act her part extremely well. "No, she did not. It would cause me a great hardship if she knew."

That Jordan could readily believe, but he just couldn't

abandon her to her own devices. "Very well. I shall take you to Vinnie's. She shall tend to you."

"I don't need tending to, thank you. If you will put me down here, I shall make my own way home. It will be better." The sooner she got away from the nearness of him, the strength of his arm around her, the faint scent of bay rum that emanated from his newly shaven cheek, the better she would be. The lean hardness of his body pressed so closely to hers sent strange shivers of an unknown discontent through her.

"Now look, Miss Chyngford, you are a delicately bred young lady who has just had a tremendous shock! You can't expect me just to abandon you here—"

"If you take me any farther, I shall be ruined, for people will be coming out for their morning airings before long. I quite assure you that I am all right. Besides, I am not a delicately bred young lady but, as you so piquantly put it, an ill-bred guttersnipe! Now, will you please put me down?" She had the satisfaction of seeing him blush at the memory of words said in strong emotion, and took the opportunity to wiggle from his grasp. It was not a particularly graceful or comfortable dismount, but at least she was free from the distraction of his nearness.

"Miss Chyngford, I must protest . . ." He fought the strange feeling that if she vanished he would never see her again. Oddly, that feeling disconcerted him very much.

"I think you for your timely rescue, Your Lordship, but please rest assured that I shall deal very well from here on without your help," a dignified Lacey said with a colder tone than she had intended, then pulled her cloak tight and vanished down a narrow street.

Lord Piedmont stared after her, trying unsuccessfully to fill the empty space in his being with anger against a harum-scarum girl from a country vicarage who had the temerity to treat him like a servant. It would have made him feel immensely better to know that an equal turmoil resided in her breast and that, after safely regaining the sanctuary of her room at Chyngford House—where she remained, feigning a headache—Lacey Chyngford cried her eyes out because she had fallen hopelessly in love with the man earmarked by her aunt to marry Elizabeth.

=12=

Sir Cicero was never at his best in the morning, and after a definitely rousing evening the previous night, that period could be extended into the early afternoon; therefore, he was most unhappy to be called from his fuzzy-headed bed of pain at a time not long past ten . . . until he learned that his untimely caller was none other than the Duke of Lowood.

With admirable courage he pulled himself from bed and dressed in a manner commensurate with the rank of his guest. Amazing that Lowood should be up and functioning so early after the night they had put in; it had been close to dawn before he had found his own bed . . . as nearly as he could remember. On closer scrutiny, it did seem that his memories of the evening were very fragmentary, save for the facts that His Grace's friends were deep gamesters and the spirits excellent.

Just how deep and excellent he did not realize until his guest, convivially joining him in a glass of port, presented a sum total of his losses the night before. The figure cut through Sir Cicero's mental fuzziness with frightening clarity.

"I do not want you to think that I am presenting a bill like some sort of tradesman," His Grace purred easily, sipping at the wine. It was at best indifferent. If this was what Chyngford was used to, no wonder he had lapped up the Lowood private stock with such enthusiasm. He looked at the gross grey creature across from him and could not

restrain a shudder. That this blob of a man was the son . . .
He stopped and shrugged; that was past history, long dead.
Now he was concerned with the present and, more properly, the future. "It is just that you seemed so unaware of it
last night and I thought you might prefer to be prepared in
private in order to arrange payment."

Sir Cicero knew the traditional forty-eight-hour limit on
settlement of gaming debts, and the pain in his stomach
became greater than the dull throb of his head. The sum
was enormous; how could he have played so deep? He
remembered writing a few vouchers, but there had been so
much good humour and so much more good liquor that he
had not remembered the amounts. By all rules of civilised
Society, he would be forever ruined if he failed to make
good his vouchers; he could just do it by selling off the
unentailed land and applying to his mother for a loan, but it
would nevertheless mean ruin. He read the figures again to
make sure his blurry eyes were not deceiving him, and
then, just to be sure, repeated it aloud.

"I didn't realise it had gotten to be so much. . . ." The
weakness in his voice appalled him and disgusted his
auditor. "Are these just to you?" Spectres of other vouchers
to the other gentlemen present in commensurate amounts
arose with horrifying vividness. The Chyngfords would be
disgraced, their name dragged in the mud. . . . Sir Cicero's
hands were sweating.

His Grace's smile was seraphic. He had read Chyngford
remarkably well. "No, no, my dear boy. I know this has
been a bad harvest year . . . we've all suffered losses. I took
the liberty of buying up your vouchers from my friends in
order to save you any possible embarrassment. . . . No,
don't thank me."

"Buy why?" Sir Cicero was well enough aware of His
Grace's reputation to be suspicious of any unprofitable
kindness.

"I once knew your mother."

It seemed reasonable. In her youth his mother had been

reputed to be something of a beauty; at least, so he had been told, for at whatever rare times he thought of her, it was invariably as that faded creature in permanent residence at Greathills and officially dead to Society.

"Thank you, Your Grace. I don't know what to say. . . . About repayment, I'm afraid—"

"There is one slight favour I would ask of you, Sir Cicero." How easy it all was!

"Name it, sir."

"Actually, it would be beneficial to both of us. . . . I speak about your . . . ah . . . niece. I would have her to wife."

Sir Cicero Chyngford blinked. "My niece? To marry? *Elizabeth?*"

It was Lowood's turn to start. "That Dunfield cow? You insult my taste, Chyngford. I meant the pretty one. Lacey."

"Lacey?" gibbered that young lady's reluctant uncle. "You want to marry Lacey?"

"She has taken my fancy. If you could . . . persuade her as to the desirability of becoming my duchess . . . well, I could scarce press my dear uncle-in-law for a gaming debt, could I?"

The interior of Sir Cicero's mouth was dry, a phenomenon connected more with greed than with the amount of liquor consumed the night before, but he was in no mood to make petty distinctions. He drained his port glass in a single gulp. "Lacey is a willful, headstrong girl . . ."

"And you are unsure of your influence on her?"

How humiliating it sounded, put in such a fashion. Sir Cicero did some quick calculating; if Lacey could be persuaded to marry Lowood—and what girl of any sense wouldn't jump at the chance of being an immensely wealthy duchess? —it would solve the problem of repayment, not to mention awarding him a definite position in Society. The uncle of the Duchess of Lowood would carry a cachet that Sir Cicero Chyngford never could. Leonora would be furious, of course, for that daughter of hers would never reach higher than Piedmont, if she could even catch him. It would be a sore trial to her ladyship to have the foundling girl take the matrimonial prize, but once the deed was accomplished he could make her see the advantages of the situation.

"She will do as she is bid," said the Head of the Family firmly.

"I am glad. The name of Chyngford is an old one; I should hate to see it dishonoured."

Sir Cicero could not resist a small shiver of pity for his niece; he had never before noticed the eagerness in Lowood's thin face, nor the clawlike quality of his hands. Still, if the honour of the Chyngford name were at stake, she would do what was necessary because she was a Chyngford; in fact, a double Chyngford, as his mother had been so quick to point out. Lacey was a girl of spirit, Cicero thought, and if anyone were well equipped to deal with the duke, it would be she; she would probably have him eating out of her hand if she played her cards right.

"When do I have the honour of telling Lacey about her good fortune?" Sir Cicero asked, not at all looking forward to the prospect.

"When I tell you to. I intend to speak to her tonight at the Carterets' ball. It would be preferable, for her sake, if she accepts of her own volition. I do not wish you to say anything until I direct you to do so."

"As you wish, Your Grace."

Sir Cicero had capitulated with no question, just as Lowood had planned. This time he would not be done out of his prize; the Chyngfords would not cheat him again! With a jaunty step, His Grace left the house and a befuddled Sir Cicero, hardly noticing the overdressed young dandy mounting the steps behind him.

Lacey was not pleased to be pulled from her room for a caller, still less to find that it was Chester Stoker. Refusing breakfast and luncheon as well as the dubious pleasure of paying calls with her aunt and cousin, she had spent the lonely hours alternating between visions of an improbably wonderful future with one whom she had always regarded as one of the enemy and helpless weeping because of its very impossibility. Though Lord Piedmont would doubtless share the amusing story about his rescue of the dreadfully *farouche* Miss Chyngford with his noble friends, she would forever treasure those few moments in his arms and the way in which he had forgotten himself so far as to call her Lacey. It would be her secret; even if the Polite World should learn of her near misadventure in Seven Dials, the real secret would remain her own.

To come from daydreams of Piedmont to the reality of Chester Stoker was depressing. Lacey had now learned enough about life in Society to see through the pretensions of the Stoker clan. The rather flashy waistcoats and overly intricate cravats young Mr Stoker thought the height of fashion now had come under comparison with the simple elegance of Lord Piedmont, against which they had no chance. Standing in the elegant hallway Chester Stoker looked every bit the Johnny Raw he was. Lacey stifled a cowardly urge to run back upstairs. It was too late to send word she was not at home, so she continued down the stairs, but stopped a few rungs up.

"Good morning, Mr Stoker."

He looked up at her and smiled. "You were not so formal once."

His intimation of a non-existent past intimacy offended Lacey and, raising her chin slightly higher, she stood her ground despite the hand he raised to assist her down the last few steps.

"Quilling implied that you were anxious to see me . . ."

The oily smile widened. "Indeed I am. Is there someplace we might talk?"

Lacey hesitated. She had no real desire to hear anything Chester Stoker might say, but knew him well enough to know that if he wanted to talk to her, he would keep at it until he did. Still, seeing him alone would be most improper. The prospect of requesting either her cousin or her aunt to act as chaperone for such an interview was daunting, but she could see no other way out.

"If you'll just wait in the drawing room . . ." she gestured toward the open doors of that stately chamber, knowing full well Quilling had left him in there, ". . . I'll request my cousin to join us."

A shadow flitted across his face, solidifying at last into a puppy-like gaze. "Please . . . cannot we speak without chaperonage . . . as we used to?"

Lacey could not recall his ever having made much of an effort to speak to her at all, with or without chaperonage, and she said so. The hurt look in the young man's eyes surprised her.

"London has changed you, Lacey. You were never cruel."

"I'll ask my cousin to come down," Lacey said resignedly. Tenacity was indeed a Stoker trait.

"But I never thought it would cause you to turn against my grandmother's principles. Or is equality of the sexes a subject fit only for the provinces?"

Stung, Lacey descended the stairs with her head held high and led the way into the drawing room. How dare that beast suggest even by the inference of a raised eyebrow that she had adopted old Mrs Stoker's principles in order to curry favour! He was indeed the most maddening creature she could imagine, completely without style or grace.

His hands were damp, too, Lacey thought with distaste as he seized her own in his, sprinkling them liberally with kisses between fulsome compliments.

"Ah, my dear Lacey, how wonderful to know that in your newfound good fortune you do not shut out your old friends who care for you," Chester muttered in honeyed tones, thankfully unaware of how close she had been to not coming down at all. He seemed to be strangely excited.

"It is nice of you to call, Chester," Lacey said repressively. She reclaimed her hands as gracefully as possible and sat in the spindly desk chair, which was hardly big enough for one, let alone two. Chester seemed loath to give up the hold their previous association had given him on her, which made Lacey quite uneasy. Chester Stoker never did anything unless it would profit him in some way, and a few minutes later, when Lacey learned his purpose, her unease turned to acute discomfort.

"You want to what?" was her blunt reaction.

"Surely you must know of my long and deep affection for you, my dear. . . ." To Lacey's horror, he knelt before her, but only after pulling at his trouser legs so they would not wrinkle and placing a handkerchief on the rug to keep his knee from being sullied.

"You certainly managed to keep it a secret at Beecham Manor!"

"Don't be bitter. . . . I had to be circumspect because of my father. Won't you make me the happiest man in the world and marry me, my darling?"

"I am not your darling!" Lacey snapped, then, on seeing her swain's ugly expression, tried to temper her decidedly negative response with a gilding of manners. "I apologise for my hasty tongue, Chester, but your offer has taken me so much by surprise . . . I never dreamed . . ." She stopped, her face as pink as her dress, making her very pretty even to Chester's jaded eye.

"Then there is hope for me?" His tone was strangely businesslike for an aspirant suitor.

"I'm very flattered, Chester, but I cannot give you encouragement. My answer is no."

Chester shrugged his shoulders in a gesture of resignation and stood up, dusting the immaculate knees of his trousers. "Oh, my dear Lacey, always causing problems no matter what."

"I don't understand—"

"Then you had better understand this: I mean to marry you."

"But I have no desire to marry you and cannot see where you have any driving passion to marry me."

"Sweet, innocent Lacey!" He laughed at her gaping expression. "I'm sorry to shatter your pretty dreams of romance, but I have very practical reasons why you must marry me—"

"Must! I must do no such thing!" In a single movement she was going towards the door to call Quilling, so that this intruder might be escorted out, but he was there before her. Now she was really attractive to him, more so that she had ever been, her face flushed with anger and her eyes aflame. He wished he had made more of an effort to woo and win her conventionally, but how could he have foreseen that she would be so difficult?

"I wouldn't; we don't want to make a scene."

"Very well. Will you leave quietly, then?"

Her courage amused him. It would be fun taming her. The thought of her pale attractiveness being subdued to his will, finally coming to crave his attentions and particular specialties, was intensely arousing. He could have happily taken her there and then, but there was business he must consider. There would be all the time in the world to indulge his whims with her after her dowry disposed of his debts.

"I have no intention of leaving until we are affianced, my sweet."

"You will have a long wait then, Mr Stoker. And I am not your sweet!"

"Perhaps you are not my sweet, but you will be my wife. Hear me," he said with a peculiar growl in the back of his throat, "my high and mighty miss, you will be my wife!"

"I will not be your wife! You cannot force me!"

Chester smiled in his most charming way, and in the circumstances it was hideous. "Not in the way you think, dear Lacey, but I can guarantee that if you aren't my wife you will never be anyone else's, at least no one with any pretensions to gentility. You lived under my family roof for more than two years. All it will take is just to mutter in a few ears that you were my mistress while you were there."

Lacey drew a deep breath. This was indeed serious business. Reputations had been irrevocably ruined by gossip coming from less provocation than this. It was as if old Mrs Stoker were standing beside her, whispering in her ear.

"He's a dangerous one," the phantom Mrs Stoker said. "Spoiled and dangerous, but a bully. Don't cave in on him. He expects women to be weak. Buy time!"

"You cannot prove it." Lacey's voice dripped with hauteur.

Although Chester was shaken, he did not allow it to show. His smile thinned and spread even wider. "You cannot disprove it, and the more you deny it, the worse it will seem. I know our world very well, my dear, and it matters not whether or not you're guilty but whether or not the ton thinks you guilty."

"I cannot believe you would do such a thing, Mr Stoker." Lacey was breathing more calmly now. Panic never won anything.

"Believe me, Lacey, I have done many things nowhere near so nice for results a lot less pleasurable." Lazily, he stroked a finger down her smooth cheek. He noticed her recoil and made a mental note to have the wedding as soon as socially acceptable. For a few months, marriage might be fun.

"But not so long-lasting. If that is your choice, Mr Stoker, go ahead and spread your filth. It makes no difference to me." At least, she thought, that would solve the problem of staying in London or going away with her hundred pounds to start a new life. . . . Besides, it would make Aunt Leonora and Sir Cicero so very happy.

Inclining her head with a graciousness that bespoke well of her breeding, Lacey stepped around a very startled Chester Stoker and left him alone in the morning room with his rather chaotic thoughts.

=== 13 ===

Pierre Carteret was the son of émigrés from the awful Revolution in France. The hospitable English had opened their shores to the persecuted aristocrats fleeing the guillotine, but what was unusual about the Carterets—at best, minor nobility in their homeland—was that they had had the foresight to bring with them a great deal of negotiable assets, which, combined with an innate sense of gaming, soon grew to be a respectable fortune. In protest against the reign of the usurping corporal, Pierre declined to use his title, a gesture which probably gained him more favourable attention than his meagre noble standing would have. He continued the family tradition for making money in acceptable ways by marrying the granddaughter of a very wealthy merchant; The money was plentiful enough to interest him, but safely removed by a generation from the smell of the shop. He and his lovely wife Martha were two of the jewels in the Society round, givers of lavish and sparkling parties. Their invitations were most prized, and as a consequence their occasions were always the most shocking squeezes, where one never met anyone who was not someone.

The Chyngford-Dunfield ménage had never been on a social level with the Carterets, primarily due to the traditional leanness of their purses, but upon seeing them at the Stanton-Hogg affair the Carterets were intrigued with the juxtaposition of the dumpy Miss Dunfield and a flame-haired goddess sprung from nowhere who was supposed to be her cousin. The Carterets had never held anything against the Chyngford clan, save their lack of sizeable fortune, so out of curiosity an invitation was duly issued and gleefully accepted.

At least Lady Dunfield was gleeful; her face was the only one unmarred by some inner anxiety. Lacey and Elizabeth stared out opposite windows of the coach, lost in their own melancholy thoughts of misplaced affection and familial duty. Sir Cicero's mind also dwelt on duty, wondering if Lacey would do hers like a true Chyngford, or become a selfish rebel like her mother.

"I vow I never saw such a collection of glumpots," her ladyship snarled. "We are asked to the Carterets' and you all act like it was an invitation to a hanging!"

"Please, Mother," Elizabeth said with surprising spirit. "Don't be so vulgar!"

Lady Dunfield would have remonstrated, had not the coach drawn up to the Carteret mansion at that moment and the door been smartly snapped open by a gaily uniformed footman. Since she wished above all to preserve her image as the matriarch of a happy family, she contented herself with a scathing look at Elizabeth which promised a dire scene later, before heaving her bulk out of the carriage and greeting her hosts with such a determinedly brilliant manner that they were left feeling slightly overwhelmed.

Even without the impact of Lady Dunfield's personality, the newcomers would have been noticed: Lacey in white, of course, and very beautiful; Elizabeth in a felicitous pale green, Lady Dunfield herself in a somewhat restrained burgundy, and Sir Cicero resplendent in yellow shot with gold thread. It was a testimony to old Lady Chyngford's training of them all that no casual observer should see any emotion on their faces but pleasure at being members of such an august gathering, yet among the family members the signals were strong.

Lacey had been in her aunt's bad looks since her suspect headache had made her miss their round of calls, a routine of boredom Lacey naturally deplored. Always quick to find fault in her niece, Lady Dunfield had not yet had a chance to find out the whole of the girl's indisposition that afternoon, but she would give her no chance for mischief. To cap off her ladyship's misery, Elizabeth was in a strange, snappish mood, given to silent tears and missishness.

By suppertime even the most fashionably late of the guests had been announced, including, to Lacey's discomfort, Lord Piedmont and the Duke of Lowood. To her relief, neither of them made a move toward her, but she thought that all she needed to make her evening a complete fiasco was for Chester Stoker to appear, though he had no hopes of aspiring so far in Society.

Unless he was married to her, quickly came the ugly little thought, which was just as quickly put down as she turned her full attention to the innocuous young lad fortunate enough to escort her in to supper. He was a nice enough young man, younger son of some obscure country squire, and Lacey found his ingenuousness refreshing. He seemed relieved to have someone with whom he could discuss country matters, and, to Lacey's relief, both Piedmont and Lowood seemed to have done with her and paid her no attention. She hoped that the attention garnered by the Chyngford prodigal had been a momentary thing and was at last over.

One scrutiny she could not escape was her aunt's; Lady Dunfield's eyes were an excellent barometer of her mood, and all evening Lacey had seen their hard glitter with a sinking heart. Since their arrival she had felt her aunt's gaze boring into her, just waiting for her to make a mistake; and judging from the warlike expression her aunt now wore, Lacey had made an enormous one.

"Lacey, my dear," said Leonora with a smile that did not rise above the lips, "forgive me if I steal you away for a moment. You will excuse us?" she said to the squire's son, who was just taking Lacey back towards the dance floor.

The young man made the appropriate comments and

with a small bow melted away into the crowd. *She's heard*, Lacey thought blankly. Already Chester's poison had begun to spread.

"What is wrong, Aunt Leonora? Has something upset you?"

Surprisingly strong pudgy fingers gripped Lacey's hand. "Smile, my child. You mustn't look so nervous."

Lacey forced her lips into a happier expression. "My apologies, dear Aunt, but you looked so anxious I was taken aback. Have I done something wrong?"

It was a sign of the depth of Lady Dunfield's preoccupation that she did not find some fault with her niece, if for no other reason than that it was her habit; instead, she laughed with a girlish trill for the benefit of nearby Princess Esterhazy. When that august lady had returned their bows and moved on, the smile on Leonora's face crystallised.

"Goodness me, Lacey," she said in a honeyed tone, should any other doyenne be lurking unseen nearby. Leonora had never given up on getting Almack's vouchers. "One would think I was going to eat you! I merely wanted to know if you had seen Elizabeth."

"Elizabeth?" Miss Chyngford smiled and played for time. Apparently her own reputation was still intact, at least for the time being. "Isn't she with you?"

"No. I wish she were. Lord Piedmont is sitting in there as big as life, and that girl is nowhere to be found. Your uncle and I thought we saw her leaving the party area after supper. Heaven knows I have tried to teach you girls the impropriety of such fast behaviour, and Elizabeth would never dream of such a thing, but I can't seem to see her. . . ."

The smile on Miss Chyngford's face remained in frozen perfection even as her mind began to spin. Until now she had seen her cousin and aunt as a single front united against her and had resented their attitude equally; now it seemed that perhaps Elizabeth was as tightly constrained as herself, which would mean . . .

Lacey's eyesight was excellent; she had seen her cousin enter the library and had had an unobstructed view of the sturdy form of Milton Litchfield as he had followed her in. Of course! All of a sudden a great number of things made a great deal of sense to Lacey, and there was only one course of action, however drastic, to be taken. If Lady Dunfield were to get any whiff of what Lacey suspected, it would go none too well for her gentle cousin; for that matter, it would go none too well for anyone who had to deal with Lady Dunfield.

"I saw her not long ago, Aunt Leonora, but I'm not sure where she might be at this moment." Lacey skated on the perilously thin edge of truth and muttered a mental apology for the facility with which she distorted facts. Her father would have been horrified at her easy duplicity, no matter the worthiness of the cause. "If I see her, I'll be sure to tell her that you . . ."

Her ladyship's dire mutterings were filtered to near inaudibility through her set smile, but the look in her eyes rendered articulate words unnecessary. Her niece waited only until the thick-set burgundy clad figure was lost in the crowd before making a direct course for the library door. Despite a personal antipathy to her cousin, Lacey felt honour-bound at least to try to warn Elizabeth. Perhaps this could break down the barriers between them.

The Carterets were not noticeably literate people, so although there was a respectable library in their house, not even the preparations for the party had been able to rid the room of its neglected air. Half-empty shelves gaped forlornly, having long ago been turned into a curio display by a lavish distribution of china atrocities only rarely interspaced with lonely clumps of books. As if in expectation that such a room would not be popular for such a gay crowd, only a minimum number of candles had been lit and it drowsed in a semidarkness just perfect for lovers.

Lacey slid into the room quickly, thinking for a moment that she had been wrong in thinking the pair were in there until she saw them in the far dimness of the window embrasure, thoroughly unaware of anything save each other.

"You do love me, don't you Elizabeth? I couldn't bear it if you didn't. . . ."

"Of course I love you, Milton. I guess I always have, since you singled me out at Lady Chislehurst's ball. . . . It was my first ball . . ."

"And you were the most beautiful girl there. Oh, Elizabeth, I love you so much! Will you marry me, my darling? You will, you have to!" Milton gathered his ladylove close. Elizabeth, pliant as always, moulded against him with a tiny sigh. One could almost hear the painful war going on inside her.

"You know nothing would give me more pleasure, but . . . oh, Milton, my mother would never let me. She is determined I shall marry that horrid Lord Piedmont! She will never give her permission."

Inspired by passion, Milton Litchfield reached heights of eloquence the Foreign Office never knew he possessed. "We do not need her permission, my beloved. I will not see you tied to that profligate wastrel, that fashionable fribble! You will be the perfect wife for a diplomat, Elizabeth. . . . I am due in Florence in a month; you will come with me. We can be married on the way."

"Milton!"

"I want you to be my wife, darling. I love you."

"And I love you . . . but an elopement . . . your career . . ." Underneath the expected nervousness she wore an expression that turned the girl's plain face into a thing of true beauty.

"My career means nothing without you beside me."

"Oh, Milton, my dearest, that's the sweetest thing I ever heard!"

"And you'll come? I'll come for you tomorrow afternoon. . . ."

Elizabeth's tone was pathetic with suppressed longing. "I don't dare . . ."

Lacey could have stamped her foot in frustration. She

would have liked to let the scene carry out to its logical conclusion, but each moment which passed meant one more closer to their discovery by Lady Dunfield, with Lacey herself in a most unenviable position. Something had to be done, and now.

"Elizabeth! Mr Litchfield!" she cried softly.

The embracing figures jumped apart in a flurry of embarrassed squeaks and harrumphs. "Cousin Lacey!" Elizabeth snapped indignantly in a fair imitation of her mother; Mr Litchfield pouted and exclaimed, "I scarcely expected to find such an example of ill-bred behaviour in you, Miss Chyngford," to which Elizabeth added, "Eavesdropper!"

"Not intentionally, I assure you, Elizabeth. Oh, do come down off your high horse! I'm trying to do you a favour. Your mother is looking for you most energetically and will not be satisfied until she finds you! Mr Litchfield, I suggest that you leave right now by that window and take a turn in the garden. Take two and come in by another door."

His ample chest measurement expanded even further in a gesture unfortunately reminiscent of a pouter pigeon. "I am not afraid of Miss Dunfield's relatives—"

"I know you aren't, but I am afraid for her, and it would make your quest a great deal easier if you were to do what I say. . . ." Lacey applied her ear to the door and tried to discern whose voices she heard in the hall.

"She is right, Milton," replied Elizabeth as reluctantly as she would take a dose of nasty medicine. "Please go."

"My dear, perhaps it is for the best," he said slowly. "We have known that this confrontation had to come."

"But it shouldn't happen tonight," Lacey hissed. "All we need is to have a public scene at this party; the story will be all over town by time for breakfast chocolate, and then do you think you'll be allowed even to see Elizabeth again before you have to leave?"

If he were surprised by a young and very beautiful debutante giving orders like a coachman, the solid young man gave no indication. "Perhaps. It was Sir Cicero who told me to go after my heart's desire, to take the young lady

I loved. That I must be firm yet tender with her and make her see it my way!"

For once Lacey and Elizabeth were of one mind. "Uncle Cicero?" they breathed in simultaneous disbelief.

"Will you answer my question, Elizabeth? I love you so. . . ."

The voices Lacey had dreaded were audible outside the door.

"She must be around here, Cicero. Piedmont will not wait all night. Oh, where is that disobedient girl?"

"It's all right, old girl. We'll find her. . . ."

Lacey turned to Mr Litchfield with a desperate look. "They're right outside. Will you *please* go?"

After a despairing look at his beloved, who silently seconded her cousin's appeal, Litchfield quietly departed the room. To Lacey's amusement he even managed a decent, if somewhat stiff, bow before exiting through the French doors with no more evidence of his passing than a quick draught of chilly air.

Her mind working quickly, Lacey reached out and twitched down a curl from Elizabeth's complicated coiffure, then, shushing the girl's squeal of surprise, calmly proceeded to roll it up again. One second later would have spelled disaster, for before the two girls could draw another breath they were joined by their uncle, who was obviously not in the best of humours.

"Here you are! Found her, did you, Lacey?"

"You make it sound as if she were hiding, Uncle Cicero. It is most certainly not approved in Society to fix a curl in public, I should think." Again Lacey sent a silent apology to her father and vowed to tell nothing but the exact truth ever again if she could get through this awful evening.

Sir Cicero watched Lacey doing arcane things with hairpins until Elizabeth's hair reposed calm again. Trust his addlepated sister to make a Cheltenham tragedy of a lost curl; damned if he would pay any heed to her alarums again!

"Your mother's in a pet about you, miss. Been looking up

and down . . . something about that Piedmont chap . . ."
Sir Cicero was definitely cooling toward Piedmont, especially considering the upcoming alliance with the Lowood camp. It might be a good thing to let Piedmont slide; if only Leonora hadn't gotten some wild-eyed determination that he was the only man in the world for Elizabeth.

"Well, we mustn't keep her waiting, must we?" Lacey said with a great deal more composure than she felt, and, lacing her arm companionably through her cousin's trembling one, sailed majestically back into the brilliantly lit hall.

The dancing had begun again. Lacey was swept from partner to partner, changing dances and young men almost without noticing as her mind vacillated wildly between elation and despair. Elizabeth did not love Lord Piedmont; she loved Milton Litchfield. That, of course, did Lacey Chyngford no good, for even if by some fluke the viscount should care for her—which he certainly showed no evidence of doing—he could never think of even the most casual social alliance with a girl whose reputation was spotted.

It was unnerving, wondering when Society, all too delighted to point a finger of scandal, would turn on her in response to Chester Stoker's poison. If only she had someone to talk to, someone to advise her. Under ordinary circumstances, a girl in such a position would appeal to her guardians, but Lacey feared that Uncle Cicero and Aunt Leonora would be only too glad to use the situation to their own benefit. That would probably mean disgrace for her anyway, and although she had developed a sincere affection for her grandmother, she held no great faith in that frail lady's ability to control her two grown children. No, she had not one to turn to in the matter of Chester Stoker save herself.

Lacey frowned; life in Potter's Ford had been much harder, but also so much simpler.

"Ah, my dear Miss Chyngford! What a pleasure to see you again."

With an effort Lacey forced herself to smile while His Grace the Duke of Lowood made an elaborate obeisance over her hand, barely brushing the back with his dry lips. Since most of the senior members of the party had departed directly after supper, Lacey was surprised and not very pleased to see him still here and soliciting her company for a dance. Though he had never been anything but gentlemanly towards her, whiffs of his reputation had reached Lacey and confirmed her innate dislike of his beady eyes and fawning manner which covered only thinly a cold arrogance.

There was no escape; the music was starting and no other contender for her presence had appeared. It would be unheard of for her to refuse, so she smiled and placed her hand on his, though to her surprise he did not look towards the dance floor.

"If you will humour me, Miss Chyngford, I should like to talk to you a moment." He indicated a small seat in a secluded alcove. "I believe this will do."

Lacey nibbled her lip. It was a very small seat, made for lovers. She didn't know if she could bear to be that close to this unseemingly eager old man. "But Your Grace, the dance is a scottische and one of my most favourites. . . ." She tried to sound winsome, but to no avail.

"If it is still going after we have had our little talk, we will of course participate, though it is so vulgarly exuberant." His hard mouth made the words an indictment against her. "Please, Miss Chyngford . . ."

With a mental shrug, Lacey sat. It was only for a dance, after all, and since young ladies were scarcely ever protected from the conversation of a duke, especially a rich, unmarried one, she would just have to bear it. He seated himself beside her, the patterned light from the greenery unkind to his face. In the alcove's narrow confines his thigh pressed warmly against hers, and Lacey could not hide a small shudder.

"Are you cold, Miss Lacey?" inquired His Grace, using her Christian name with consummate effrontery, knowing that she would not venture to correct one so much her senior both in years and rank. "That is your name, I believe? So lovely and so unusual."

"It is a nickname, Your Grace. I was christened Louisa Anne."

Lowood drew a deep breath and quite alarmed his companion with his sudden pallor. That name . . . it was retribution arranged by Fate, it had to be! She had to be his; she was destined for him in repayment . . .

"Sweet, beautiful Louisa Anne . . . I have not been able to keep my eyes from you since the affair at the Stanton-Hoggs'. It is not my habit to speak precipitately, but you have driven all caution from my heart. Miss Lacey—Louisa Anne—will you be mine?"

Stunned, Lacey opened and closed her mouth a few times before the words would come. "I beg your pardon?"

"I am asking you to be my wife . . . to become the Duchess of Lowood!"

For a moment even the floor seemed to shiver insubstantially. Whatever Lacey had thought he was going to say, this most certainly was not it! The idea of being a duchess was no longer distasteful to Lacey, but the idea of marrying this man was abhorrent no matter what the benefit. Her grandmother and Aunt Leonora would, of course, be furious if she rejected this excellent opportunity to advance herself, and Uncle Cicero's reaction at losing the smallest chance of access to Lowood's fortune and stable was not to be thought of! They would all be so anxious for her to marry him, but she would be the one who would have to share her life with him, to become his property. Better to find a new life with the legacy from Mrs Stoker than to be sold like so much meat, although it would be interesting to see how His Grace might react to the rumour Chester Stoker was doubtless already putting around. The future Duchess of Lowood's name linked with that of a parvenu squire's son like Chester Stoker would really knock Society back on its heels! Lowood would stop the talk, of course, but Lacey decided that she would really prefer the scandal to the alternative. The thought of his hands and lips on her, with inalienable rights to invade her privacy anytime he should desire, made Lacey nauseous.

"You flatter me, Your Grace, but I cannot see where we should suit."

For a fraction of a moment the duke's face turned very ugly. "You are refusing me?"

"It is a great honour you have offered me, sir, but I must decline," Lacey murmured, alarmed by the intensity of feeling in the old man's face.

"No . . . not again! I must have you! I will have you! Louisa Anne . . ."

Scrawny but surprisingly strong arms went around Lacey, pulling her against the half-crazed duke's thin chest. His mouth, agape in passion, left a moist trail across her cheek.

Lacey did not protest; she knew that no mere words would have any effect at all on such a creature. Instead, she dealt him a blow to the ear, which left him unbalanced, and used his momentary disconcertment to escape. It didn't seem likely that His Grace the Duke of Lowood would come hare-footing it down the hallway after her, but then very little of what had passed during the last few hours had seemed likely.

In her flight, Lacey looked over her shoulder to see if she was being pursued and so ran unseeing into an imprisoning pair of muscular arms.

$=14=$

LACEY CLOSED HER eyes and wished fervently for the gift of swooning at will, an art, highly perfected by young ladies of Fashion, which she had heretofore scorned. How nice it would have been just to sink into a graceful faint, to be revived later with cries of concern and offers of hartshorn and burnt feathers, with no memory of any embarrassing moment.

If it is Lord Piedmont again, she thought despairingly, *I simply cannot bear it!* It was bad enough to be indebted to that arrogant landowner for one rescue, but two and on the same day?

"Miss Chyngford! Whatever is the matter?"

"Mr Litchfield . . . Thank Heaven it is you," Lacey murmured with heartfelt sincerity. Never had the sight of the young diplomat's unprepossessing features been so welcome.

"Are you all right? Has anything happened to Miss Elizabeth?"

"No, no, she's fine," said Lacey hastily, alarmed by his warlike expression. "It was just that I . . . I heard a sound and was frightened."

It was a lame explanation, but apparently Mr Litchfield possessed no critical faculties about the courage of women. Lacey could forgive him even that. Before this evening she had dismissed Milton Litchfield as merely a dull office-holder, but now she could see the fineness of him, how much he loved the girl of his choice and what good care he would take care of her. Elizabeth would probably be very happy with him; they were a good match, and if Lady Dunfield had not been more infatuated with title and fortune than with her daughter's happiness, she would have blessed their union.

For a moment Lacey thought how wonderful life could be if Piedmont felt the same way about her, if he were sweetly attentive and loving. . . .

But to dream so was sheer fantasy. She should be planning instead what she would do when young Stoker's poison began to spread through Society. Bleakly, Lacey came back to the present and forced a smile at Mr Litchfield's earnest face.

"A momentary fright, I assure you. Might I beg your escort back to the ballroom?"

"But of course. I am only too happy to be of service. Rest assured that you are safe while with me." He tucked her arm through his with a brotherly pat. He would stolidly defend her from any traditional or normal danger that might threaten, but what would this upright and steady man say when word reached him of Chester Stoker's allegation? Would his smile turn to scorn? He and Elizabeth would avoid her, deny any knowledge of her, and Piedmont . . .

And Piedmont. Lacey's heart wrenched. heaven only knew he thought little enough of her now; after that loathsome Stoker creature started talking . . .

In sudden anger Lacey bit her lips. She could do nothing, nothing! Once Chester Stoker told his story no one would believe that she was pure as could be. Society fed on such gossip; there was no way to counteract it at all, unfair though it may be! Well, Lacey thought with surprising militarism, she might be going down, but she would go down with all flags flying!

She walked into the ballroom as proudly as a queen and turned a dazzling smile on her companion. "I thank you for your escort, Mr Litchfield."

"Might we dance, Miss Chyngford? Have you no partner for this number?"

He wants to talk about Elizabeth, Lacey realised. He must talk about her, and I'm the only one who knows. "This is not a card dance, sir. I would be happy to partner you."

With measured precision, they moved onto the floor. Despite his chunky solidarity he was a surprisingly graceful dancer, Lacey had remarked. They made an excellent and noticeable pair to Society's watching eyes—Miss Chyngford both beautiful and happy, Mr Litchfield pink with some inner joy.

"May I speak to you in confidence, Miss Chyngford?" His tone was just loud enough to reach her ears alone.

"About your chosen lady? But of course." Although her tone was equally low, Lacey knew euphemisms would be safer. She smiled.

"It is such a relief to have someone to whom I can confide. I fear losing her. She is so good, so gentle . . ."

"I agree that she has very little pluck when it comes to defying her family," Lacey replied bluntly. "She has always been taught that the idea of marriage without fortune and title is heresy. It will not be easy for her to act contrary to principles she has been taught all her life."

"That is my fear, Miss Chyngford. I can only influence her so far, but I do love her deeply, and I think she loves me. I could give her a good life. . . ." Carried away by his own ardour, Mr Litchfield forgot himself and squeezed his partner's hand until she was forced to squeak a protest.

"Oh, I'm sorry. Please accept my apologies, Miss Chyngford. It is just that I am driven half to distraction by the fear that I may lose her."

Despite all good intentions not to be drawn further into this imbroglio, Lacey was touched by the throb of emotion in his voice. "Would you like me to speak to her? I cannot guarantee that my word will carry any credence, but—"

"Would you, Miss Chyngford? I hesitate to ask, but if

you could only convince her that a loving heart is worth more than a king's crown or ransom. . . ?" A smile of hope illuminated his face. Lacey could not help smiling in return.

"I will try, Mr Litchfield."

Although Society might have looked approvingly on the pairing of the new Chyngford girl and the young man who was rising so quickly in the Foreign Office, Sir Cicero definitely did not. He stood by a towering column morosely watching the pair. A very icy Duke of Lowood had just informed him that it was his duty to apprise Miss Chyngford of her forthcoming marriage and ensure her cooperation.

It meant, of course, that that stupid chit had refused the duke's offer, giving His Grace no choice but to display his whip hand. Which meant, Sir Cicero reflected sourly, that he himself would have to do it, and a pretty scene that would be. Heaven only knew why Lowood wanted such an ungrateful wildcat as Lacey, but he intended to have her, and Sir Cicero had to make sure he did. It was not a task to which he looked forward, especially now that it seemed her heart beat only for that Litchfield fellow, the one who had hung around Elizabeth so much last Season, driving Leonora to extremes of displeasure.

With a sinking heart, Sir Cicero remembered the conversation in which he had counselled Litchfield to speak for Lacey. It had seemed such a perfect solution at the time; he was leaving for Florence, it would have removed that girl from underfoot—which would, in turn, have made living with Leonora much easier—without reflecting badly on the family. Heaven knew it would be profitable to have a wealthy duke in the family, but why could his eye not have lighted on nice biddable Elizabeth, who never entertained a rebellious thought?

Another onlooker was not pleased with the obvious rapport between the dancing couple. Jordan, Lord Piedmont, was flagrantly ignoring the flirtatious wiles of his partner to scowl at the exchange of smiles between that other pair. What on earth was Lacey Chyngford doing with that mealy-mouthed paper pusher? She had made it very clear that morning she wanted none of Piedmont's company or protection, which had not made him happy, but to discover that she obviously preferred the company of that Foreign Office lackey was a blow to the viscount's pride. He never thought about his attraction for women; as one born to wealth with more than an average share of good looks, he had taken the adulation of the fair sex for granted. It was not pleasing to find that a young lady—however unconventional her behaviour—who held such a strange fascination for him seemed to prefer the pleasure found in the company of a worm like Litchfield. It was a situation which needed investigation.

"May I have this dance, Miss Chyngford?"

Lacey tried to hide the treacherous flush of emotion that flowed through her at the sight of Piedmont's handsome figure beside her. Tonight he was resplendent in a rich black evening suit, relieved only by the whiteness of his linen and a great emerald signet ring. His figure showed to advantage in the long stove-pipe trousers and closely fitting coat. Lacey could remember all too well the strength in that body, the way he had held her close while rescuing her from the gang of cutpurses, the way his heart had beat so steadily beneath her cheek, pulsing to an echo in her own secret being. . . .

She tried to tell herself that he was an arrogant nobleman, one of a breed she hated, that he was conceited and shallow and interested in women only as playthings, but no amount of argument could slow the pounding of her heart at the sight of his handsome face and golden curls. This could easily be the last time she saw him, for one of a class who put so much importance on a female's market value instead of her worth would disclaim any proper association with a female who had the reputation that snake Chester Stoker intended to give her.

"With pleasure, Your Lordship."

The orchestra was striking into a particularly lively country dance. Jordan frowned; he had intended to talk to his chestnut-tressed Amazon, an exercise not easily accomplished in the patterns of a quick-moving dance. With courtly grace, he placed her hand on his and gave her his most enchanting smile. "Might I beg the favour of a few minutes' conversation instead? I believe the Carterets' picture gallery is to be especially admired."

Despite all good intentions, Lacey's heart thudded harder. The gallery was one of the showplaces of fashionable London. There could be some impropriety in visiting it, since this late in the evening it was likely to be deserted. Lacey didn't care; soon it wouldn't make any difference.

"I have heard so," she agreed, but later could remember seeing none of it.

The music was faint up there, an intruder in a well of quiet. The silence affected both of them. It was the first time they had been alone together in a place of privacy since their first meeting in the secluded garden at Greathills, and such intimacy placed a constraint on them. They walked the length of the panelled gallery without saying a word, their footsteps hushed on the Turkey carpet. It was enough just to be together, each thought, and blessed the disinterested forbearance of the other.

"I trust you are unharmed after your unfortunate experience this morning?"

"Yes, thank you. I was more shocked and saddened than hurt. It pains me that those people would act so. . . . If only they could be helped."

"Some people do not want to be helped, despite your pretty beliefs. What about the woman you went there to see?" It was not the direction he wanted the conversation to take, but how could he tell her how beautiful her hair was in the shimmering candlelight, or how lovely she looked, when her mind dwelt on the filth and poverty of Seven Dials? He should have started out with something else;

imagine the urbane Lord Piedmont unsure of himself in a conversation with a mere chit of a girl! He devoutly hoped Vinnie would never hear of this, for she would tease him unmercifully.

"Mrs Feeny is a decent woman, as different from those other poor creatures as possible. She was let go from her job at a dressmaker's simply because she was ill. . . . That's an inhumane practice. The work is incredibly demanding and the hours are so long . . ."

The genuine pity and distress in her eyes touched Jordan's heart in a new way. He was unfamiliar with anyone who would feel such sorrow for an unknown, insignificant woman. He was concerned about the plight of the farmers, but it was a selfish interest which motivated him—the desire to stop a possible revolution and increasing production, not a concern for the people as individual persons. Hers was an unusual and not an altogether comfortable sort of care.

"And now you are going to take on the entire seamstress industry?"

His rallying tone annoyed Lacey. It was easy for him to be frivolous about the misery of Heaven only knew how many women condemned to a kind of slavery. Safe behind the wall of his wealth and privilege, he had never known cold or hunger or want, Lacey thought, completely unaware of his adventures and deprivations during the American campaign.

"I just might," she replied with fire.

How beautiful she is, he thought. What a wonder it would be to kiss her. . . . Piedmont was an accredited man of the world; to be so aroused by an unfledged first-Season chit was unprecedented, but he knew he had never felt this way about any girl before.

"I have already arranged for Mrs Feeny to make some handkerchiefs for me at her own speed." Lacey was babbling and she knew it. "I never mastered the art of fine embroidery . . ." Did he have to stand so close and be so handsome? For one glorious moment Lacey thought of the delight of being close to him always, of knowing him as she knew no other human being, and her breath became erratic.

"You are very beautiful, Miss Chyngford . . . Lacey." He gave her a look so intense she thought her bones would melt. With a gentle finger he traced the firm line of her jaw, then his hand slid to cup the pearly angle of her shoulder.

"Do not tease me, my lord." Her voice was low but steady. Could he not see the tiny tremors running through her, how she longed to throw herself at him without shame or restraint?

"I have no intention of teasing you. . . . My God, Lacey, you're driving me mad!" Without any conscious effort, she was in his arms, her soft body moulded against his muscular one in a passionate embrace. Her lips pressed against his, returning the fervent kiss with equal ardour.

The open gallery where they might be discovered any moment, the party below, the very world of rational thought all disappeared in a multihued swirl of lights and colours and sensations where Louisa Anne Chyngford ceased to exist as an individual and became instead pure feeling. It was a new sensation and a very pleasurable one. She thought of nothing more than the feel of his lips against her or the circular pressure of his hands against her back, pulling her ever closer to him.

"Lacey, Lacey . . ." His voice was a husky growl. He could think of nothing but her alluring nearness. "You're beautiful . . . so desirable . . ."

The desire in the rough voice reminded her of the Duke of Lowood and his pawing and grasping; suddenly there was no difference between them. She was only an object to satisfy their momentary lust, a plaything, not a person at all. At least the duke had offered marriage, but then Piedmont had probably heard of young Stoker's story by now and felt he was offering her a step up the peerage in the only way she would be permitted to take it.

With the last of her strength, she shoved him away. Her anger brought additional height to her queenly carriage, and sparks fairly flew from her glittering eyes, the outward signs of outraged pride to cover a strange hollowness inside her.

"You are all alike, you noblemen!" she spat. Her words were an indictment.

Jordan, Viscount Piedmont, ladykiller, Pink of the Ton, war hero, stood and watched the fleeing Miss Chyngford with an odd sense of loss, never guessing that she was running from herself as much as from him.

Going to the Carterets', the family had been a glum enough party, but it was a positively funereal group who returned. Elizabeth was lost in struggles of her own, and Lacey had withdrawn into a sullen shell, both replying only in grudging monosyllables. Sir Cicero, while telling himself he was no coward, was in no way looking forward to the ordeal yet to come. He would have put off his confrontation with Lacey until the next day and gotten quietly foxed, if Lowood had not insisted on coming by Chyngford House that very night to settle things. When Sir Cicero had pointed out that it was nearer dawn than night, Lowood replied that he had waited long enough for the proper lady and intended to wait no more. Sir Cicero had sighed and consoled himself with thoughts of the Lowood racing stables.

Leonora, Lady Dunfield, was the most beset of the party. Informed by her brother as to the status of things, but enjoined from speaking a word of it until all details—informing Lacey, for one—were settled, she sat and steamed in a ponderous silence. It was bad enough to have this cowbird foisted upon her family, but to think that this wild and ungrateful child should walk off with the matrimonial prize was bitter gall. That the child of her disgraceful and hated sister Charlotte, who had run off to marry a penniless clergyman, should descend on them and then marry one of the richest dukes in the kingdom right from under their very noses outraged every fibre of her being. Her own daughter, the gentle Elizabeth, had been trained from childhood in the responsibilities of an advantageous marriage, but now even if the Piedmont connexion were pulled off, she would still have to curtsey to Lacey's strawberry leaves. There was absolutely no justice!

Understandably, Sir Cicero put off the moment of truth for as long as possible, waiting until Lacey was almost on the staircase before saying, "Lacey, my dear, could you please step into the library? I wish to have a word with you."

Not without a little apprehension, Lacey followed him. After Chester Stoker's visit, she had been expecting denunciation momentarily, so of course her first thought was that he had gone to her uncle.

When Sir Cicero explained the circumstances to her, she was unable to assimilate her position until he, thinking her positively feeble-minded, had to explain in detail a second time.

"I won't do it! Marry that horrible old man?" Feel his embraces after having been kissed by Piedmont? Explore the mysteries of the marriage bed with that dried-up old lecher? Carry a part of him in her body as a child? Never! She would disappear first; vanish to the country or, if need be, abroad.

"That 'horrible old man' is as rich as Croesus. You'll have jewels, carriages, several fine estates, a title of your own . . ." Sir Cicero was trying to be persuasive. He was also sweating and inwardly cursing Lowood for not choosing Elizabeth. If it had been Elizabeth, he merely would have told her, she would have said, "Very well," and that would have been that. This hell-born independent brat of Charlotte's was just as likely to chuck the family over and pursue her own desires, just as her mother had done.

"And him for a husband. No!"

Their eyes locked. It was he who had to turn away.

Sir Cicero checked his watch; Lowood would be there almost any minute. As Head of the Family, he must do something!

"You will listen to me, Louisa Anne Chyngford! Your mother brought disgrace on this family—but we will not go into that now," he added hastily on seeing the martial light rising in her eyes. He made himself continue to speak gravely, as befitted such an occasion. "The truth is, you have been brought here and given all the advantages a girl could desire, and nothing has been asked of you. We are an old and noble family, and now the honour of the Chyngfords lies in your hands. I have told you that Lowood has certain markers of debts against the family assets; if he calls them due, the family is ruined." It was only a slight exaggeration, and Sir Cicero was beginning to feel desperate at the persistently mulish expression on his niece's face.

"What you are saying is that I should be sacrificed to pay for your poor gaming," Lacey all but snarled. The spectre of His Grace was still too much with her. Despite the warm fire and the comforting library, she shivered.

Sir Cicero decided to ignore her remark. "You must learn that being a member of a great and old family entails responsibilities as well as pleasures. So far you have tasted only the fruits of gentility—the clothes, the parties, and the rest. Now we are asking you to shoulder part of the responsibility. A great family is built and sustained by advantageous marriages."

"But I do not love the Duke of Lowood."

"Love has nothing to do with marriages in our class of people. I do not know what scurrilous standards you learned in that damned vicarage, but young ladies of good families know that love comes after marriage. His Grace has offered you a very good life and seems to care for you a great deal. In fact, he is determined to have you." Sir Cicero could not keep the bewilderment from his voice. Lacey was attractive, yes, but there were many other girls equally good-looking and much more convenable.

"Just like a prime piece of livestock."

It was too much. Here the chit was offered the most advantageous match she would ever be likely to receive and she treated it like a stable transaction!

"Listen to me, Louisa Anne Chyngford! You are in a position which most girls would give their eyes to be in. One of the wealthiest peers in the land is paying you court, offering you a king's ransom for the taking as well as a chance to save your family—the same family that rescued you from a life of servile obscurity and gave you all the benefits of a young lady of Fashion—from certain disgrace and you turn up your nose!"

Lacey began to protest, but her uncle spoke on, carried away by his own unexpected eloquence.

"Do you wish to repay our kindness to you by seeing your grandmother cast out from Greathills, where she has lived since she was married? Do you wish to see Helvetia, who has been raised with the expectations of her class, become a workhouse slavey? Your aunt and cousin beggared? I should have thought you would have more pride of family than to be so selfish!" Sir Cicero smote the table with fervour. He was just getting in the rhythm of his speech and could have gone on with even more plummy rhetoric, had not Lacey given a convulsive sob and buried her head in her hands.

Feminine hysterics made Sir Cicero extremely uncomfortable, as did any form of emotional outburst not his own. He looked toward the door as if gauging the possibility of obtaining feminine assistance before the storm broke and his niece started shrieking.

The silence of the room remained unbroken, save for the crackling of the fire. Lacey pulled out her handkerchief, gave an almost inaudible sniffle, then raised a dry and composed face to meet her uncle's.

"Very well, Sir Cicero. So be it."

She had neither changed expression nor moved when His Grace was announced a few minutes later. Seeing his volatile niece turn into a composed young lady only slightly less animate than a marble statue was highly disconcerting to Sir Cicero. What was she thinking of? Rebellion? An attack against His Grace? Suicide? None was unheard of in cases of forced marriages, and Lacey was capable of almost anything! If he could get the chit safely married to Lowood, she would be the duke's problem from the moment of the ceremony and he would be welcome to her!

"Your Grace," Sir Cicero said effusively, "you're here at last."

"Chyngford." Lowood dismissed him with just enough attention to be called civil. His aged eyes were only for the still loveliness seated in front of the fire. "And you, my dear? Has your uncle explained everything to you?" With scant effort, Lowood smiled. For the first time in years he was happy, or, at least, felt as he remembered happy to be. He would love and cherish this unexpected gift from the gods, lavish on her every material comfort within his power. "Louisa Anne," he murmured, almost to himself.

Lacey raised cold eyes. "The transaction has been settled. I am bound over to you as prescribed in your dealings with my uncle."

"My sweet girl!" His Grace cried, and all present heard the distress in his voice. "It is nothing like that. It is marriage, a partnership, that I am offering you."

Her gaze did not waver or warm. She had been raised in a hard school, where obligations were kept, no matter the cost, and everyone knew their place. It would seem that old Mrs Stoker's dream of a world where a woman could have a place and a will of her own was only the fantasy of a bedfast crone, for in the real world outside of books and freethinkers' ideals it seemed the only place for a woman was as the possession of some man, not even granting her the choice of which man. Disappointing as it might be, she was a Chyngford—the daughter of Barton and Charlotte Chyngford, all the family she wished to claim—and she would do her duty.

"Hardly. What you offered me earlier this evening was marriage, when I had the freedom of choice. Now you offer me a business transaction, already settled with my guardian, which I cannot refuse, legitimised by marriage. I cannot see where it is the same thing at all."

At that moment Sir Cicero could happily have strangled his niece. Where had she gotten such damnable ideas, anyway? She was crazy, that must be it . . . the result of inbreeding; her parents had been cousins. After all, what sane young lady would cavil at a chance to become a duchess?

His Grace was also taken aback. The face and form might be that of his dead darling, but no such heretical idea would ever have come from her lips. The woman he loved had been gentle and passive, as she should have been, with no wild notions in her pretty little head.

"You wound me to talk so, and I will endeavour to change your mind. I realise my reputation is not all that it should be, but that is in the past. Here; I have brought you a symbol of our plighted troth."

Lacey opened the velvet box with slow deliberation, unnerved by the duke's transformation from a notorious rake to ardent and tender fiancé. The ring was a ruby, fully as large as a peach pit, cunningly encircled with a fringe of multicoloured stones. She sat silent as he took it from the box and fitted it to her finger.

"This has been in my family for generations . . . some say since the Crusades. Does it please you, Louisa Anne?" His voice caressed the name as if it were a trophy.

"If you insist on such informality, Your Grace, I should prefer to be called Lacey. It is the only name I have ever known."

"Henceforth it pleases me that you will be called Louisa Anne. It is your name. You will be Louisa Anne, Duchess of Lowood!" The old voice rang with triumph.

Lacey bit her lips. She would not even be allowed her choice of name. "In the interest of honest and fair trade,

Your Grace, I feel I must tell you that a disappointed suitor is spreading rumours about me. They are not true in the slightest, but I doubt if anyone will believe that."

Haughtiness became the duke. "No one will believe anything about the Duchess of Lowood, save that which I wish them to believe."

"Louisa Anne, you never mentioned any problem to me. . . ." Sir Cicero was once again Head of the Family—until a speaking glance from his niece silenced him effectively.

His Grace stood and placed a lingering kiss in the palm of his chosen one's cool hand. "It is late, Louisa Anne, or perhaps I should say early, and you must have your rest. Sweet dreams, dear girl. Day after tomorrow I shall guard your slumbers myself."

That startled Lacey. "Day after tomorrow?"

"Yes. I have already sent instructions that Saint-Martin's-in-the-Fields is to be ready for us at ten in the morning the day after tomorrow. Already my man of business is on his way to Canterbury to procure a special license. I do not wish to live without you any longer than absolutely necessary, Louisa Anne," he said with shocking simplicity.

"But my bride clothes . . . my linens . . . ," Lacey babbled desperately, knowing full well that they were only excuses. If it were Piedmont in front of her, she would have happily gone with him that moment in the clothes she stood up in, or, if it were necessary, without them.

"That's too soon," sputtered Sir Cicero. His vision of weeks as the duke's prospective uncle, squiring the happy couple to all their engagements, riding high as one of the principals in Society's newest drama, faded. Once they were away on their honeymoon the whole thing would be a nine-days' wonder, all too quickly buried by some other tidbit, and Heaven only knew when they would be back in London! "It's not decent."

"It is as I wish it," Lowood replied evenly, with the air of one who is never challenged. "After we are married, you may have every frivolity your heart desires, Louisa Anne, and there is no need for you to bring any linens or other folderols, save your personal treasures. All my houses are fully furnished with every possible need and we shall take great delight in buying you every feminine frippery you could conceivably want."

"You overwhelm me, my lord," she murmured faintly.

== 15 ==

LORD PIEDMONT HAD never spent such a night—or very early morning—in his life. Abandoning the dying party, he had dismissed his carriage and walked home, borne company by his thoughts, all of which seemed to centre around the highly delectable Lacey Chyngford.

He had acted like a cad and a cur in the gallery, kissing her like that, as if she were a girl from the demimonde, but the memory of her enthusiastic response still generated a queer feeling all the way down to his knees. She was a girl of the Quality, for Heaven's sake, and he was treating her as if . . . as if she weren't. Quality or no, he had to admit that he had never wanted a female so much in his life as he wanted that fiery, chestnut-haired beauty, in spite of her family, in spite of her damned blue ideas, in spite of everything. He wanted to talk to her, to make love to her, to be with her. . . .

I must be in love, he thought suddenly. *This is what Vinnie and Bernard were each trying to tell me about. God forgive me, I thought they were crazy, but it's true.*

He thought about appealing to them for advice; it was barely four, so they would probably have just gotten home . . . No, this was something he would have to wrestle out himself. Taking the long way home, he proceeded to do just that. It was past dawn before he crawled into bed and fell into a justly deserved slumber.

Lacey did not see her bed until just before dawn, either, but the encircling arms of Morpheus eluded her for some time thereafter, as her brain busily played again and again the night's seemingly unending dramas. It had not stopped with her stunned departure from the Duke of Lowood— dear Lord, soon to be her husband.

An unusually animated Elizabeth had lain in wait for her cousin to come upstairs at last, slamming the bedroom door behind her and demanding to know the truth.

Lacey had looked wearily at the plump girl sprawling across the chaise and felt a thousand years older than her cousin. Elizabeth even looked younger, for her dressing gown was of sprigged wool, trimmed with lace as if designed for a child still in the nursery.

"Mama is in a tremendous pet and sent the maids to bed. I'll help you. Is it true you're going to marry the Duke of Lowood?" Fear and excitement in equal parts mingled in her eyes as she jumped up to help her cousin.

Wincing as much from the thought of the day after tomorrow as from her cousin's enthusiastic but inexpert removal of her hairpins, Lacey quietly answered in the affirmative. Elizabeth picked up the hairbrush and began to run it through the flow of chestnut waves with surprising delicacy. When she spoke, it was gravely.

"I must tell you something, Lacey. I've never liked you. Mama said you were an usurper and an intruder bent on destroying us for what happened to your mother. She warned me against you and I believed her. I—I'm sorry. What you did tonight was magnificent! If Milton . . . Mr Litchfield and I had been caught in so compromising a position . . . !"

"Do you love him?"

The hairbrush faltered. "Mama would never accept him."

"I didn't ask you that; I asked if you loved him."

Elizabeth sobbed and hid her face in her hands. the brush fell unnoticed to the floor. "Yes, yes I do, more than anyone will ever know. It will kill me when he leaves, because I know I'll never see him again!"

By Heaven, someone was going to come out happy in all this imbroglio! Lacey grabbed her cousin's shoulders in a singularly ungentle shake. "And why must that be? Elizabeth, he loves you. He's asked you to go with him. Why don't you go?"

For a moment Miss Dunfield's face lit with an animation born of longing. "I've dreamed of doing it, of being with him for always—"

"Then do it!"

"Do I dare? Mama would never let me."

"Your mother doesn't have to rule your life, Elizabeth!" Lacey took a deep breath and told her spellbound cousin the story of her parents' love and elopement, which, as Lacey had suspected, Elizabeth had never heard. "They never had worldly wealth, but no couple was ever happier or more in love."

"I never heard of such." Elizabeth's face glowed with a newfound hope. "Mama always told me an advantageous marriage was a young lady of good family's first duty."

"She would!" Lacey snapped. "You have a right to happiness! There's no need for more than one of us to be sacrificed for the sacred Chyngford name!" Her voice was bitter enough to make the other girl look up at her in amazement.

"Sacrificed? I don't understand."

"I didn't think they would tell you the whole truth," Lacey murmured, and proceeded to enlighten her cousin as to the true circumstances of her engagement.

"Mama always said that to people of our class love comes after marriage," she replied slowly. The lessons she had been taught all her life were crumbling before her eyes.

"Usually because they have no choice," Lacey said bitterly. "But you do, Elizabeth. Take it! Mr Litchfield is an admirable young man and he loves you. Don't you understand? All the jewels and titles and fortunes in the world won't replace a love that's true and lasting. They're just things, while love . . . love is everything!"

172

Elizabeth had never seen her indomitable cousin weep before. Gently, she stroked the bright head and asked, "And who is it you love, Lacey?"

"Piedmont!" It was a relief to share her burdensome secret with someone. "He is arrogant, overbearing, opinionated . . . and I can't help it!" Lacey raised a tear-stained face.

"Piedmont! Lacey, he is a frightening man, so cold and remote. . . ." To think of that man in conjunction with the tender emotion of love was alien to Elizabeth, yet even her simple mind could see where he and her fiery cousin might make a match of it quite well. "Does he know how you feel about him?"

"No." She tried to erase those few passionate moments in the gallery. "He doesn't care for me, of course, so it makes no difference in what happens now . . . or later."

Elizabeth was alarmed by the look on her cousin's face, but that same look precluded any questions. Lacey had no intention of telling anyone her plans, let alone rattle-pated Elizabeth. Lacey was a Chyngford, and she would do her duty to the family, but after that was over, her life would be her own. It would be dangerous, of course, for it was against the law for a wife to leave her legal husband, but nothing could be more odious than remaining as the wife of that horrible old man. The risk would be worth it.

Lacey had planned her strategy during that awful time in the library. After the gaming markers were destroyed and the honor of the Chyngford family was safe again, she would simply disappear—perhaps to the country, perhaps even abroad. She had a hundred pounds, an adequate mind, and courage; it should be enough to build her own life. The thought stayed with her long after she talked more to Elizabeth, trying to pump courage into that frail vessel— and finally even into her restless slumbers.

Another member of Society went to an uneasy rest that night, though Avery Melsham's sleep was disturbed more by excitement than by disquiet. Purely through the accident of a late-night drink at the Cocoa Tree, he had stumbled on what promised to be the most spectacular *on-dit* of the Season. Properly played, it would result in his acceptance as a Power of Note in the Polite World.

He all but wriggled with excitement. No more shabby lodgings in the unfashionable end of Barrett Street. No more raised eyebrows from haughty dowagers. No more snubs from higher reaches of the ton. Once he proved himself as worthy of ducal confidences, his reputation would be unassailable.

After all, hadn't the Duke of Lowood himself told him that he was going to marry Louisa Anne Chyngford? It had taken only a moment's cogitation to realise that he must mean that changeling goddess the Chyngfords had produced at such short notice, though he distinctly remembered her being called Lacey. No matter.

They had met at the Cocoa Tree, where apparently His Grace was biding time in expectation of his lady's answer. Melsham had first been attracted to the table by the unprecedented event of seeing the Duke of Lowood smiling, and then, on being asked to sit and drink to the health of his future bride, could not refuse, despite the fact that the duke was not one of his favourite people.

Remembering the painful disappointment of the duke's previous hopes for a certain Miss Winterthorpe the previous season, Melsham—ever a cautious man with a high regard for his own skin—was hesitant to mention the *Times*'s notices, but when it accidentally slipped out, His Grace seemed positively grateful for the reminder and, in an unfamiliar spirit of bonhomie, asked him to the ceremony.

And the wedding was the day after tomorrow! His future secured by happy circumstance, Avery Melsham, Esq., slept soundly.

In her calculations Lacey had made one possibly fatal mistake; she had overestimated Chester Stoker's courage, or perhaps underestimated his debts and consequent cunning.

Her refusal to knuckle under to his threats of spurious exposure as his mistress had taken young Stoker badly by surprise. The Chyngford chit had never exhibited that much courage at Beecham Manor, and who would have thought any girl with social aspirations to be so cavalier towards her reputation? He knew the Chyngfords had to be filthy rich, but not all the money in the world would protect a girl in such a situation from the vicious tongues of the ton.

Well, he decided, it made no difference; it was too late now for him to find any other means of relieving his financial obligation, so it had to be Lacey Chyngford, no matter what other plans she had made.

He had spent most of the night in wakeful plotting and at last had evolved a plan which he thought should do the job. It was weak and had holes, but given the situation and the pressing financial problems, he dared not take the time to create a better one.

With his goals firmly in mind, Chester Stoker, armed with a book of poetry and a sizeable posy of very expensive flowers, presented himself at Chyngford House. Quilling was reluctant to admit him, being mindful of Miss Chyngford's displeasure at Mr Stoker's last visit, but after a long and soulful tale of a lovers' quarrel and a broken-hearted suitor's wishing to make amends, the butler relented. Like most of the servants at Chyngford House, he was fond of Miss Lacey and wished a better life for her than her aunt and uncle seemed prepared to offer. Mr Stoker had apparently loved Miss Lacey before she became an heiress, and he was a squire's son to boot. Although Quilling would have wished a higher rank for the young lady, he was a romantic at heart and found it not too difficult to smooth the path of true love.

After a night of weeping, Lacey was in little humour for Quilling's announcement of an unnamed visitor, much less inclined to see this mysterious personage, but, on being informed that he intended to stay until she did, went down to make short work of such an unmannerly creature. Of all the people in the world she had expected to see, Chester Stoker was not one of them.

She closed the drawing room door quietly behind her, knowing she was committing a solecism that was all the worse for being a repetition. So far no one had learned of Chester's first visit—or its dreadful course—but she wanted to take no chance of her aunt or cousin finding out about either. Quilling would certainly keep silent for fear of his place and Lacey herself had no desire to have the situation known, so with any sort of good fortune she should be able to resolve everything with no one the wiser.

"I can see why you forbade Quilling to tell me who was here, Mr Stoker. What inducement did you offer to keep him from his duty to the family?" Lacey's tone was sharp. She had been ill-used by all of Society, and now it seemed that even the family servants were in conspiracy against her. She had slept ill, and the crimson-striped lutestring morning dress Bailey had laid out for her only served to increase her pallor, making her look undeservedly fragile.

"Only the truth," Chester lied with convincing humility. "I told him we had had a misunderstanding and I would make amends." Without ceremony, he handed over his offerings. "Here."

"For me?" Lacey asked in some confusion. "Lord Byron! I *am* fond of his verses . . . and tuberoses!" She sniffed at the small, highly scented blossoms. The trailing white ribbands draped gracefully over her fingers.

"Was that what they were? I asked the woman at the stall for the best she had. . . . They are none too good for the woman I wounded with my thoughtlessness. Lacey . . . Miss Chyngford, I have come here to proffer my apologies. I was an unspeakable brute at our last meeting."

"Yes, you were," Lacey said with devastating frankness. "Won't you sit down, Mr Stoker?" Her grandmother had impressed on her that a lady was a lady at all times; she never expected him to take her offer, and she was not disappointed.

Seemingly overcome by emotion, he turned to the window and fumblingly drew out a handkerchief, which he ostentatiously applied to his eyes before turning to face her again.

"No, I do not wish to outstay my welcome, Miss Chyngford. It . . . it is not easy to apologise, but please believe me, I meant you no harm. It's just that I care so much . . ." His expression would have melted a stone, a much harder substance than Miss Chyngford's heart, which was feminine enough to be somewhat flattered by such desperate devotion.

Muffled by the thick morning-room doors came the sound of the doorbell and Quilling's measured step. Chester—to Lacey's extreme embarrassment—dropped to his knee with extended hands.

"Please say you forgive me, Miss Chyngford. I was just driven mad by the thought of losing you. At home at Beecham Manor, I thought there was all the time in the world to woo you properly, after we had decently mourned my grandmother's passing, but then without warning you were gone. . . ." He imprisoned her hand in a fervent clasp. "I thought I'd never see you again, until Mother happened to hear that you were in London. I never stopped to think that you might not feel as strongly as I. . . ."

"I never knew of your feelings," she murmured, unsuccessfully trying to free her hand, but the volume of poetry and the white-streamered flowers hampered her.

"I know that now, but when I saw you here that afternoon, so beautiful and desirable—and in London, where I might lose you at any time . . . I went a little mad. All I want to say is that I'm sorry if my outburst caused you any discomfort. Please believe me when I say I am yours to command. Do you forgive me?"

"Mr Stoker, this is not necessary—"

"But it is! If you would only say you forgive me! Do you? Please say yes. . . ."

Well, Lacey decided, he really hadn't done anything, and forgiving him seemed to be the only way to retrieve her hand. Besides, he seemed to be sincere; he hadn't even waited to place a protective handkerchief for his knees.

"Yes, Chester," she said in all good fellowship. She had, after all, been very fond of his grandmother.

His light knock unheard in the fervour of Mr Stoker's plea, Quilling had taken the liberty of human curiosity and opened the door just in time to hear young Miss Lacey's soft reply. Once aware of his presence, the young couple blushed in confusion and sprang apart; he wished he could tell them to be sure of his discretion, but rules could be bent only so much. He extended a sealed note.

"This just came for you, Miss."

"Thank you, Quilling," Lacey replied with as much dignity as possible. What a coil! That she should be caught in a compromising position by the butler . . .

Chester waited until they were alone again before speaking. Lacey seemed not to notice his continued presence; having rid herself of the book and flowers, her attention was now captivated by the thick paper and sizeable wax seal of her missive. The red wax looked like gouts of blood against the creamy paper.

"Please . . . read your note," Chester murmured. "I should hate to stand in the way of your business."

It was a graceful speech, but went largely unheard. The writing on Lacey's missive was crabbed and uneven, as if an elderly person had scribbled it in a hurry. The superscription did not give a feeling of confidence, either: *Miss Lacey Chyngford, Chyngford House, London. Personal. Urgent.*

Lacey broke the seal with a well-deserved sense of unease.

Lacey—You must come at once. There has been
an accident to Helvetia and she is calling for you.
There is no need to alarm the others yet, so please

tell no one, especially your aunt or uncle, as they would just be in the way. Please, you must come as soon as possible while there is still time.

Your loving grandmama

Unable to restrain a squeak of shock, Lacey was glad for the strong arm and instant attention of Chester Stoker. He seated her on the sofa, made a ceremony of procuring a glass of water from the desk carafe, and gently chafed her wrists.

Helvie! Injured! During her time at Greathills, Lacey had tried diligently to reach the little girl, to make friends with her, and had achieved some minor success; now that she was injured, Helvie was calling for her. Grandmother had been quite right to send for her, but she wondered about not telling Aunt Leonora or Uncle Cicero; if things were serious, they should know. . . . However, as she could imagine, and as her grandmother probably knew, there could be no two more nerve-wracking in a sickroom. On the other hand, if it were really too close to being too late—

"Lacey! Lacey, dearest . . ." Chester's voice came as if from far away. He was dampening her forehead with more water from the carafe. "Speak to me, sweet Lacey. What is wrong?"

Pushing away his dripping handkerchief, Lacey struggled into a sitting position. She felt oddly fuzzy-headed. "My cousin . . . she's injured."

"How horrible! What must we do?" His heavily handsome face creased into a frown of concern.

"I must go to her. . . ." Lacey stood. Only yesterday she had been wishing for the gift of swooning; now it seemed she had it in a half-hearted sort of way, save that she continued to function. Chester's supporting arm was comforting.

"Of course you must, the poor little tyke. My dear Lacey . . . allow me to prove my goodwill. I'll take you anywhere you need to go. My carriage stands right outside."

"I couldn't put you to so much trouble—"

"But you said that you forgave me! That is not Christian to go back on your word. Besides, I can get you wherever you want to go more quickly. . . . Please allow me to prove myself."

If only she could think clearly! Chester's words had a slipperiness that her befuddled brain could not quite grasp securely. Poor little Helvie . . .

"Very well. But first I must write a note. . . ."

"A note? But you mustn't . . ."

She was still alert enough to catch that, and a sharp glance brought a flush to Chester's face.

"When you were so stricken and I rushed to your aid . . . the note was lying face up on the carpet. . . . Please let me help you, Lacey! Think of that poor child in pain, calling for you. . . ."

Oddly enough, Lacey found his argument convincing; she had never known Chester to be so strong. It was quite pleasant to let someone else make the decisions.

"I understand, Chester, but I must leave a note for Elizabeth." She sat at the desk, alarmed at how scrawly her hand seemed. "I don't want her worrying about me."

Chester frowned; he had not counted on such devotion between the two elder cousins. In fact, he had thought there was a definite antipathy there. He leaned forward in all solicitude, but it was too late. With brisk and only slightly shaky motions, Lacey had folded the paper.

"Shall we go now? I'll just leave this with Quilling." She seemed to feel better now, being in motion and actually doing something. It must have been the restless night and the emotional turmoil which made her feel so fuzzy and weak.

"Your flowers," Chester said, scooping up the white-ribbanded posy. "They might cheer the child."

Lacey agreed and held out her hand to him. She would feel even better in the fresh air, she hoped, for now she felt a slight nausea beginning to rise. Chester seemed to understand, for he hurried as much as humanly possible, allowing her barely enough time to accept her cloak from a startled Quilling, and press the note into his hands with express instructions to give it to no one but Miss Elizabeth, before she was down the steps and safely bundled into his old but serviceable travelling berlin.

—16—

HER DECISION IRREVOCABLY made, Miss Elizabeth Dunfield awoke feeling quite alert from a surprisingly restful night. Even though she opened her eyes to the room that had always been hers, it was like waking into a completely new world. She ate the light breakfast brought her, dressed in a becoming frock of fawn silk that her mother had condemned as being sadly dowdy, and wrote a short note, which she sent to Mr Milton Litchfield's hotel by the underfootman. She had expected that it would not go unanswered, and the boy returned in record time with a scrawled note in which Mr Litchfield replied he could not believe what she had written and intended to call upon her at three.

By the time Lady Dunfield was awake, Elizabeth was sufficiently composed to join her for morning chocolate, as was her custom. She sat on the chaise, and since she was a quiet person by nature, no comment was made on her reticence. In fact, her ladyship was in such a pet about her niece's expected aggrandisement that she heard no voice but her own, endlessly complaining about the injustice of life.

"Just imagine that jumped-up vicarage brat as a duchess! It is enough to make your blood run cold."

"As Grandmother said, she is a double Chyngford."

"I will not have you being impertinent, young woman. When I think of how you have been so carefully nurtured and trained to take your place as one of the great hostesses of the land . . . it just makes me ill. Even when you are a viscountess, she will still have precedence over you. I vow it gives me a fit of the vapours!"

Seeing her mother through new eyes, Elizabeth sipped her chocolate and sat in watchful silence.

"Poor darling. I can see it makes you sick, too, as it would any person of real sensibility. For all that His Grace is a duke, he must be close to insane."

"I am glad to see my cousin so highly advanced in life."

Her ladyship's eyes, always somewhat puffy in the morning, narrowed even more, as if being pushed down by the weight of her prodigious lace nightcap. "Nonsense! You'll have to be bowing and scraping to her for the rest of your days. To think of that . . . that foundling a duchess! How Charlotte must be laughing at us. Besides," she added in one of her notorious conversational redirections, "if you felt yourself, you would never have chosen that awful dress. Can't think why we ordered it at all. It makes you look like a governess."

Elizabeth ran her palm down the smooth silk, uninterrupted by bows or ribbands or ruching. "I think it makes me look dignified."

"Dignified!" Leonora snorted. "And what makes you think Lord Piedmont wants anyone who looks dignified? Last night I was appalled at the amount of time he spent with that Remington hoyden, and you . . . you had to be searched out! It will serve you right if that chit snaps him up from under your nose."

The only reply to that remark was silence. The newly aware Elizabeth drained her chocolate cup and, not wishing to draw attention to herself by walking to the table to put it down, sat there holding it.

"Elizabeth, the sight of you in that makes me think of those prosing Methodys. Go put on that pretty dress with the blue bows. You and I are going to Lady Tewksbury's."

Having been present when the invitation was given and knowing that her cousin was included as well, Elizabeth could not help asking, "Is Lacey not well?"

"That scheming chit! I have no idea and don't intend to find out. She will have her time as the Duchess of Lowood, and I must admit I'll be glad to see it. How can a brat from a vicarage hope to run some of the biggest and most palatial households in the country? Fine figure of fun it will make her. Lowood will discover his mistake. 'Her Grace' indeed! Her Gracelessness is more like it. When I think of how you have been trained to all the duties of a lady while that upstart . . . It makes me ill!"

Unaccustomed to pity for others, it was amazing how easily Elizabeth could feel for her cousin. That bright personality, condemned to live with a man she found repulsive; while the man she did love seemed to care naught for her. It was a cruel joke which Society played on women, just as Lacey had always said, but the saddest thing of all was that she would have to bear the brunt of it, while Elizabeth . . .

Taking a deep breath, Elizabeth rose and, depositing her cup on the tray, moved gracefully to the door. The fawn dress did become her, adding the illusion of height to her dumpy figure and decreasing the unfortunate ruddiness of her skin. "I will leave you now, Mama, and let you get dressed."

Never before had her darling child left her presence without first asking permission and then kissing her cheek. Lady Dunfield stared after the self-contained girl and finally decided that she must be eating her heart out with jealousy, as well she might. Charlotte's child a duchess! It was outside of enough!

Her ladyship was a slow and meticulous dresser, so when she was finally ready for the afternoon's outing, it was with surprise that she found Elizabeth stretched full length on her bed, still clad in the fawn silk. Her eyes were closed and her face pale, as if she were labouring under strong emotion.

"Elizabeth! We must leave at once and you aren't even changed! I will not have Lady Tewksbury and her friends see you in that dowdy dress! She's so aware of what is fashionable." With misguided pride, Lady Dunfield straightened her gown of India muslin striped in three startling shades of green and picked with yellow ribbands.

Despite her frail appearance, Elizabeth's voice was strangely firm. "I do not wish to go, Mama. I have the headache."

"The headache! I vow this household has had an epidemic of headaches, not the least of which is that cousin of yours, but—"

"Please, Mama! I do not want to go."

"I understand, my precious, but you just can't hide because you're embarrassed over your cousin's putting herself forward in such an unseemly way."

"It's not that, Mama. . . . I have just decided I do not wish to visit Lady Tewksbury."

Lady Dunfield had never heard such a decisive tone from her daughter, and it went as another black mark against Lacey. Before her disruptive presence in the household, Elizabeth would never have thought of disagreeing so vehemently with her mother. Still, Lady Tewksbury was waiting—the old doyenne was a stickler for punctuality—and short of physical means, there seemed to be no way to move Elizabeth.

"Very well, Elizabeth," she said at last. "I realise your disappointment over the unkindness of Fate, so I will humour you today, but tomorrow you must pull yourself together and act properly."

"I will not be a charge on you tomorrow, Mama."

Lady Dunfield, content that she had discharged her maternal duty, left the room, only to be stopped at the bottom of the stairs by her daughter's cry. She did hope the child was not going to have a tiresome bout of hysterics, for she did not want to be late to Lady Tewksbury's.

"What is it, Elizabeth?"

"I—I just wanted to tell you I love you, Mama." Elizabeth leaned over the rail, her face taut.

"Silly child, of course you do. Go back to bed and I'll see you this afternoon." All too conscious of the presence of Quilling, Lady Dunfield was more brusque than her wont. What had gotten into Elizabeth? She had been taught better than to display emotion in front of the servants; her mama would have to straighten a few things out with that young miss when she returned!

Elizabeth took a heavy heart back to her room; the best things were not always the easiest, but she persevered with only the faintest qualms and was sitting composedly in the upstairs sitting room when Mr Milton Litchfield was announced promptly on the stroke of three. He immediately went to his knees in front of her, unmindful of the effect on his new and very correct brown trousers.

"My dear Elizabeth . . . when I received your note this morning, I could not believe it! Are you sure?"

She allowed him to clasp both of her hands securely. How could she ever have even considered any other course? "If you still want me, yes. Yes!"

No other words ever sounded sweeter to Mr Litchfield. In his heart he blessed Miss Chyngford for her support in this miracle, since his beloved would never have taken such a step without her aid. With the prerogatives awarded a fiancé, he rose and took Elizabeth in his arms, vowing silently that she should never regret the magnitude of this step.

"Ever since I received your missive this morning, I have been making plans. We board the *Evening Star* at Dover and sail on tomorrow's tide for Calais. From there we take the land route to Florence and can be married at any place along the route that you fancy."

"It sounds wonderful. 'Mrs Milton Litchfield.' "

"I regret having no title or fortune to offer you, dearest heart."

"Being your wife is all that I could ever desire. Your name for a title, your love for a fortune . . ." For perhaps the first time in her life, Elizabeth was completely happy. She gave a small sigh of contentment and laid her head against her beloved's ample chest, then for a full moment enjoyed the pure sensation of love before more practical matters intruded. "We had best be gone, Milton, my dearest. Mama might return early. I told her I had the headache. I fear I bring you no dowry . . . I dare not pack much—I do not want to excite any notice." She indicated a smallish bag which might have contained nothing more than needlework. "I fear you will have to take me with little more than I stand up in."

"Just taking you with me is enough, Elizabeth." Pausing just long enough for the luxury of one more quick kiss, Milton adjusted a cloak about his beloved and lifted the bag as she took one last, somewhat sad look around the room. "I will love you no less if you change your mind, dearest."

It was just what she had wanted to hear. Smiling, she took his arm. "No, dear, but we must behave as if we were going to do nothing but drive around the park. We must act as if we always took a bag with us. Quilling will notice, of course, but I will trust his discretion."

Their demeanour in the front hall aroused no suspicion, even in the romantic butler. One elopement in the family that day was quite enough and very much in keeping with the dramatic Miss Lacey; Miss Elizabeth was too much of a lady to be involved in such goings-on.

"Mr Litchfield has been kind enough to offer to take me for a drive in the hope it might alleviate my headache, Quilling," Elizabeth said easily. "I should be home before her ladyship, but in case I am not and she should start to worry, please give her this." It was only a small lie, she thought guiltily. Surely Heaven would forgive her when so much was at stake.

Quilling took the heavily sealed envelope and nodded; trust Miss Elizabeth to be so considerate of her mother's feelings. "Beg pardon, miss, but your cousin left this for you. I did not feel that you should be disturbed when you felt badly. . . ."

"Lacey?" A faint premonition of oncoming disaster creased her brow. "I did not know she had gone out."

As if in echo to Elizabeth's pounding heart, a resonant tattoo shook the front door and sent it smashing back from Quilling's hands. "Well, is she in yet?"

"Your Lordship . . ." The butler quailed visibly before the magnificent figure. Quilling was not a particularly brave man, and there were certain dangers not to be endured; at least, not in the service of Sir Cicero Chyngford. "I'm sorry, sir, but Miss Chyngford is not at home."

His face a study in wrath, Jordan Piedmont strode into the hall. It had been a trying night and a long day, and he was in no mood to be brooked, especially by a titian-haired chit. He had wrestled with himself until dawn before finally admitting that he loved Miss Lacey Chyngford, regardless of her wild ideas, her bluestockinged attitudes, and her dreary family. She was unlike any other girl he had ever known, gently bred or not, for no other female of any class had ever excited him this much or intrigued him quite so completely.

With that question settled firmly in mind, he had presented himself at the earliest possible hour for calls, set to make her a formal offer, only to be told she was not at home. Three successive calls had garnered the same unproductive answer and, not being used to such cavalier treatment, his temper had worn down in direct proportion to each negative. That girl *would* be gone when he was ready to make a declaration!

"Sir, I must protest—" Quilling made a valiant effort but was forestalled by Miss Dunfield's cry.

"Your Lordship! Oh, thank Heaven you are here!"

There was something different about Miss Dunfield

today, something that vaguely pleased him, but he was in no humour to refine on it at the moment. With easy grace he swept her a bow. "Miss Dunfield. A pleasure. How may I serve you?"

"You have come here to see my cousin Lacey?"

"Indeed! I have been trying to see her the better part of this day, and she is always not at home! I would gain the impression that she is not anxious for my company!"

"And are you for hers?"

"Elizabeth!" Milton sounded horrified.

"Please, dearest, let me handle this. Oh, please forgive my bad manners." Early training ran deep, and having been trained by her mother and grandmother in the niceties, Elizabeth quickly sketched an introduction between the two gentlemen and went ruthlessly on. Lacey had been kind to her in helping her find true love and happiness; it was the least she could do to return the favour. "I asked you a question, Lord Piedmont."

Part of the art of staying alive in war was having an instinct for whom you could trust; Jordan sensed that Miss Dunfield was now an ally. "I came here to request her hand in marriage. Does that answer your question?"

In the background, Quilling quietly choked.

"Admirably."

"Well, where is she, then? Won't she see me?"

"She thinks you don't care. I've been afraid she would do something crazy. . . . Here, read this."

"She thinks I don't . . . That abominable girl!" Piedmont snatched the letter and then felt a rush of unease, equal to that which had passed through Miss Dunfield. He had never seen Miss Chyngford's fist, but even in moments of strong emotion he would have expected her to produce something quite different from this lopsided, uneven scrawl.

> Dear Elizabeth—Please don't worry. I have gone with Chester Stoker on a matter of utmost urgency. I can tell you nothing, save it is for the

good of the family. I will contact you as soon as I can.

Lacey

"I don't know what it is, Your Lordship, but something is horribly wrong." Her face was desperate. "Please, please help her."

There was darkness and light and a sickening, swirling sense of motion. There was a hard place where she was bunched up like a garble of washing and two arms that were not strong enough to hold her securely; she might fall . . . and then a great softness and she could sleep. . . .

The ceiling was old and cracked; not even the flickering rosy light from the hearth could take away the patina of squalour and age. Lacey was lying on her side. Her mind was still fuzzy, but that was lessening. She had been dimly awake for several minutes, lying completely still, like an animal when the hunter was abroad. Although she wasn't quite sure why, she was afraid.

There was nothing in the room itself to inspire fear; she had been in many worse. It was old, with flaking plaster and heavy, time-darkened timbers. From her limited point of view, she could see a great chest against the wall. Two heavily draped windows flanked it, the colour of the hangings indistinguishable in the faint pinkish light. The fireplace must be behind her. She was lying in a bed, a heavy, testered thing from many generations past. It smelled musty.

Now she was sure of it.

There was someone else in the room with her. She hadn't been certain before, for the old building was full of creaks and rattles, but now there was a definite sound behind her, like someone shifting in a chair, and if she listened very carefully, she could hear breathing.

Lacey was fully awake now, testing her faculties, cau-

tiously wiggling fingers and toes. She was not uncomfortable, though a bit cramped from lying so still in one
position; someone had covered her with a warm cloak.

Deciding that she could not stay there indefinitely,
Lacey chose surprise as her best defence, and sat bolt
upright.

"So, my dear wife, you are awake at last," said Chester
Stoker.

=17=

LACEY GULPED AND swallowed heavily. "Your wife?"

"I thought that drug I gave you should be wearing off about now. Does your head hurt?" He was sitting in the chair by the fireplace, but rose with some stiffness to approach her side and bend gallantly over her hand. "Most uncomfortable chair I've ever had the misfortune to sit in. Did you sleep well, dear?"

"Curse the chair," Lacey snapped inelegantly. "And I'm not your dear. You called me your wife. Please explain that."

"Always deucedly practical, dear Miss Lacey! Well, to be precise, we are not married yet . . . but have no fear, we will be! It is but a few days to Gretna Green. I apologise for the poor accommodations, but at the moment my slender purse does not allow for the niceties of life, and my creditors refuse to extend an ounce more charity until I have your fortune firmly in hand. I should add that a great number of my creditors are counting on that happening quickly. Yes, you should be proud to know that the mere mention of the mighty Chyngford fortune is enough to stay the most blood-sucking of moneylenders, especially if they think they are going to get any part of it." Chester spoke with a certain bravado, not expecting his quarry to be able to tell the difference between courage and bombast.

He had prepared himself well with an arsenal of hand-kerchiefs and smelling salts, anticipating anything from tears to hysterics to personal attack, but nothing he could have dreamed of would have been more unexpected than Lacey's heartfelt laughter.

"So you think you're going to marry me? And for my fortune?" Her laughter increased until Chester, fearing a different form of hysterics, raised his hand, but Lacey stopped him. "No, please don't slap me. I'm not in the least out of control. It's just that it's so funny!" She dissolved into a giggling heap across the bedclothes.

No planned insult would have angered Chester more. A deeply drawn breath of indignation puffed his features, and he proceeded to turn a choleric shade of red.

"I'm glad you seem to see such a matter for amusement, Lacey. Rest assured that I do not find it so! Had our debts not been so troublesome, I wouldn't have bothered with such an elaborate plan of action."

The dancing lights in Lacey's eyes dimmed a little. "So you were behind everything. Helvie is all right?"

"So far as I know," Chester said with callous dismissal.

"Very clever, Chester. You wrote the note and signalled your confederate somehow . . . your handkerchief at the window, of course . . . and then you drugged that glass of water you were so kind as to procure for me. You really have gone to a lot of trouble for nothing, I'm afraid. Now stop this charade and take me home. You'll have to find some other way to settle your problems."

Young Mr Stoker snarled with long-suppressed rage. "Easy for you to say. We are not all of us fortunate enough to fall into great inheritances; some of us, in order to maintain a decent standard of living, have to find our fortunes as best we can."

Lacey had been keeping her mirth under control, but to Chester's utter fury that set her off again.

Chester's tone became dangerously icy. "Stop that laughing at once! The situation is anything but funny."

"Oh, but it is!" Controlling herself with an effort, Lacey

sat up and wiped her eyes. "I wonder if this is how horses and cows feel at auction. I vow I shall never feel comfortable purchasing anything again!"

"What is all this about horses and cows? You must be demented! There is nothing at all amusing about being up against the wall, I assure you."

"Sit down, Chester. I know there is nothing amusing, because I am in that same situation." In a few well-chosen words, Lacey enlightened Chester as to the state of the Chyngford finances and her subsequent engagement to the Duke of Lowood. Chester's face grew paler and tighter as he began to understand the full seriousness of the situation.

"So you see, Chester, unless I marry the Duke of Lowood tomorrow morning, there is no Chyngford fortune. And, quite frankly, I can't say I relish being sold to either one of you."

"That sounds like my stupid grandmother. Neither one of you cares a hoot about what happens to me." Chester sat forward in a defensive crouch, his brow furrowed with the unaccustomed exercise of thought.

"Your grandmother was a wonderful woman, and she cared a great deal for you. She just hated to see you become a wastrel."

"Don't you go preaching at me the way she always did. A woman's place is to be quiet, have sons, and bring a fortune to her husband. I was prepared to *marry* you!" The last was a scream of accusation. "In spite of your fancy family, you're nothing but a parson's daughter who used to be a servant in our house. I was going to make you the lady of Beecham Manor!"

Despite her perilous position, Lacey's unruly tongue would not behave. "An honour I could certainly do without! If I am to be sacrificed to save a family's fortune, I would certainly rather it be my own. Now, if you are quite finished with this farce, I should like to go home!"

With a graceful movement, Lacey slid from the bed. He had not bothered to remove her shoes, but the floor felt gritty even through the soft soles. She would have made a dignified move towards the door, but Chester placed an iron grip on her arm and pulled her close.

"Yes, I wager you would, my fine miss, so you can marry that rich duke of yours. . . ." His face was distorted with anger. "But what about me? What about my debts? Everyone granted me a stay on payment because I was going to marry into the Chyngford fortune!"

Against her will, a giggle bubbled up and was stifled only with a great deal of effort, but this time it was closer to hysteria. Lacey was beginning to be frightened by Chester, who seemed increasingly irrational, and as usual, her fear was transmuted into a masking anger.

"Despite my affection and respect for your grandmother, I don't give a groat for what happens to you! You incurred those debts. Before you expected me to rescue you, you should at least have consulted me. Now, will you please take me back home?"

Chester's eyes glittered. Lacey could see all reason leave his expression. "Very much the duke's lady, aren't you, my fine, jumped-up hired companion? Well, you may not have a fortune, but I deserve something for the way you've wrecked my life! Let's see how much his noble lordship enjoys his bride when he discovers he's got damaged goods!"

With arms of steel he pulled her close, his loose wet mouth stifling Lacey's angry protest. After the initial paralysis of shock, she moved to fight back, but he was stronger, his natural strength further increased by his mad fury. One arm held her upper arms all but immobile while the other pawed madly at the front of her dress; the crimson ribbands of her bodice were meant primarily for show and not to stand up against such assaults. They gave way, exposing the linen underdress, which only enhanced, rather than concealed, the soft swelling of her breasts.

Outrage and anger gave Lacey strength. Chester was trying to tip her over onto the bed, but although he had the advantage in weight and bulk, she was almost his equal in height and that made his task difficult. His struggles loosened his grip and Lacey took instant advantage to break away. There was no chance to make the door and no guarantee of help beyond it, so with a cunning born of desperation she grasped the aged candlestick and brought it down on Chester's skull with sufficient force to bend the heavy brass. He slipped to the floor without even a groan.

Lacey's first fear was that she had killed him, then—on hearing his regular, if rather ragged, breathing—that he would awaken before she could make good her escape. Chester Stoker had always had a lively temper; she could not imagine it improved by the events of this evening. Her best defence against him would be to return to Uncle Cicero's protection as soon as possible. After all, she thought with just a touch of bitterness, it was in his best interests to guard the duke's property!

To her despair, the door was locked most firmly. The key was most likely on Chester's person. Despite her situation, Lacey could not bring herself to touch him, key or no key. She had no choice but to try the window, yet as she approached it, she heard, to her utter terror, the unmistakable sound of breaking glass coming from that very casement. This sent Lacey back to the questionable defence of the brass candlestick.

The only light in the room was the reflected glow of the grudging fire, which threw deep shadows in which Lacey could hide. She sheltered in the lee of the massive bed, the turned brass of her makeshift weapon cutting cruelly into her hand.

The intruder worked with consummate stealth; the ancient casement made barely a protest. The heavy drapes bellied out sightly on the draught, then farther and more solidly as the tall form slipped into the room. Gnawing her underlip, Lacey took a step forward and raised the candlestick, only to have it knocked ruthlessly from her grasp.

"Lacey Chyngford! Why in the name of all that's holy—"

"Jordan!" Lacey cried in a maelstrom of emotions she

was unable to comprehend, before flinging herself into his waiting embrace.

"Lacey," he answered in a husky tone containing a passion quite equal to her own.

Without a qualm, Lacey abandoned herself to the exquisite sensation of being in his arms. She buried her head in his shoulder and breathed deeply of the mingled scents of bay rum, horse, and the indefinable sweetness of his skin. How wonderful it was to lie quietly against his strong body, to feel his arms encircling her as protection against any dangers, to be so close to him whom she desired with all her heart. If only it were he to whom she were to be wed on the morrow, she would be the happiest woman in the world! To know that his would be the face to greet her each morning . . . she caught her breath with a little sob.

"Are you all right? Did that swine hurt you?"

"No . . . I'm all right." She leaned back to feast on the glory of his features, her state of disarray forgotten.

Jordan noticed, and a cloud passed over his face. "He did! That filthy cur . . ." Even as he felt a flood of anger for the senseless violation of an innocent lady, a different, stronger tide was rising in him at the sight of her indisputably feminine attributes gently rising and falling beneath thin linen and the soft white flesh scored with four thin red lines from Chester's careless nails. Hesitantly he traced one of the angry weals with his finger, divided as to killing the cad immediately or bending to heal the hurts with his loving lips.

No! He was Lord Piedmont, not a slavering beast like that Stoker offal; he would teach Lacey the delights that could occur between a man and a woman, but not in some hole-and-corner fashion. He loved her, and the highest tribute of love he could give her would be to marry her and protect her with his name for the rest of their lives. He would not defile his love for her; it would not be easy, but he would take the honourable course and wait until their love was sanctioned by God and, more important, Society, which was much harder to please.

Lacey was aware in every nerve of the trip his finger took over her breast. She had never felt this sensation before, this warm burning within her that threatened to destroy her. He was too near, too much of a power to resist, and she knew she would go with him anywhere under any circumstance. Despite a country upbringing, she knew very little of the actual physical rites between a man and a woman, but she could think of sharing them happily with no one but Jordan. She wanted to belong to him in every way for the rest of her life, and when he suddenly tensed and removed his stroking finger, she felt as if she would faint from loss.

"We must get you back to London as quickly as possible," he said in a strangled voice. "Can you fix . . . that?"

Lacey blushed; somehow his words made her feel dirty and common. Powered solely by pride, she pulled free of his encircling arm and stood—however shakily—alone. Her fingers fumbled with the crimson ribbands and soon brought a semblance of order back to her person.

"How did you find me?"

"Your cousin Elizabeth showed me the letter you left." His instincts under firm control, Jordan knelt by Chester's prone body. Nothing would have given him greater pleasure than to smash that ugly face, but no Piedmont could ever violate the code of sportsmanship so as to hit a man when he was down. "Did you hit him with the same candlestick you were going to use on me?"

"Yes. The blow bent it." Lacey struggled with a knot.

"If you say anything about the Stokers being hard-headed, I shall beat you."

"I have had enough of physical assault for tonight, thank you, but I still should like an explanation of how you came to be here. I told Elizabeth nothing of my destination. . . ." Lacey blushed at the memory of her gullibility. "In fact, I didn't know it. Where are we?"

"Not far from King's Langley. When Miss Dunfield told me you had gone with Chester Stoker, I merely applied to his stableboy. As I had surmised, the lad's master is not overly generous with him, and consequently, I found that the application of a few pounds made him more than happy to talk. Knowing young Stoker's reputation and route brought me here. I've checked every little-known inn along the way, ostensibly seeking a cousin. When the landlord here said that there was only a young couple here, the wife taken with the travel-sickness, I decided to investigate. I assumed you had been drugged. Are you ready?"

"Are we just going to leave him here? When he awakes . . . He's been threatening to spread scurrilous rumours . . ."

"And what would you have me do with him? Wait until he wakes and challenge him to a duel? No, I think you needn't worry about him. From what I've heard of young Master Stoker, when he awakes he'll have so much trouble from the moneylenders and duns that he will be unlikely to have any time to think, much less to say anything about you." There was a hardness about Piedmont's mouth which indicated he would enforce that scenario if necessary. "It is well past dusk, and we have quite a drive ahead of us. And I think it would be prudent if we left by the window."

He was almost brusque and impersonal as he helped her out of the low casement, through the shielding rosebushes, and into a lightweight curricle, the hood raised against the bright moonlight.

Lacey was glad for his coolness, since it helped put the nearness of him into perspective. She would never share her waking and sleeping with him, she would never be allowed to be alone with him again; for that matter, she might never even see him again. In only a few hours she was to marry the Duke of Lowood, and her life as she knew it would end forever. Even if she managed to escape from Lowood, she would be a married woman and as such could never expect to belong to another, let alone one as honourable as Lord Piedmont. She sighed and stared out into the lowering night.

Being considerate of her quite understandable nervous condition—any other woman would have been in shrieking hysterics after such ill usage—Jordan remained quiet, content just to be near her, until it was full dark and they were nearing London.

"Are you cold?"

A delicious image of pleading a chill to get his arm placed comfortingly around her danced in Lacey's mind. "I'm fine, thank you," she replied with painful honesty.

"How did he get you to go with him? I cannot see you voluntarily eloping with such a creature, nor can I see him carrying your drugged form out of the house under the very estimable Quilling's nose."

"A note purportedly from my grandmother, saying that Helvie was ill and calling for me. If I had not been so . . . so distracted, I would have questioned the validity of the letter, but he manipulated me, gave me drugged water, though I did not know it at the time. He had come to apologise for an impertinence and seemed so anxious to help. . . ." She was all too aware of how pathetically stupid her story sounded and tried to keep her voice as even as possible. It would be too low to try to gain emotional support or sympathy. She had been shamefully silly and certainly deserved anything that happened to her.

Jordan heard the restraint she so ably commanded, and it pulled at his heart. How many ladies could be so beautifully self-controlled after enduring such an ordeal? His admiration for his chosen lady grew. "The letter was his doing, of course."

"Of course. I should have known if I had only examined it more closely. . . ."

Trying to put a smile in his voice, Jordan decided to bring the conversation around to a subject of his choosing. "Well, such an emotional message coming at a time when you were so occupied with other matters . . . I do know everything, let me assure you. Miss Dunfield told me."

Lacey's heart skipped a beat. This was the cruelest load of all. He knew her fate and took it so calmly that there was no question of his ever caring for her; he had rescued her solely as an act of disinterested chivalry. It didn't matter to him at all that she would marry the Duke of Lowood in mere hours. She felt as if she might weep, and could not resist the urge to heap coals on her own suffering head. "And you don't care?" she asked with a tiny sob.

"Care? Of course not! You can't think that I really cared for Miss Dunfield? That was all a piece of drivel cooked up by that monomaniacial mother of hers—sorry, your lady aunt. Oh, I think Miss Dunfield is an estimable young woman, and I wish her every happiness with her Foreign Office chap, despite their unconventional start. . . ."

Lacey's eyes flew open. "What are you talking about? Do you mean to tell me my cousin Elizabeth actually eloped with Milton Litchfield?"

"Of course. What did you think I was talking about? She gave me a message for you; that you were right, that she was taking your advice, and that you should as well."

Jordan was silent a moment. It was slightly ridiculous for a man of the world, a hardened veteran of battles with savage Red Indians and scarcely more civilised Americans to feel such nervous flutterings at the thought that a young lady's answer—a single choice between two words—could determine his future happiness.

He harrumphed. The best approach was a direct one. "Miss Chyngford, I . . . Lacey . . . when I came to your house this afternoon, it was to ask for your hand in marriage."

There! It was said, the fateful words dropping like stones in the silent, chilly moonlight. Lacey sat like a ghost, her mouth forming a small "O" of amazement. Her heart was gyrating wildly in her bosom. He loved her! He loved her enough to marry her! And she . . .

"You want to marry me?" Her voice was bleak.

"Yes. Very much, if you must know." His own heart was thudding erratically now, powered by the alien emotion of fear. "What is it? Don't you like the idea of marrying me?"

"Oh, yes, I like it," Lacey breathed with sterling sincerity. "I like the idea of marrying you very much!"

His lordship had always been a casual man, given to

getting the outlines of a situation and allowing the details to fill themselves in as needed, usually by a staff of well-paid and devoted underlings. This was one thing he had intended on doing alone, and that had been his downfall. Accepting the matter as settled, he stopped the horses, embraced an enthusiastically willing Lacey, and kissed her as he had really wanted to do since that first evening in the garden at Greathills, though he hadn't realised the cause of his unaccustomed restlessness until his lips met the eager firmness of Lacey's.

With only a slight twinge of guilt, Lacey abandoned herself to the voluptuous pleasures of Jordan's embrace. Surely it could not be wicked to steal a few moments of innocent pleasure, when the rest of her life was so rigidly planned? She knew she would risk anything, lose anything, for any amount of time she could have with Jordan.

She leaned back easily, as far as the limited interior of the curricle would allow, revelling in the weight of his body on hers. His breath was soft against her neck as his lips nibbled the tender flesh beneath her ear, travelling upward to claim the soft willingness of her mouth again. Her fingers stroked his head, threading the hearty curls into a handle to hold him a willing prisoner.

There was no estimate of how long they might have remained in their own private world of innocent passion had not a rabbit, fleeing some nocturnal predator, so alarmed the horses that they demanded in no uncertain terms the immediate and undivided attention of their master. Breaking off the embrace with an interior promise of a lifetime of such delights, Jordan tightened his grip on the reins and started the horses once more on the road to London.

It was fortunate that the animals had had the edge taken off their friskiness, for they were a spirited pair and normally would have taken advantage of their master's using only one hand for the reins. This time, however, they were content to keep a crisp pace along the deserted road while

Lord Piedmont devoted the majority of his attention to the lovely lady cradled in his arm.

". . . and the gardens were once a true beauty spot, but they've been sadly neglected since my mother died. Aunt Harriette kept the house up because of a sense of family pride—and the things in it are valuable, I suppose—but she regards the gardens as a useless vanity. She's a bit of a Puritan, I suppose."

"She sounds a bit intimidating," Lacey said carefully. She must tell him the truth, but his plans for a rosy future were so lovely to hear. Later, this night and its lovely fantasies would be all she had.

"She is, but she'll just love you. I can't wait for you to meet her. She raised my brother and me after our mother died. We must name our first daughter after her. . . ."

Lacey surprised herself by blushing. How wonderful it would be to bear his children, to feel a part of him moving and growing within her body! Odd how with him such a thing seemed right and natural, yet how that very same thing put in context with the Duke of Lowood became a loathsome duty.

"I love you," she said.

He gave her a meaningful squeeze. "And I love you. I suppose I have since that first afternoon in your grandmother's garden. Heaven knows my life has never been the same since. I guess I wanted you for my own and I've just realised it only recently."

"I tried so hard to hate you because you stand for what I've thought was wrong all my life, but I couldn't. . . ."

"I'm glad you couldn't, and I'm glad you are such a dogged little crusader. There are things wrong in our world, Lacey, and we're going to lose everything if something isn't done soon. You've made me see that. Vinnie says I'm a different person since you entered my life."

"I like her quite a bit. Do you think she approves of me?"

"She does indeed. Why else do you think she arranged that meeting in the park? We didn't cooperate though.

When I think of how close I came to losing you . . . I couldn't bear it. Oh, Lacey, do let us be married quickly!" His voice was a husky throb.

"Jordan, there's something I must tell you. . . ."

"Darling, I want to hear everything you have to say for the rest of your life, but we're in town now and I don't want to risk your being seen. I don't want any gossip to disturb you. Why don't you put up your hood? It's just after midnight and the streets will be crowded." He gave her a quick squeeze before releasing her to put both hands on the reins. While his horses were well-mannered enough to put up with scant attention on a deserted county road, he would not put their temperament to the test in a city street.

Lacey put up the hood of her cloak and sat far back in the shadow of the curricle's raised top. If anyone did see her, it would be impossible to tell her identity from just a shapeless shadow.

That's what she was to become, Lacey thought: just a shapeless shadow called the Duchess of Lowood, completely the possession and plaything of His Grace the Duke. By the time they pulled to a stop before the brightly lighted facade of Chyngford House, she was so downcast as to cry, which an attentive Jordan misinterpreted.

"Are you afraid, my darling? Perhaps I should go in with you and explain. I can speak to your uncle tonight as well as tomorrow." In the uncertain light, his face was full of concern and so very handsome; Lacey studied it, memorising every plane so that she could remember it the rest of her life. But now she must tell him everything. Discretion about her family must take second place to honesty with the man she loved—and would always love.

"Jordan, I do love you. Please remember that."

"I love you too, darling." He kissed her gently. "I intend to love you the rest of my life."

"No, you don't understand. I have not been quite honest with you. In the morning I am going to be married by special license to the Duke of Lowood." It wasn't going to make it any easier for Jordan to accept her position, Lacey reflected, that the man she was marrying was his arch-rival and the defiler of his father's honour.

"You are going to do what! The *duke?* Why ever—"

"My Uncle Cicero was unwise in gaming. His Grace bought up the vouchers and says that he'll call them due unless I marry him."

"I'll pay them! How much are they?" Jordan demanded, and was severely shaken when Lacey named an impossibly high figure. "That much?"

"If we have to pay, the Chyngfords will be ruined."

"And so you are to be sold!" His voice was bitter.

"It is my duty to help my family, and I will do it, but please believe that it is you I love, you I have always loved, and I will love you to the end of my life!" Lacey planted a last, desperately passionate kiss on Jordan's astonished lips and then, without waiting for assistance, jumped from the curricle and ran into Chyngford House.

═18═

LEONORA, LADY DUNFIELD, had never been renowned for her stability of temper even in the best of times; when she was thwarted and outmanoeuvred in something dear to her heart, her rage knew no bounds. Petulant about Elizabeth's refusal to come with her to Lady Tewksbury's, she had not enquired about her daughter until that young lady failed to appear for supper. After all, Elizabeth had offended her; it was up to Elizabeth to apologise. When Lady Dunfield's questions produced only a letter and no daughter, she became alarmed. When the letter proved to be a tearful good-bye from her child, saying that she had eloped with her true love, Milton Litchfield, her ladyship promptly went off into strong hysterics.

Sir Cicero, more alarmed by the seeming disappearance of the duke's affianced bride, subjected Quilling to an intensive questioning which revealed not only that Miss Dunfield had left with Mr. Litchfield but that Miss Chyngford had departed in the company of Chester Stoker and had been followed—at Miss Dunfield's request—by Lord Piedmont!

The fact that her own daughter had sent the viscount out after her cousin was almost as upsetting to her ladyship as Elizabeth's elopement with that Litchfield creature. Leonora all but howled with rage and indignation, sending injudiciously offered vinaigrettes and hartshorn flying. She established herself in luxurious misery on the first-floor sitting room couch and kept the staff on the run with requests for restorative wine and chocolate.

It was there, in the midst of a magnificent round of hysterics, that a preternaturally calm Lacey found her family. At one time the idea of facing her aunt and uncle under such inflammatory conditions would have terrified her; now, after having sent away the only man she would ever love and knowing what awaited her on the morrow, Lacey felt only contempt for their puny anger.

"There she is! Ingrate! Vile and wicked girl! My daughter would never have defied me unless you goaded her into it! It was a sad day my mother ever made the mistake of bringing you into the family!"

Lacey stared with cool detachment at her aunt, who was clad in a startlingly brilliant yellow morning dress. How could she ever have been unnerved by such blustery bad manners? "Good evening, Aunt Leonora. Are you feeling better?"

His niece's calm composure made Sir Cicero uneasy. She was still an unknown quantity and probably quite capable of fouling his careful plans even at so late an hour. "Be quiet, Leonora. I should like to know where you have been, young lady."

"Thank you, Uncle Cicero. I thought you might be worried about your investment." Lacey's voice was flat. During her slow walk up the stairs, she had derived faint pleasure from the thought of wielding the whip hand over her relatives, but it was a hollow triumph. "And as for you, Aunt Leonora, believe that I regret my being dragged into this family much more than you ever shall."

"Ungrateful hussy!" her ladyship shrieked.

"As for my actions this afternoon, I was drugged and abducted by Chester Stoker and rescued—at the direction of my cousin Elizabeth, to whom I wish the most happiness—by Lord Piedmont. Now I am tired, and since I am to be sold in the morning, I wish to retire. Good evening."

Sir Cicero was struck wordless, as if attacked by a dainty sparrow, but Leonora was made of sterner stuff. She leaned forward from her couch of sorrow and pointed an accusatory finger. "Tell me something, my fine miss! Did you know my daughter was running off with that no-account man?"

"Mr Litchfield is a fine gentleman with a promising future, Aunt Leonora. Yes, I knew about it. In fact, I encouraged it."

Lady Dunfield shrieked, "I knew it! You were just out to humiliate me and my girl. He has no title, no fortune—"

"He and Elizabeth are in love, and he will probably prove to be a better son-in-law than you deserve, dear aunt. Oh, also—if any attempt is made to interfere with them, I will refuse the duke at the altar tomorrow! Is that clear, Uncle Cicero?"

Sir Cicero nodded. Leonora had demanded that outriders and Bow Street Runners be sent in all directions to apprehend the runaways, but he had ignored her ravings, as his attention had been more occupied with Lacey's whereabouts. Litchfield was not as good a catch as Piedmont, but he certainly might be more politic, as the duke and Piedmont were such enemies. Leonora was already furious, but she could be dealt with later.

"I understand completely, Lacey."

Even as her aunt's voice rose in raucous protest, Lacey moved into the hall, shut the door behind her, and went dry-eyed to bed, where she could lie staring at the ceiling until dawn. Her parents would have been so ashamed of her behaviour; she had been cruel and unkind and manipulating. At last she had truly become a Chyngford of Greathills, though not in the way her grandmother had originally intended.

Louisa Anne, Lady Chyngford, had lived apart from the ways of Society for many years, but she was still a lady. So when a gentleman came and wakened the household in the wee hours of the morning, she was not pleased. Only when he identified himself as Lord Piedmont and said that it was a matter of utmost importance concerning her granddaughter did her ladyship relent and come down.

Lady Chyngford had met the viscount on his single visit to Greathills only months before, but the change in his appearance shocked her. He was haggard, as if sleep were only a word to him, and his once-exquisite clothes were rumpled and travel-stained. She was glad she had ordered refreshment, for while she had been donning her dressing gown and making herself reasonably respectable he had downed most of a pitcher of ale and a sizeable chunk of meat pie.

"Your Lordship . . ."

"I apologise for disturbing you this late . . . this early, rather, Lady Chyngford. I assure you it is urgent."

With a graceful motion her ladyship indicated that he should resume his seat, and she took the one opposite him. Even in the faint light of the single candelabrum, the room was much happier than it had been before; Lady Chyngford had had it redone in a sunny yellow, and though Piedmont was not one to notice minor changes, especially under such trying conditions, he had thought the house somewhat nicer.

"There is no need to apologise. Please tell me what is wrong with Elizabeth?"

Well-shaped eyebrows shot up. "Elizabeth? I have no idea. I suppose she is all right. . . . It is Lacey about whom I need your counsel and help."

"Lacey? Forgive an old woman's lapses of memory, but I distinctly remember being told that you were on the verge of offering for Elizabeth."

"Only in your daughter's mind, I assure you, ma'am. Lady Dunfield did her best to bring it about, but Lacey is the one I love."

Inwardly, her ladyship smiled. Leonora had always been foolishly single-minded about that girl. Elizabeth was a good child, but she would have had no more idea about handling a man of Piedmont's stamp than the man in the moon. Lacey . . . It was a possibility they might make a good match.

"And you woke me up in the middle of the night to ask for her hand? Romantic, but scarcely practical, as I fear her uncle is the man to whom you must apply."

"I cannot, ma'am. He has promised her to another. They are to be wed in the morning." It was not Jordan's custom to be so blunt with ladies, especially those of a certain age, but time was short. He regretted such tactlessness, for her ladyship's fragile skin went the colour of old parchment. Lacking any other restoratives, he applied the ale mug to her lips and was relieved when she took a healthy swallow.

"Lacey to be wed? I had heard nothing of it."

"Apparently, Lady Chyngford, there is quite a bit you don't know."

"I think, my lord, that we are both going to need some fortifying." She stood and stepped for a moment into the dining room, returning with the brandy decanter and two glasses. Jordan was quick to relieve her of this burden and, at her direction, poured them both a generous tot.

"I was not aware that the fairer sex ever developed a taste for brandy," he said with a smile.

Lady Chyngford raised her glass. "We do a great number of things which we take care to keep from masculine ears," she said almost flirtatiously; Jordan could see both the ghost of the great beauty she must have been in her youth as well as an unmistakable resemblance to Lacey. "And apparently my family is involved in several matters which they wish to keep secret. I pray that you enlighten me."

"The rôle of tale-bearer does not sit easily with me, ma'am, but my fondest hopes are caught in this snarl . . . First of all, your granddaughter Elizabeth has eloped."

"Eloped? Elizabeth? Impossible. She never had the spirit the good Lord gave a goose."

"I believe she had encouragement."

"You mean Lacey? Well, if it is, it is. Who is my new grandson? Is he a man of good character?"

"I believe so, ma'am. He is with the Foreign Office, I believe. His name is Milton Litchfield." Jordan sipped again at the brandy, which was exquisite.

"Milton Litchfield." Lady Chyngford murmured the name, examining each syllable. "Singularly uneuphonious, but as I recall that young man seemed to figure prominently in Elizabeth's conversation after her first Season. And they eloped!"

"Yes. You see, Lady Dunfield had it in her head that no one would do for Miss Dunfield except me. . . ." He had the good grace to look embarrassed. "It sounds so arrogant, said like that."

Her ladyship's voice was dry. "Believe me, young man, I know my daughter quite well. Leonora is . . . Leonora. Well, it seems that Elizabeth is felicitously disposed, although in a rather crude way. I must do what I can to smooth their path. Now, tell me about Lacey, as you have been dying to do."

"First of all, let me tell you I love Lacey with all of my heart. She is the dearest, most wonderful girl . . . I want to marry her."

"I gathered that, since you pulled me from my bed at this unholy hour. But is she not to be wed this morning? To whom? How did this come about?"

Go carefully, Jordan told himself. *You are criticising her children; you have a right to be bitter and angry, but you must have her as an ally.* He spoke slowly.

"You son Cicero is a bit of a gamester—"

"He is notorious, as was his father before him," her ladyship corrected sharply. "Please go on."

Jordan did, this time more easily. "He was taken into a high-stakes game where he lost a great deal of money. This person . . . encouraged him to wager beyond his depth and then bought up the vouchers." He knew this was pure speculation on his part, but it was the only chain of events which made sense. He had thought of little else on his long and desperate ride to Greathills. "The amount is crippling. . . . He demands instant payment or Lacey's hand in marriage, in which case the vouchers will be destroyed."

Her ladyship's mouth tightened. A great cold wave passed over her as if in presage of an event she did not wish to face. "This . . . er . . . person is apparently very wealthy. Is he respectable?"

"He is accepted in most of Society."

"Does Lacey care for him?"

"She loathes him, and with good reason. You remember our conversation that evening about the Duke of Lowood, ma'am?"

Lady Chyngford's eyes filled with tears. Again! It was happening again—the unhappiness, the misery—just because she had tried to help her grandchild by giving her the birthright she should have had. It was almost as if some malignant fairy had cursed the first Louisa Anne in her cradle for all succeeding generations.

"You've got to help her, ma'am!" Viscount Piedmont was on his knees before her, gripping her ice-cold hands in his travel-stained ones. "You're her grandmother. Tell Sir Cicero you forbid the marriage. Tell the duke . . . he'll have to listen to you. The debt will be paid, it will just take a little time. . . . I'll be able to raise the cash as soon as I sell the stables—"

"I can do nothing. Cicero will never listen to me."

"You must try!"

"I cannot. He's just like his father. Neither of them ever took any notice of aught I said. Arranged marriages . . . yes, arranged marriages for financial gain are traditional in the Chyngford family. It has been so for centuries."

His lordship's contempt was swift. "Like breeding cattle!" he roared in final, if unconscious, capitulation to his beloved's precepts. "Don't you understand, ma'am? Lacey and I love each other!"

A tear welled over and fell down the furrows of Louisa

Anne's soft cheek. "Don't *you* understand, My Lord? I can do nothing for Lacey, any more than I could do anything for myself." She drained what was left in her brandy glass with a most unladylike gulp, extended it, and waited for a refill before she spoke again.

"You never heard of Charlotte, I suppose. She was the youngest and most beautiful of my children. She became Lacey's mother. She had spirit . . . all the spirit in the family. She was the only one who ever broke free of the Chyngfords. And look what it cost her . . . alienation, poverty . . . because I gave in. I didn't have the courage to intervene and keep my daughter, my Charlotte, just as I hadn't the courage to flee with the one *I* loved." She looked up into his lordship's startled face and, despite the depth of her grief, felt a shimmer of amusement. Why was it that the young always thought every emotion their own discovery and their private prerogative?

"Does it strike you as shocking that I should once have been in love, Lord Piedmont? Of course it does. Youth never imagines that such a delicious emotion could have existed before they discover it personally. Believe me, I know the . . . the hellish ecstasy of love and the utter despair it brings when you are forced to accommodate others instead of your own desires." *It still hurts,* Lady Chyngford thought with some surprise. *All these years and it still hurts!*

"We were so much in love, we two," she went on in a dreamy voice. Piedmont listened, amazed. "The whole world was golden that summer. I knew we'd never be wealthy, for though he was well-born, he was not rich, being the son of a younger son; but we had each other. He went away one day, to ready his house for my coming to it as a bride." Her voice caressed the words as she slipped back into those long-gone days of happiness, then hardened to icy slivers.

"While he was gone, my father informed me that I was to marry Sir Homer as soon as decently possible. I was not even permitted to write a letter of explanation or apology to my beloved. They thought I might make some plans to slip away and join him, they told me later. What a joke, because I had been taught my duty so firmly that the idea never crossed my mind. I did what I was told!" She turned ravaged eyes to his. "You think me a contemptible and spineless creature, don't you?"

Ashamed that his emotions should be writ so plainly on his face, Jordan had the additional embarrassment of an uncontrollable blush. He rose and walked to the fireplace, scattering a fine trail of dried mud.

"There is no need for you to answer, and you are correct, but that was a different world, sir, so different that you could scarce comprehend it." Lady Chyngford's voice softened until it was barely audible. "My father was wrong, you know. He said that we were just children, that I would forget him and come to love Sir Homer."

"And did you?"

"No, I never did either. I still remember Alastair, though from the day he left me in the garden of my father's house I never saw or heard of him again. And the title of 'Mrs Crewes' still sounds sweeter to my ear than 'Lady Chyngford' ever could."

"What did you say?" he rasped, starting forward. His face was ashy pale. "What name?"

"My pitiful first and only love? Doubtless he's been dead and gone a score of years. His name was Alastair Crewes. Alastair Llewellyn Crewes." Her lips lingered over the syllables as if savouring every taste of a forbidden sweet.

Lord Piedmont's face bore an alarming expression. "Ma'am, we must act quickly if anything is to be done. Please order your travelling cloak, and I will see about having a carriage set to."

Lady Chyngford started forward. The young man seemed quite mad. "I don't understand—"

"Your Ladyship . . . ," he began in a voice pregnant with import. "Alastair Crewes is the Duke of Lowood!"

—19—

"AND I TELL you, Cicero, I will not attend! That horrible creature encouraged my daughter to run away, to elope with that Foreign Office man! She is a disgrace to the name of Chyngford."

"Leonora—"

"I will have nothing to do with that female!"

Sir Cicero stamped his feet and swore, earning yet another darkling glance from his sister, ensconced most immovably in her big bed. What had he ever done to deserve such a pack of irrational females? So Elizabeth had run off; she had been so quiet when she was at home that he never noticed her presence, so since she had married a respectable enough—though lamentably dull—man, why cavil? Lacey was set to marry a duke, one of the richest men in the kingdom, and she was acting as if she were going to her execution rather than her wedding. Leonora had set herself up as a wronged tragedy queen who threatened to keep to her bed indefinitely just when she should be her happiest; her plain daughter was happily married, and she was about to become the aunt of a duchess. Thank Heaven his mother was safely out of mischief at Greathills, though he would probably have the devil to pay with her later.

"Listen, Leonora, 'that female,' as you so quaintly term her, is going to be a duchess and save both of us in the process as well as the sacred name of Chyngford! You are her aunt and you will be at her wedding!"

"I will not!" As if to enforce her determination, Leonora burrowed back in among the pillows.

"If you do not come, Lacey's wedding will certainly be commented upon. His Grace may even cancel it, and we will both be ruined, my dear sister. If he calls in his vouchers, the house will have to go, as will most of Mother's personal fortune. We'll have Greathills, but precious little else!" It was not so far from the truth that Sir Cicero had any qualm in claiming it, especially when it served to make his sister think. "We will be leaving for the church in half an hour. I suggest that you be ready!"

Sweating like a man who has just done violent physical exercise, Sir Cicero escaped from Lady Dunfield's cloyingly pink room. He went in there seldom, finding the proliferation of pinks offensive even to his undiscriminating taste, but perhaps he had accomplished his aim. Behind the cupid-adorned doors, he could hear his sister moving about. Was any man ever so cursed simply for a few injudicious gaming debts? If only he could hold everything together for just a little while longer . . . Now he had to talk to Lacey, a task he did not relish.

The morning had come fair and clear with no hint of disaster, somewhat to Lacey's disappointment. At least it could have been cold and grey and rainy, to suit her mood. She stood silently still as Bailey fastened her into what would be her wedding dress. With so little time before the wedding, it had been impossible to obtain a proper gown, so one of Lacey's least spectacular evening dresses had been denuded of its silver lace to conform to a semblance of matrimonial propriety.

"Good morning, my dear," gushed Sir Cicero. "Don't we look lovely!"

In his own case, "lovely" would have been an exaggeration. He had a new suit in the long-trousered style, which most unfortunately emphasised his protruberant girth. It was a distinct improvement, however, over the dressing gown he had been wearing when he had burst in earlier, happily surprised to find that Lacey had not fled during the night. She thought contemptuously that he still felt her incapable of keeping her word as befitted a Chyngford.

"Good morning, Uncle Cicero," she replied dully.

"Your aunt is just dressing. We'll be ready to leave before long." Made uncomfortable by her cold stare, Sir Cicero lounged against the door jamb, wishing he did not feel quite so much like a gaoler delivering a prisoner.

The last button was fastened now. Lacey studied her reflection in the mirror with a distant interest. She was making a pretty bride, but on what was supposed to be the happiest day of a girl's life, Lacey felt nothing but misery. If only it had been Jordan who awaited her at the church, she could have floated to him on a cloud of joy. . . . No, she would not, could not let her thoughts wander so, for in that way surely lay madness. Bailey deftly twisted and curled her hair into a style both flattering to Lacey and fitting for the heavy magnificence of the Lowood wedding veil.

It was a tradition that the Chyngford brides should wear the Chyngford veil, a long concoction of spiderweb silk and lace, but that was in storage at Greathills, and Sir Cicero had been reluctant to stir up his mother by demanding it. There was just no telling what wild hare that news would start; he had no intention of letting anything go wrong until Lacey was married to the duke and his vouchers were safely back in his own hands. Surprisingly, the duke himself had offered the solution in the form of the Lowood veil, saying somewhat shyly that he had sent for it after seeing Lacey for the first time.

"Well!" his lordship said in a voice that was too hearty. "You will be the prettiest bride to grace Saint-Martin's-in-the-Fields, I wager. It's hard to consider that by this afternoon you will be a duchess of the realm. Quite an idea, that!"

It was odd, Lacey thought. She moved, she spoke, but it

was as if someone else were doing it in her place, or as if a huge wall of impenetrable glass had been set up around her, like that unfortunate princess in the fairy story. Was the rest of her life to be lived in this dull detachment?

"My thoughts have been on Helvetia," she said suddenly. She had vowed inwardly not to be ugly or vindictive, telling herself that what was done had been of her own free will, but the words were out before she could stop them.

Sir Cicero was not a sensitive man. His niece's barb went right past him without notice. "Helvie? Why?" he asked in all innocence.

"I am wondering what her situation will be on her wedding day," Lacey replied, looking straight at her uncle, who had the good grace to look somewhat abashed. "My pearls please, Bailey."

"Oh, miss, you sure aren't going to go and wear pearls on your wedding day! It's always said that pearls on a wedding day mean tears!"

Lacey found the pearls in her drawer and extended them inexorably, dismissing her maid's outburst with a mere "How apt."

Once the necklet had been fastened, the great Lowood veil was securely pinned into place, the magnificent spill of lace doing the seemingly impossible job of dwarfing Lacey. Bailey snuffled, as was suitable for a wedding, and said how lovely her mistress was, for which Lacey thanked her kindly before turning to her uncle, the cold, empty look in her eyes not at all softened by the masking lace.

"You are beautiful, my dear. Shall we go join your aunt? She should be ready by now, for we really must be leaving."

"I should not have thought that Aunt Leonora would come."

It was almost over now. Sir Cicero could see the end, to his utter relief. "I just talked to her awhile. She's quite upset with you still about the part you played in helping

Elizabeth rebel so against her, but Leonora is a Chyngford and will do her duty. It's a Chyngford tradition," he could not resist adding. No matter how near done they were, it was not over yet!

Lacey did not pretend to misunderstand his inference. She stopped and faced him, her skin almost as pale as her veil. "Yes, Uncle Cicero, there seem to be a number of Chyngford traditions. The men gamble away fortunes and the women have a duty to marry well. Don't fear, I will do my duty as is expected of a Chyngford, but that will not stop me from hating you the rest of my life."

Never having heard such strong emotion expressed in such a serene way, Sir Cicero was taken aback. "My dear girl, what a way to talk—"

"Don't worry about that, either, for I never intend to talk to you again." Holding her head proudly up and disdaining the questionable support of her uncle's shaky arm, Lacey walked from the room to meet her waiting aunt, who was clad in a striking new cerise gown she considered just perfect for a wedding.

His visions of a life gloriously enhanced by being the uncle of the Duchess of Lowood shaken to the core, Sir Cicero rushed alongside his niece to talk about it further, but she steadfastly refused to speak to him. She was as one mute until the church was reached, where she gave a civil greeting to the vicar and the aged sacristan.

Saint-Martin's-in-the-Fields was a smallish church, not given to fashionable weddings, but it was pleasingly made of old stones and had been lovingly decorated for the occasion with masses of fresh flowers, enough to make the air giddy with scent. With a flourish of old-fashioned courtesy, the vicar ushered Lacey into the choir vestry, apologising for the lack of such modern conveniences as a bride's room. The groom, he said, was waiting in the church office, and the ceremony could begin at any time.

The vicar was no end impressed with the quiet grace of

the bride as she nodded her assent. He hurried away, assuring the party that everything would start just as soon as he could don his vestments.

The departure of the verbose vicar left the room in a thick silence, one which made Sir Cicero somehow nervous. Desperately, he snatched up the elaborate bouquet left on the table and extended it.

"Look at what His Grace has gotten you. Orchids and roses!"

Silently, Lacey took the posy, allowing her mind to drift back to the last white-ribbanded posy she had accepted and to its outcome. . . .

"When the music starts, you and I will start down the aisle, Lacey. Leonora, you will follow as Lacey's attendant . . ." Sir Cicero paused as a lightning glance from his sister told him exactly what she thought of that. Only minutes now, he thought; just minutes . . . !

Muffled slightly by the closed door, an asthmatic organ began to play an appropriately stately piece. Sir Cicero looped his niece's arm through his own and breathed a silent "At last" just before the door flew open.

"Stop this at once!" demanded Louisa Anne, Lady Chyngford.

"Mother!" gasped Sir Cicero. He had never seen such a look of absolute fury on his mother's face and was frantically thinking of some way to explain the situation without making himself sound a selfish fool. Leonora, Lady Dunfield, did the only sensible thing she could think of, which was to fall into an all-too-real and painfully ungraceful swoon on a convenient bench.

"Grandmother!" Lacey cried. "How did you get here? How did you find us?"

The doorway was filled with a bristling hulk of a man whom Sir Cicero, cringing, recognised as Piedmont. Jordan, however, had eyes only for Lacey, looking so odd in a shroud of enveloping white lace.

"Lacey! Are we too late?"

The tremor in his voice convinced her of his reality more than her eyes ever could. Regardless of hairpins, she snatched off the Lowood veil and flung herself enthusiastically into his waiting arms, thus answering the one faint, lingering question her grandmother had.

"Jordan! Oh, Jordan, darling, I thought I'd never see you again!"

"Cicero, I should like an explanation."

The element of surprise was gone. He had hoped to present his mother with a *fait accompli;* failing that, he had to see that everything went according to schedule no matter what a dust she kicked up. Sir Cicero took a deep breath and became once more Head of the Family. It was only his mother, after all, and he was still Lacey's legal guardian.

"Lacey is about to be married, Mother."

Lady Chyngford stiffened haughtily. "I did not expect my permission to be asked, but I would have thought that as the child's grandmother I should have deserved the courtesy of an invitation! And why such a hole-and-corner affair?"

The music, less breathy now, continued to pour from the church.

Perhaps this could be salvaged, Sir Cicero thought. Above all, His Grace must not see his bride locked in a passionate embrace with a younger man, let alone a younger man who was his arch-rival on the Turf!

"There are valid reasons, Mother, which I will explain to you after the ceremony. I am pleased that you are here, but time is short. If you will take your seat in the chapel while Lacey—Lacey!—replaces her veil, we can get on with the ceremony."

The man was a cool one, Jordan admitted to himself even as his lips were enjoying the delicious contours of his beloved's mouth. With regret he broke the embrace, though his left arm stayed firmly anchored about Lacey's waist, as if she might be snatched away at any moment.

"There's not going to be a ceremony," he said. "Lacey is

not going to marry anyone but me! I'll get a special license or we'll flee to Gretna Green or—"

Lady Chyngford waved a languid hand. "Don't be silly, Jordan, you'll do no such thing. You and Lacey will be married in Saint George's, Hanover Square, with all due circumstance after a proper announcement and a suitable time of engagement."

"Grandmother!" whispered Lacey, sounding so much like Charlotte had when she was promised an especial treat that Lady Chyngford's eyes misted over. She had been wrong to let them keep her from Charlotte, wrong and weak and wicked, for which she had been duly punished, but now there was Charlotte's child, a gift she was not going to lose. With a new emotion, she embraced Lacey.

Sir Cicero, feeling the need of allies, shook his sister roughly. "Leonora! Wake up!"

Heavy-lidded eyes fluttered open. "Where am I?"

"Good Heavens, Leonora, sit up!

"Don't snap so at me, Mother. I've had an awful shock. Elizabeth has eloped, and that girl—"

Lady Chyngford surveyed her daughter and shrugged her shoulders. Leonora would never learn to take responsibility for her own actions. But—perhaps she was being unjust, as she was a great deal older than Leonora and just now learning a few lessons herself. "I know all about it, and it's probably the best thing that ever happened to Elizabeth. One of my cousins does something with the Foreign Office; I must see what he can do to look out for young Mr Litchfield."

Bereft of her last court of appeal, Leonora applied herself to dusting off her skirts and snuffling dolefully as the organist bravely switched to a third tune.

Lacey and Jordan had heard little beyond the beating of their own hearts. From her grandmother's arms, Lacey had turned back to Jordan's, where she buried her face against his coat to hide her sobs.

"Crying, my Amazon? Don't you want to marry me?"

He had intended it as jest, but the fierce look of loving passion in Lacey's eyes seared him to the core.

"Yes, oh yes, more than anything, but I was so afraid that you didn't want to marry me!"

His gaze bathed her in love. "Why not? I did an awful lot of rushing around to rescue you from this marriage. . . . I just couldn't let him have you without putting up some sort of a fight. . . ."

"I'm an awfully uncomfortable person. . . . We'll be sure to argue . . ."

"And there'll be the pleasure of making up."

"There are things in the world I must do. I'll probably use your fortune and your name in a great number of ways you don't like."

"Charity baskets?"

She caught the humour in his eyes and returned a smile that lit up the room. "Nothing so small. I was thinking of standing for Parliament!"

Jordan gave a roar of laughter. "Bluestocking wench!" he cried in quite good humour, giving his beloved another healthy kiss. There would be no predicting what their future would be like, save that with Lacey beside him he could face anything. How wonderful life could be!

Lacey snuggled close to her darling's chest, revelling in the muscular warmth of him. Those arms would be around her always. . . . She smiled in the secretive way of women in love.

The organ music had stopped. This time the door was filled by a smaller but much more menacing figure, and Lacey could not resist shrinking closer to the solid presence of Jordan.

"Precisely what is delaying the ceremony, Chyngford? I warn you . . ."

It was Lady Chyngford's turn to go pale. That voice, rough with anger, so similar and yet so changed. . . . Was she strong enough? Squaring her shoulders, she stepped directly into the duke's path.

"Hello, Alastair."

Uncharacteristically united, Jordan and Sir Cicero had been taking the duke's measure, trying to anticipate his next move, both literally and figuratively. Neither had expected him to go pale and slump against the table, murmuring, "Louisa Anne!"

"Leave us," Lady Chyngford said brusquely, groping for her vinaigrette as she inwardly cursed her clumsiness. As she knew all too well, he was not a young man; shocks would be dangerous. "Wait for us in the chapel."

After being helped to a seat on the unyielding old bench and to several liberal applications of her ladyship's vinaigrette, the duke's colour began to return to the sour shade he called normal. None of the younger people would have recognised the expression in his eyes, nor the hesitant way in which he clasped Lady Chyngford's fingers.

"Is it really you, Louisa Anne? Am I dreaming?"

"I am quite real, Alastair."

"I thought you dead."

"My late husband found it more expeditious to forward a social life in London if he were thought a widower. I preferred to have as little to do with him as possible, so I permitted his careful rumour to go unchallenged," she said simply.

"I did come back for you. Your old nanny told me how you had been coerced into marriage."

"And you would have done the same to my granddaughter?"

He searched her face, and his eyes held no shame. "She is so very like you. I couldn't lose you twice."

"Alastair—"

"Let me finish. How different things might have been had I known you were alive! Some five years after our parting, my uncle and his son were both drowned in a flood in Ireland. My father and then I ascended to the title. I never married, you know."

Lady Chyngford caught her breath. "Never?"

"I never forgot you. I was so miserable I took pleasure in making others unhappy as well, to my shame. As the years passed, vice became my way of life—"

"Please . . . You don't—"

"No, let me tell you. You should know it all. By that time I had heard Homer Chyngford was parading around town as a widower. I could stand the thought of your being married to him and hope that you had found a little happiness. But knowing that you were dead while he walked the earth almost drove me mad. I tried to ruin him and your son too, and never knew that in doing so I was hurting you. Forgive me!"

Gently, Louisa Anne kissed the wrinkled forehead. "There is nothing to forgive. Had I not been such a coward, none of this would have happened. It is for you to forgive me."

He sighed as if the burden of a lifetime had been removed. "Is Louisa Anne . . . no, Lacey . . . is she to marry Piedmont?"

"They're very much in love."

"As much as we were?"

"Yes, but it's different, Alastair. They've lived more than we had. Jordan fought in the Americas, Lacey grew up in that dreadfully poor parish. . . . They're stronger than we were, better equipped to handle life as it will be. Our time is gone forever."

The duke took her thin hand in his, interlocking the fingers. They were both old hands, with prominent veins and age spots, but there was a warmth between them which had nothing to do with the temperature. "Perhaps you are right about them, Louisa Anne, but . . ." To her ladyship's intense disappointment, he gave his head a shake, then rose and walked across the room. "Funny. You always think you care nothing for the opinion of Society until something happens to make you a fool."

"What are you talking about?"

"Avery Melsham. The worst gossip-monger in London.

He knows about the wedding; he is even sitting out there this moment as my guest. I was so sure of my hold on Lacey, I had notices put in the *Times*." A funny little smile which made him look almost handsome flitted across his face. "I have a special license," he added in a completely different tone of voice, changing the conversation altogether.

Her ladyship's heart began to thud erratically. *It isn't possible*, she thought. *I can't be feeling his thoughts, nor he mine, as we used to so many years ago!* Still, webs of love, fragile and beautiful as moonbeams, stretched out between them, unbroken by the passage of years.

"And what is the name?" she asked hesitantly. "Louisa Anne Chyngford?"

His extended hand was an invitation. She rose and walked to him, their eyes exchanging a question and answer forty years old. With a smile of triumph, he raised his lady's fingertips to kiss them, then tucked her arm gently through his. They walked into the chapel together, closing the door softly behind them.

If you have enjoyed this book and would like to receive details of other Walker Regency romances, please write to:

Regency Editor
Walker and Company
720 Fifth Avenue
New York, NY 10019